MASTER OF PUPPIES

SPELLBOUND HOUND MAGIC AND MYSTERY BOOK 4

JEANNIE WYCHERLEY

Master of Puppies
Spellbound Hound Magic and Mystery Book 4
By

JEANNIE WYCHERLEY

Bark at the Moon Books

Sign up for Jeannie's newsletter:
www.subscribepage.com/JeannieWycherleyWonky

Master of Puppies was edited by Christine L Baker
Cover design by Cover Affairs.

Formatting by Tammy
Proofreading by Johnny Bon Bon
Please note: This book is set in England in the United Kingdom. It uses British English spelling conventions as well as English and Welsh idioms.

AUTHOR'S NOTE

In January 2020, my husband and I took an incredibly special trip to Sri Lanka. I'd visited once before, a very long time ago, and fallen in love with it. So much so, I wanted John to share the experience.

We travelled for part of the time with a small tour group and, on one fateful afternoon in the middle of nowhere, were pulled over by the police. The driver had been travelling slightly over the speed limit.

Sitting in the back of the minibus waiting for the driver to have his fine issued, I spent time observing the dogs on the side of the road. As with many countries throughout Asia, there are street dogs everywhere, playing, running, foraging.

One particular dog caught my eye. Young. Injured. A wonky dog.

It broke my heart.

I cried for that dog right there and then. I felt hopeless.

When we reached our hotel much later that evening, I dedicated several hours trying to reach a couple of English-speaking, Sri Lanka-based animal rescues so that I could get him help. It was a long shot. I was fully prepared to pay his veterinary fees and have him moved to a safe kennel somewhere.

Sadly, despite their best endeavours, the one rescue that did respond to me couldn't find him.

I have never forgotten him. Or the many other dogs I have met on my travels. I try to honour those who touch me by taking photos and thinking of them. Their existence matters.

I vowed on that day that I'd dedicate Spellbound Hound Book Four to that anonymous young Sinhalese dog and that I'd donate all profits from this book to dog charities.

It has been a long time coming but finally, here is Master of Puppies, and I will get to keep my promise.

Young man, wherever you roam now, you are in my heart and enshrined in the spirit of this book forever.

Jeannie Wycherley
29th May 2022

CHAPTER ONE

Toby was minding his own business.

This wasn't as innocent as it sounds. Being a schnauzer-collie-whippet-terrier-thingie, Toby was of the opinion that anything that took place within a mile radius just so happened to *be* his business and therefore, wherever necessary, he needed to know about it, sniff it, explore it and bark at it.

Sometimes he even needed to cock a leg on it.

And *that* sorted *that* out.

For this morning at least, Toby was preoccupied with loitering at the front gate—the one Clarissa liked to close and bolt just to keep him from straying, as if he would!—trying to outstare the cat from across the road.

It wasn't working.

The problem with cats, Toby found, was that they

had an infinite amount of patience, whereas Toby could be instantly distracted by the slightest thing. The thud of a dustbin lid somewhere down the road. Mrs Crouch opening her back door. Clarissa inside their house in Chamberlain Drive behind him, chatting away on her mobile. The buzzing of an insolent fly that had located a discarded crust of pizza in the gutter, left over from some child's walk home from school the previous evening.

Toby regarded the bluebottle with some jealousy, half considering banishing it to fly Armageddon, but he'd promised Clarissa he would stop doing that to things that annoyed him. She was forever telling him that all creatures had a right to life and he mustn't hurt any of them.

And she was right, of course.

Any sensible dog wouldn't want to snaffle fly-blown, maggot-infused, half-eaten remnants that had lain on the ground all night anyway.

But Toby wasn't 'any' sensible dog and, to add insult to injury, breakfast had been served over an hour ago and he was feeling peckish.

He sighed, wondering, *How long till lunchtime? Perhaps there'll be a sammich—*

"You're drooling."

Toby tore his gaze away from the pizza crust and

the bluebottle. The black cat, young and pretty, with wide slanted eyes, stared back at him.

"Did you say something?" Toby asked, trying not to growl. He wasn't usually an unfriendly dog by any means, far from it. He was inquisitive, loving, boisterous and intelligent but, like all dogs, he needed to show newcomers their place in his world.

And this cat *was* new.

Very new.

Its humans had only moved in the previous week. Toby, from his vantage point at the gate, had observed their car arrive, with the enormous removal van following behind it, and had seen the new lady owner take the cat carrier inside—in fact, it had been the very first item she'd moved into the house, which probably said something about the esteem in which the cat was held—but until this morning he hadn't caught a glimpse of the cat itself.

Well, here it was. A large black feline with white paws and a white stripe between its eyes. Cute, if you liked that kind of thing. Toby could only imagine it was called Flash, or Socks, or something equally sweet.

The cat strolled across the road towards the pizza crust, her hips swinging elegantly, her tail high with a little kink in the end. She certainly didn't lack confidence. Toby watched her approach, cocking one of his fluffy eyebrows, uncertain as to her motive.

She slowly repeated herself. "I said you were drooling."

"That's because I'm hungry," Toby explained.

"In my experience, your type always is."

"My *type*?"

"You ... dog things." She floated past the pizza crust, her tail wafting at the flies—which buzzed off, at least temporarily—and stepped onto the kerb not three feet away from Toby's face.

Toby blinked. The brass neck of her! "Ah. Right." Toby couldn't help what he was. Faced with the proximity of this cheeky creature, he had a go at raising his hackles but, unfortunately, they seemed to be on strike. The distinct lack of snacks in his recent history was surely to blame. He gave up. "Aren't you scared of me?" he asked.

She regarded him in astonishment. "You're not very fierce."

"I am, too." In order to prove it, Toby began to bark. Deep, excited little barks accompanied by a front paw jig.

The cat became still, watching him, then sat neatly down and began licking the underside of her paws.

For fluff's sake! Toby huffed. She could at least try

to look a little wary of him, fearless and world-renowned hound that he was! Renowned in the nearby forest at any rate. Several thousand squirrels knew his name there. Didn't the cat realise this?

"You look like a teddy bear," she told him. She wasn't looking at him anymore though, being far more interested in her personal grooming.

"Appearances can be deceptive ... although it's true I need a bit of a furcut," Toby admitted. "But Clarissa—my hooman—likes my scruffy look."

"Does she?" The cat sounded bored now.

A few seconds ago he wouldn't have been remotely bothered if the cat had chosen to ignore him, but now he found himself worried she might be considering walking away. He blurted out the most interesting thing about himself, to his mind at least. "I'm magick."

The cat glanced up and Toby read a little more interest in her expression. "Magick?"

"Yes." Toby wagged his tail a little. He didn't like to boast, but he knew he was special.

"How magick?" The cat gently replaced the paw she'd been cleaning down on the pavement.

"A witch cast a spell on me and it went a little bit wrong—"

"Not much of a witch, then," the cat sniffed.

Toby, thinking back to The Pointy Woman and all

the chaos she'd wrought, privately disagreed. Miranda Dervish was still out there somewhere. Perhaps their paths would cross again one day. He shuddered. That didn't bear thinking about. "Maybe," he said.

"Can you do spells yourself?" the cat asked.

Toby suddenly came over all bashful. He scratched at the dust beneath his claws. "I can," he said. "Yes. I'm practising lots."

The cat sized him up. "I suppose it would be bad form to ask you to do something to, you know, prove it?"

Toby squared his shoulders. He enjoyed a challenge. Wrinkling his nose, he barked softly once. "Arf!" The bolt securing the gate slid back. He moved backwards, and added, "Yip!" It swung open. Toby trotted through it, as sweet as you like.

The cat seemed to be reconsidering her life choices. Her safety had been a different matter when Toby had been securely tucked behind the fence, but now he was free, all bets were off.

Sensing the cat's sudden consternation, Toby plonked his furry bottom down so that he and the cat were eighteen inches or so apart. "I'm Toby," said Toby.

"Moriarty," said the cat.

"Isn't that a boy's name?" Toby asked.

Moriarty glared at him. "Do I look like a boy to you?"

Toby, unsure, held his tongue, although not literally because it's difficult for anyone to hold their tongue, let alone a dog. As far as he was concerned, cats were cats. They all looked ... like cats ... and although he was close enough for a quick inspection, he didn't feel it would be right and proper to duck his head to check for dangly bits.

"Hmm." Moriarty wasn't impressed by his silence. She lifted her rump, curled her tail and prepared to stalk away.

She certainly *sounded* like a female, though.

"Welcome to the neighbourhood," Toby said before she could fully abandon him.

Moriarty lifted her chin in a haughty little manoeuvre that Toby found rather fetching. He stowed it away to practise later. "Thank you. We've downsized," she said, and he heard the note of disapproval in her tone.

Toby wasn't sure what downsizing was, but he imagined it meant shrinking. "How big were you before?" He tried to imagine Moriarty being twice the size she currently was. That was a scary thought.

"Not me, you nitwit. The house."

Moriarty's house was exactly the same size as it

had been before she moved in, but Toby decided it would be rude to contradict his new acquaintance, so he nodded as though he understood.

"Our previous house was big," said Moriarty. "Enormous! No other houses within a hundred metres and a garden perfect for endless exploring."

"Gosh." Toby scanned Chamberlain Drive and the long line of semi-detached houses with their small front gardens and larger back gardens. A big garden he could appreciate—perfect for those post-dinner zoomie sessions he was so fond of—but he couldn't imagine living anywhere without neighbours. How dull that would be! "Weren't you bored?"

Moriarty blinked. "Cats don't get bored."

"Oh." Toby would have gone out of his mind. "But that's great because if you didn't get bored there, you certainly won't here! It can get quite lively at times," Toby told her. "Between six and eight in the morning, lots of big hoomans rush by. They're always worth watching. And then, between eight and half past in the morning and half three and four in the afternoon, the little hoomans walk up and down the road dropping snacks. That's my favourite time of day." He wagged his tail. "And next door to me, Mrs Crouch bakes her own cheesy biscuit snacks. Perhaps she'll offer you some."

Moriarty raised a perfectly arched eyebrow.

The cat was definitely interested, Toby decided.

He reconsidered his generosity. If Mrs Crouch gave away snacks to everyone willy-nilly, that would leave fewer for him. That would never do! "Or *one*," he corrected himself. That would be a perfectly generous portion of treats and leave plenty for him.

Moriarty licked her lips. "Does she do fish flavours?"

"Do you like fish? I love fish. Tuna sammiches are my favourite." This morning, at least. "See? We have so much in common!" Toby pranced around with enthusiasm. "I can tell we're going to be besties."

"We're not going to be besties," Moriarty replied, her tone flat and matter of fact.

Toby stopped dancing. "We aren't?"

"No. You're a dog and I'm a cat. We *won't* be besties."

"Aw." Toby deflated like the football he'd managed to savage to death in the local park the previous week. That had been awesome fun, but the kids whose ball it had been weren't happy, and Clarissa had been a little red faced and frustrated with him, so in the end that had proved to be a challenging couple of minutes.

She could never stay cross with him for long though. His natural charm overrode her annoyance.

"We should stick to our own kind," Moriarty told him. "It keeps things simple."

"But—" Toby protested. He'd have happily made friends with anything—even goldfish—and everything. It didn't matter to him who or what things were. If they were a creature and they wanted to hang out, he was game.

"Speaking of which—" Moriarty began to slide away. "It seems like I'm outnumbered."

"Outnumbered?" Toby peered up the road. A medium-sized dog, graceful and fluffy in cream and grey, trotted towards them. Behind her, a smaller, darker dog struggled to keep up.

"Pippin?" Toby barked in surprise.

"Catch you later, sugarpaws." Moriarty didn't break a sweat, but she did skulk with a little more purpose back to the safety of her front garden, where she disappeared into the bushes. Toby wondered whether she would spy on him from there. He really hoped Moriarty was the spying kind. It would be smashing if they could form a league of neighbourhood spies!

Fun, fun, fun!

"Hey, Pippin!" Toby wagged the back half of his body in ecstasy. Pippin had been his first friend at the Sunshine Valley Pet Sanctuary. Without her calm whisper in his lughole, he'd never have made it out of there and found Clarissa. Losing Old Joe, his previous owner, had been the worst event of his young life so far, but discovering Clarissa? That had been the highlight.

Excluding the time he'd once stolen—he preferred the term borrowed, but she hadn't got it back—Clarissa's roast beef and gravy sammich, maybe.

"Good to see you again," Pippin said, maintaining her air of grounded calm. Pippin's hackles were never raised. She was the most Zen-like dog he'd ever met, with the possible exception of his friend Star, an enormous Leonberger.

"Who's your friend?" Toby wagged politely in the young dog's direction while preparing to exchange butt sniffs once the cordial greetings were out of the way.

Pippin snuffled in amusement. "Don't you recognise him?"

Toby took a step back and cocked his head. Tan and brown fur. Pointy ears that were far longer than they had been. Lifting his nose, he took a deep sniff.

Familiar.

The dusky, sweet smell of Rich Tea biscuits. Mmm. And ... the scent of a dog who relished hanging around markets, especially the fruit and vegetables stalls. A dog who enjoyed rummaging in crates of potatoes and swedes and most specifically ... beetroot.

"Troot?" Toby gaped in wide-mouthed astonishment. Of course it was. Not a baby anymore, but not fully grown either. Toby could see that by the size of his pointed, semi-floppy ears and his enormous paws.

Still, he was growing into a bigger boy *fast*!

"Hey, Toby!" Troot scampered about in excitement, all legs and clumsiness, then lunged at Toby's tail before rolling over and offering up his slightly grubby belly for inspection.

Toby examined the puppy's undercarriage and blessed him with a sloppy great kiss. "But why are you guys here?" he asked when he was finally able to extricate himself from Troot's attention.

Troot sobered at once.

"My friend's in trouble, Toby. I really need your help!"

CHAPTER TWO

"You've come to the right place," Toby said, rather grandly, as he led them up Mrs Crouch's drive. "I mean, this isn't the right place because I don't live in this house, so it's the wrong place, but in terms of general area, you came to the right place. I'm only next door."

"Such a lovely garding," Troot said, staring wistfully at the flowers in Mrs Crouch's borders.

Pippin corrected him. "Garden. The problem with not living with humans, I find, is that speech development is delayed."

"Don't you live with hoomans, Troot?" Toby asked. "I thought you'd found a home?"

"So did I." Troot sighed. "But I was the right

puppy at the wrong time and ended up being sent back to Sunshine Valley Pet Sanctuary."

All three dogs shuddered.

"Selma didn't take you?" Toby asked. He'd been certain the wonderful kennelmaid would have rehomed Troot.

"She thought I had a decent place to go to. By the time I went back to the kennels, it was too late. I don't know where she is now."

"Didn't they close it down after the fire?" Toby asked.

"They did, but a temporary rescue centre was set up in its place," Pippin answered. "Only a fraction of the size of the old one, but not somewhere any pup wants to be."

"Pippin rescued me," Troot sang happily.

Toby nudged Pippin in appreciation. "So brave!"

Pippin shrugged but looked pleased all the same. "Much easier than last time."

They'd reached Mrs Crouch's back door. Toby climbed the single step and turned to his friends. "I find this works better if you sit and do the puppy dog eyes thing. Look suitably pathetic—"

Troot instantly obeyed, although he mixed up his sits with his downs and ended up somewhere between the two, unsure where to fold his paws or his tail.

Pippin needed a little more convincing. "I don't do pathetic." She rolled her eyes.

"Take my word for it, you do today," Toby told her. "Mrs Crouch's cheesy dog biscuits are the best thing since eau-de-badger poop."

"Pffft! I don't believe that," said Pippin, but, after a moment's consideration—it had been a while since she'd had any dog treats *at all*—she plonked her furry butt down.

"Watch and learn," Toby instructed them, and, lifting his front paw, scratched at the door and whined a little. Then he sat neatly, rolled his shoulders back and waited.

"This is taking a while," Pippin complained, instantly bored.

"Mrs Crouch is an old lady who hasn't been well," Toby explained, glancing over his shoulder. "She's getting better, but it does take her time to—oh!" He resumed the position and whispered, "Here she is!"

Mrs Crouch swung the door open. "Is that you, Toby-oby Tobester? It's about time you visited me, you little scamp." She peered down at him, sitting so beautifully on her step. "And how lovely. You've brought some friends to meet me!"

"Good morning, Mrs Crouch!" Toby stood and wagged his tail. "This is Pippin, and the little one is

Troot. They've come to ask for my assistance. We're going to have A Meeting."

"I see." Mrs Crouch's smile widened. "A Meeting, indeed? Am I to assume that young Clarissa is busy?"

Toby nodded. "Tippity-tapping away on her computer. No time to sort out the hospitality for what is sure to be a Very Important Meeting."

"Gotcha!" Mrs Crouch tittered gently. "Give me a moment, boys." She ran a careful eye over Pippin and Troot. "And girls? Let me see what I can find. You make yourselves at home on the lawn."

Stepping inside her cool, clean kitchen, she disappeared from view. Toby jerked his head. "Come on."

He led them onto the lawn and underneath a large cherry tree where they could bask in the warm shade. Mrs Crouch's back garden was in much better shape than Clarissa's, mainly because Mrs Crouch didn't have a schnauzer-collie-whippet-terrier-thingie using it as a racing track even on the wettest of days. Toby had perfected the art of landscaping. Well, it was perfect if you wanted to live in a bog, anyway.

"She can understand you?" Pippin asked.

"Yes. Since I became spellbound, all witches can understand me and me them. It's really cool having proper conversations with hoomans, although some of their subject matter is dull, dull, dull."

"For example?" Pippin sat down on her haunches.

"Their obsession with why someone would want to rip a slipper to bits—"

"To extract every ounce of scent, of course," said Troot. "And for pure mischief!"

"I know, right?" agreed Toby. "Or, and this is a really stupid one I get asked *alllll* the time ... why did you tear up the post?"

"Well, der!" Pippin sighed in exasperation. "We don't have opposable thumbs, so how else are we supposed to see what's inside?"

"I've tried explaining this to Clarissa, but she doesn't appreciate the wider complexities of canine behaviour."

"Or misbehaviour, I think you mean." Mrs Crouch appeared behind them carrying a tray.

Troot jumped on her slipper-clad foot, tugging at the decorative bow.

"Excuse me," she scolded.

"What did I tell you?" Toby asked, nudging Troot away from Mrs Crouch. "She doesn't appreciate your redesigning skills. If I were you, I wouldn't bother, otherwise you may be out of luck with the treats."

"Can she understand what *we* say?" Pippin asked, gazing up at Mrs Crouch thoughtfully.

"No, but I can translate," Toby said.

Mrs Crouch stooped down to deposit the items she was carrying. A bowl of clean, cold water. A plate with an assortment of home-baked goodies. "I made some fresh dog biscuits this morning, Toby, just for you. I must have known you'd have friends coming." She held one up. About an inch high, it had been cunningly shaped like a fish. "These are tuna, and these"—she held up a more familiar round one—"are cheese."

"You're the best, Mrs Crouch! Thanks so much."

"Any time, young man, any time."

Toby imagined she would leave them to it, but she remained where she was, holding out the tuna fish biscuit in Troot's direction. Troot eyed her with an element of suspicion. "She's luring me to my death, isn't she?"

Pippin snorted. "I don't think so."

"She just wants you to eat the treat," Toby said, his mouth beginning to water. *Get on with it*!

Troot edged away from Mrs Crouch, all his previous interest in her slipper now completely forgotten.

"You're very young, aren't you?" Mrs Crouch cooed. "And no collar."

"Uh-oh," said Pippin.

"What?" Troot shot backwards and hid behind the tree.

Mrs Crouch giggled in appreciation. "What a big silly you are. I won't hurt you."

"She won't hurt you," Toby reiterated.

"Why is she interested in his lack of a collar?" Pippin asked.

"Because she cares!" Toby answered and turned to Mrs Crouch. "Troot doesn't have a home. He lives in the market, but you won't tell anyone, will you, Mrs Crouch?"

"He doesn't have a proper home? Aww, the poor wee mite."

"You can't say anything, though," Toby repeated. "He's spent most of his life in and out of the horrible rescue kennels, and you know what they're like."

Mrs Crouch nodded. "From what you've told me they are remarkably unpleasant. I won't breathe a word." She jiggled her finger at Toby. "But only as long as he's healthy and happy and isn't in any danger."

"He's not!" Toby wagged his tail. "We look after him!" Not strictly true, seeing as Toby hadn't seen him since he'd escaped from Sunshine Valley Pet Sanctuary, but perhaps the promise could apply from now on.

"Alright then." Mrs Crouch stood and edged around the tree trunk. Troot tipped his head back to stare up at her. "See you later, cutie." She dropped the treat at his feet. "If you're ever in need, you can always come and visit me," she told him and retreated.

The three dogs watched her go, Toby barely able to prevent the line of dribble sliding from the side of his mouth.

"One of the good ones," Pippin decided and stared expectantly at Toby. "Let's convene this meeting, shall we?"

They shared the biscuits out equally, even though Pippin was the bigger dog. She didn't seem to mind, and was much taken with the clean water. "Beats puddles any day," she said as she licked the bowl dry.

Troot came out from behind the tree to examine the biscuits. He daintily chose a fish shape to nibble first. Wrinkling his nose, he chomped down on the biscuit. It crumbled as he did so, releasing the tang of tuna. "Oooh," he laughed, chewing faster. "It melts on your tongue!" The remainder of his biscuits disappeared in two point five seconds.

"Are you hungry?" Pippin asked, pushing a couple of hers over to him with her nose.

Toby, who until this moment had had no intention of sharing his spoils, cocked his head.

"I'm always hungry," Troot replied.

"Me too," Toby agreed. The realisation that he

had unlimited access to biscuits—as long as Clarissa and Mrs Crouch would share them—dawned on him. He added several of his own to Troot's pile and watched with some satisfaction as the puppy snaffled through them. *That's my boy*, he thought, like a proud father.

"That deals with the first order of business," he declared. "Now onto the second item." He munched thoughtfully. Tuna this time. *What was it again*?

Pippin's bushy eyebrows shifted around her forehead like caffeinated caterpillars. She didn't say anything, but Toby had a feeling she was judging his temporary memory lapse.

He cleared his throat in a gruff doggy kind of way. If the postman had been anywhere close by, he'd have run a mile. "Yes. Yes." That was it. "What brings you both here to see me?"

The three dogs formed a loose circle, all the better to share their secrets and pool their fishy breath.

Pippin nodded at Troot. "Go ahead. You tell him."

Troot, who had polished off his extra treats even faster than the first batch, gave himself a good shake, crumbs escaping from the fur around his mouth. "It's like this, Toby. I have a friend—"

"That's good." Toby nodded in approval. *We all need friends*.

Troot's eyes were downcast. "Maybe I should say, I *had* a friend."

"Oh." Toby didn't like the sound of this. "May he walk beside his hooman forever in a meadow of sunshine—"

Troot wailed in alarm. "Is he dead?"

Toby reared away in shock. "Isn't he?"

"Hang about." Pippin tutted. "We're getting a little ahead of ourselves here." She meant Toby and Troot, but she was too polite to say so. "Start at the beginning," she told the puppy.

"Hokay." Troot planted his bottom on the floor and scratched behind his ear for a moment. "Once upon a time—"

"Perhaps not that far back?" Toby suggested. "Just cut to the chase. We all like a chase, don't we?"

"We do," Pippin agreed.

"I love a good chase!" Troot jumped up and began to sprint around the picnic area in shallow circles. The more he ran, the more he wanted to. Seconds later he was running laps of the whole garden, with Pippin looking on in exasperation and Toby seriously considering joining in.

Pippin sank into the grass and buried her nose beneath her paws with a sigh. "I sometimes wonder why I bother."

Toby pulled himself together. "Troot!" he barked, and the younger dog slid to a halt, carving tramlines into Mrs Crouch's good lawn.

"Sorry." Troot hopped around for a few more seconds, then had a good shake, all the better to work the buzz of adrenaline out of his paws.

"About your *friend*?" Toby prompted him. It was good to see these two, but he had a feeling that his pre-lunch naptime was approaching.

"He's disappeared," Troot blurted. "He used to play with me around the market, but just like that he went missing."

"Are you sure he didn't—" Toby didn't want to use the words again. *Die*?

"He was just a baby!" Troot said. "Like me. But more so."

"It's possible he found a home, then," Toby said. *Isn't that what happened with puppies*?

Pippin intervened. "The point is, he already *had* a home. He was much loved by the guy who runs the hardware stall."

"I think he was taken," Troot said, and now his tail was tucked between his legs. "And Lionel, his daddy, thinks so too. I heard him say so. He was really sad."

"He's been putting up reward posters," Pippin said.

"There's a reward?" Toby liked the sound of that. "In money?"

"One hundred pounds." Pippin wagged her tail. "For Bourgie Bourgie's safe return."

Troot had started to sniffle. "I miss Bourgie and I hate to see Lionel sad. He's a nice man. A good hooman."

Pippin arched an eyebrow. "There aren't enough of those around."

"More than you imagine." Toby couldn't help but disagree. Clarissa and Mrs Crouch, Dom and even DC Plum—they were good hoomans. Not to mention Selma. Toby wondered where she was now. Surely she would have considered adopting Troot?

"Troot came to me, but I thought you, with your connections and your magick, might be better placed to help him out than I am," Pippin said. "What do you think?"

Toby gave the matter some thought. But only for a nanosecond. One hundred pounds would pay for a shedload of sammiches. He'd be able to afford all of his favourites! Roast beef! Salmon and cream cheese! Banana!

"I'm your man," he said. "Spellbound Toby's Investigation Services at your disposal!"

CHAPTER THREE

"Who do we have here?" Clarissa had paused her tippity-tapping on her laptop and, clutching her coffee mug, had joined Toby, Pippin and Troot in her kitchen. She glanced at the other two dogs in surprise.

Troot squeaked and hid behind Pippin. "Is she a witch?" he whispered.

"I believe so," Pippin answered in her nonchalant way. Did anything phase Pippin? Probably not.

"These are Pippin and Troot," Toby explained, without extracting his head from the cupboard under the sink. "They're my friends."

"I see." Clarissa, raising her eyebrows, flipped the kettle's switch on. It started to hum straight away.

"Is she going to turn us into frogs?" Troot whimpered.

"She's not that kind of witch," Toby told them, his voice muffled as he searched among the dusters and floorcloths.

"What kind of witch am I not?" Clarissa asked. She didn't understand what Pippin and Troot were saying, so was only hearing Toby's part of the conversation.

"An evil kind," Toby answered. *Like The Pointy Woman.* He shuddered.

"Hmmm." Clarissa didn't sound convinced. "Come out of there, Toby. What are you looking for? And what, pray tell, are you up to?"

Toby belatedly pulled his head out of the cupboard, the kitchen torch clamped between his teeth. "Rrrr rrrr-rrr rrr rr rrr-rr-rr-rr," he said.

Clarissa retrieved the torch. "I beg your pardon?"

"I said, we're going on an expedition," Toby repeated.

"Why do you need a torch?" Clarissa wanted to know.

"Don't all great investigators have torches?" Toby had watched enough reruns of *CSI* and *Law and Order* and other great police drama series to know that any detective worth their salt carried a torch.

"Since when were you an investigator?" Clarissa wasn't buying into this.

"Since ..." Toby rolled his eyes up, thinking. "Just now."

"You can't take the torch," Clarissa told him. "It's the only one we have. What happens if there's a power cut?"

"But—"

Clarissa deposited the torch on the countertop, way out of Toby's reach. "But nothing. Some of the best detectives ever didn't have torches."

"Like who?" Toby grumbled.

"Sherlock Holmes? Hercule Poirot? Miss Marple? When did you ever see them with a torch?"

"Mainly because batteries weren't invented back then." Toby was no idiot. He watched plenty television while Clarissa was out playing at being a journalist.

"Alright. What about DCI Barnaby in *Midsomer Murders*? You never see him with a torch."

"Hmmm." Toby wasn't convinced, but the softly spoken, gentle John Nettles was his favourite favourite detective. If it was good enough for DCI Barnaby—

"Besides, you're only able to carry the torch in your mouth. What happens when you need to interrogate a suspect? You'll open your mouth and it will fall out." Clarissa, suddenly amused, giggled to herself.

Toby cut his eyes up at her, feeling cross. Why hadn't he thought of that?

Clarissa reached for the jar of coffee and snickered again. "We'll have to get you a little backpack if you're going to be out and about solving mysteries."

"Harrumph!" Toby pouted. "I don't think you're taking me seriously."

Clarissa had turned away and was spooning ground coffee into the cafetière. Now she paused, cast a look over her shoulder, opened her mouth to say something, reconsidered, closed it and returned to the coffee pot. After filling the jug with the hot water, she turned back to Toby and, folding her arms, stared down at him.

"Should I be?" she asked, her tone more serious.

"Troot's friend has gone missing. I'm going to help find him," Toby told her.

"I see." Clarissa studied the other two dogs more carefully. "Which one is Troot?"

Troot peeked out from behind Pippin. "Me, miss," he whispered.

"And Troot's friend is another dog?" Clarissa asked.

"A puppy. Yes." Toby nodded. "He went missing from the market in town."

Clarissa sucked in a breath. "You can't just go gallivanting about town, Toby."

"Why not?" He knew his way around. He'd often accompanied Clarissa on shopping trips.

"There are rules about stray dogs—"

"She's not wrong," Pippin chipped in.

"I'm not a stray dog, though!" Toby pointed out the flaw in their argument.

Clarissa was having none of it. "If you're not with your owner, then you're a stray."

"That doesn't make any sense!"

"You're not allowed to walk around town willy-nilly," Clarissa told him, her voice becoming firm. "You have to be with me."

"Ah!" Now Toby understood. "Get your lead then, and we'll be off."

"I've told you before, it's not *my* lead, it's *your* lead."

"I lead you. You follow. I know where I'm going. The lead is for your benefit."

It was an old argument. "The point remains, you have to be with me, and I'm afraid I can't go anywhere till much later this afternoon, or possibly this evening. I have a looming deadline and a zoom meeting with my editor."

"But—"

"But nothing, darling. We'll go out later and have a look around the market then." She smiled down at Troot. "We'll see if we can find your friend, don't worry."

Taking the cafetière and her mug, she nodded at Toby. "You wouldn't want the dog warden coming after you now, would you? Catch you in a bit, sweetheart."

Sweetheart! Toby stared after her retreating figure. He loved Clarissa to bits, but lately she'd become a little one-minded about her job. Several times she'd disappeared up to that there London, leaving him in Mrs Crouch's care. When she was home she was on her laptop or phone, always typing and chatting and printing things out. He understood how important her career was to her. For the first time, they were making ends meet. They weren't wealthy, not by any means, but at least they didn't have to scrabble about for loose change any longer just so they could buy bread and milk.

"Oh dear," Pippin said.

"Does that mean you can't come, Toby?" Troot wailed. "What will we do now?"

"What do you mean what will we do now?" Toby was most put out. "We'll carry on regardless!"

Pippin smirked. "Aren't you afraid of the dog wardens?" she wanted to know.

"Spellbound Toby is afraid of no-one," Toby announced, throwing his head back, a grand gesture of foolhardy confidence if ever there was one. "If any dog warden interferes with me, I'll cast a spell and turn him into a dog flea."

"You can do that, can you?" Pippin asked. She didn't sound altogether convinced.

"I've never tried," Toby conceded. "But there's always a first time." Turning tail, he headed for the dog flap. "Let's go!"

"Yippee!" Troot cried, his long, thin, awkward legs becoming tangled as he tried to navigate the flap. "Bourgie! We're coming for you!"

Pippin nudged him through with her nose. "We're coming for something," she said. "But who or what is yet to be made clear."

CHAPTER FOUR

Like most British markets, Sunshine Valley's pannier market was busiest at lunchtime. The food stalls, the artisan bakery and deli, and the nearby burger and pizza vans attracted those looking for fast food on their lunch breaks at the same time as most shoppers were finishing up their purchases.

Both Pippin and Troot knew their way around the market square with their eyes closed and were able to navigate through the stalls without drawing attention to themselves. Toby followed them, periodically checking for wardens, Clarissa's warning ringing in his ears now that he was out here on his own.

However, the rush he experienced from being free was exhilarating! Had it been up to him, and he hadn't been investigating A Very Important Case, he would have thoroughly enjoyed exploring the market and surrounding area. The smells were intoxicating. Sizzling beef and fried onion. Cheese! Pork! Fish! Even the shoe repair stall had a delicious fragrance that Toby wanted to acquaint himself with—all that leather and polish. Mmm-mmm mmm! Other things were slightly less interesting—the musty scent of second-hand books, the clean smell of new clothes, pots and pans and plastic utensils—but they would have been worth investigating if he didn't already have a job to attend to.

"This is Lionel's business." Troot pulled up beside a double-width stall, the roof covered in a gaily striped tarpaulin, with buckets and mops and brushes and dustpans hanging from hooks above the dogs' heads, boxes of screws and nails arranged on the tables in front of them, along with displays of lightbulbs and tools, packs of batteries and—ooh!—torches.

Toby stored that information away for a later date.

Troot pointed out a wooden crate. The three dogs moseyed over and sniffed it. Lined with newspaper and then covered in an old woollen blanket in yellow and orange, this held the scent of a puppy not much older than Troot. Toby took his time, his olfactory prowess investigating the undertones of the puppy's individual fragrance notes.

Satisfied he would be able to pick the youngster out among a field of identical puppies, Toby stood back and considered his surroundings. "When was the last time Bourgie was seen?" he asked Troot.

"I can't tell the time," Troot confessed, "but it was while the stallholders were clearing up. Later in the afternoon. That's always the best time for scavenging and scrounging. I was wandering around by the butcher's stall. He usually tosses me a chop."

"Really?" Toby, momentarily distracted, quickly fantasised about a nice lamb chop for dinner. Clarissa didn't eat much meat so, even had they been able to afford lamb chops, he had little chance of enjoying such a delicacy.

"That would make it sometime after four," said Pippin. "Most stallholders are long gone by five."

"Is that a busy time of day?" Toby wanted to know.

"Not in terms of customers," Pippin told him. "Just the stallholders loading up their vehicles."

Toby nodded. "Is it possible Bourgie simply ended up in the back of someone's van by mistake?"

Pippin pursed her lips, her fluffy white moustache twitching. "I suppose it is."

Troot's mouth dropped open. "You mean Bourgie could be trying to find his way back from wherever he ended up?"

"All things are possible," Toby replied, rather grandly. He could quite see himself as the John Nettles of the canine world. "That doesn't explain why whichever stallholder mistakenly took him hasn't already brought him back though. But we mustn't rule anything out." He led them to the edge of the market-place. "It's equally possible that someone puppy-napped him on purpose when his hooman wasn't playing close enough attention."

He hummed and hawed for a few seconds. "That would make equal sense, wouldn't it?"

Pippin shrugged. "It would, but I'm not sure how far that gets us."

Toby peered left and right, turned in a circle, swung back and repeated the process. The market square was surrounded for the most part by small shops and cafés, a couple of national bakery chain franchises, a newsagent and a sweetshop. But on one side of the square was a row of Victorian terraced houses, most of which had seen better days. Worn wooden gates had replaced the original iron ones, and chains and padlocks spoke of the kind of visitors the residents were not happy to attract.

"What, Toby?" Troot asked. "What are you looking for?"

"Not a what ..." Toby took off at a fair pace; Troot

dashed after him. After a moment, Pippin ambled more calmly in their wake.

They didn't go far. Toby pulled up before a beaten wooden gate, the paint flaking off and one large chunk of the corner nibbled away. An enormous pair of dusty paws poked out in their direction.

"Excuse me, sir? Madam?" Toby called, polite as you like.

Loud snuffling preceded the appearance of a large, shiny, black nose and an orange-ringed eye.

Troot backed away.

Toby sank to his belly. "Good morning!"

"Is it?" a doleful voice replied.

"It's certainly glorious!" Toby maintained his enthusiasm.

"It's too hot for me," the voice replied. "They leave me out here without any shelter, and at this time of day there's no shade. What's a girl supposed to do?"

Toby frowned. He didn't like the sound of that at all. "Wait here," he told the others and scampered off, threading his way between people's legs, straight through to the centre of the marketplace and a small stall he'd spotted as they'd walked through earlier. Hanging from the scaffolding were handbags for every occasion—although none that he imagined Clarissa would like to be seen dead carrying—as long as those occasions involved you sporting a faux crocodile leather monstrosity with a cheap gold-coloured chain that wouldn't look out of place in a prison. Or an oddly mute popular 'designer' pattern with brown piping that had already started to become unthreaded. Or a large shopper with cheap plastic fabric covered in enormous blousy flowers in garish colours.

However, it wasn't the bags that Toby was interested in; it was the accessories. And not even all of those. Only the umbrellas. He sidled up to the stall, waited until the middle-aged woman with crazy flyaway hair turned her attention to a new customer, then snaffled the brolly nearest to him and, without batting an eyelid, turned tail and skulked away, flitting easily among the busy legs meandering this way and that without any awareness of the magickal dog in their midst.

He arrived safely back with the others in no time at all, the umbrella clamped between his teeth.

"What have you got there?" Pippin asked.

"Did you pinch that?" Troot asked in a scandalised whisper.

Toby dropped his prize. "I liberated it. The same way that you liberate lamb chops from the butchers," he said. "Here. Help me get this plastic off, will you?"

Between them, Toby, Pippin and Troot were able

to shred the wrapping and expose the umbrella without causing too much damage to the fabric. Pippin pulled the sheath free and discarded it to one side and then Toby, who hadn't a clue how Velcro worked, proceeded to chew through the tab until the umbrella unfurled.

"What are you doing?" The baleful orange eye stared out at the trio of dogs who had taken it upon themselves to interrupt her snooze. Not that she minded. Snoozing was pretty much all she did in this weather. It could get mighty dull.

"I've found you some shade!" Toby wagged his tail with excitement.

Pippin frowned. "How are we going to get it to do that ballooning thing the hoomans do?"

"And how do we get it over the fence?" Troot sounded worried.

"Relax! I've got this," Toby said, swaggering. He pushed the umbrella through the gap in the gate, nearly taking the big dog's eye out.

"Oi," it grunted. "Do you mind?"

"My apologies," Toby said. "Please stand back, madam."

He lay down on his belly again and pushed his nose right up to the hole. "Please don't bite me," he told the dog when she growled at him. "I mean no harm, I just want to be able to see what I'm doing."

And what you're doing, he thought.

Now that he could see her, he could appreciate her size. Perhaps not as big as his friend Star, the Leonberger, but certainly this lady had to be crossed with a St Bernard or something similar. She had a St Bernard's face and colouring but more of a retriever's body. Toby had a feeling that if she wanted to, she'd be able to do him some serious mischief.

"If you wouldn't mind standing back?" he suggested. The St Bernard-retriever-thingie regarded him with scepticism but moved back a foot or so.

"Further?" Toby pressed.

"What—"

"That's fine." Toby lifted a paw to hold the big dog where she was, then concentrated. He had been studying magick with the help of Dom and Star and Clarissa and Mrs Crouch and anyone who would share the time and skills he wanted to learn, but he was intelligent enough to understand he'd only scratched the surface. What action would be needed to make the umbrella open up the way he'd seen it working?

If he ordered it to 'open', would that be too generalised? Would all the doors and gates in the vicinity open as well? Not if he deliberately targeted the umbrella. He decided to go with a word that he felt best represented what happened when an umbrella was opened.

"Flower!" he demanded, aiming a claw directly at his target. Instantly it sprang open, the spokes scraping along the concrete before clicking into place with pleasing snaps. Unfortunately, the dog behind the fence was ... well ... a big girl, and this wasn't a very large umbrella. He'd have been better off sneaking away with a golfing one if he could have managed it.

But you can't keep a magick dog down. Toby lifted his paw again, and his eyes focused hard, settling on a spot inches above the big dog's head. "Float!" he demanded, and the umbrella floated into the air, the curved handle parking itself exactly where Toby had wanted it to. It cast a satisfying shadow around the small yard.

The big dog surveyed the area, then peeked at Toby. "Hey, thanks!" she said.

"Any time," he said. "I'm Toby, by the way."

"Moira." Moira lay down under the shelter of the brolly and sighed happily.

"Move over," Troot demanded, slipping between Toby and the gate. "I'm Troot!" he called, pushing his nose through the gap and wagging his tail in a frantic, happy greeting.

"And I'm Pippin," Pippin said, making no move to

join the other two. There wouldn't have been enough room anyway.

"Pleased to meet you all," Moira said.

"We were wondering if you could help us with a small problem we have?" Toby enquired.

Moira cocked her ears. "I can hardly say no, can I? Not after you've been such a gentleman."

Pippin made a strangled noise in her throat. Toby glanced round at her. "Bit of fish bone," she said, and coughed.

"I could fix that for you, if you like?" Toby offered.

Pippin took a step away from him. "No, really. I'm fine." She cleared her throat. "*Ahem hem hmm.*"

"Okay." He returned his attention to Moira. "We're looking for a friend of Troot's by the name of Bourgie. Do you know him?"

"Bourgie? Can't say the name rings a bell."

Troot elbowed Toby out the way. "You'd know him if you saw him. He's little, like me. Friendly. Also like me. He's a Pomeranian cross Border terrier."

"Ah! Yes, I have seen him around, but only from a distance. He doesn't wander far. Not like you." Moira's big orange eye regarded Troot with a hint of envy.

"I like to get out and about," Troot acknowledged. "I'm a bit of an expawer."

"The canine version of Bear Grylls, eh?" Moira asked.

Pippin and Troot looked at Toby, the only one of them with access to a television. "He's a hooman expawer," Toby explained. "Does derring-dos, goes to wild places and eats strange things. Just for the fun of it."

"That's me!" Troot tossed his head back proudly. The fact that he'd never been out of Sunshine Valley in his short life was by the by.

"Guys?" Pippin intervened.

Toby instantly understood. At this rate they would take all day just to interview one potential witness. Time was marching on and they hadn't had any lunch yet.

"The thing is ... Troot's friend—"

"Bourgie," Troot reminded him.

"Bourgie has disappeared," Toby told Moira.

"And not of his own accord—" Troot interrupted.

"We don't know that for certain," Pippin piped up from the rear, "but that's the scenario we're working with."

Scenario. *What a great word*, Toby thought to himself, wishing he'd used it first. He quickly ran through the spelling of that in his head. *S-C-E-N-A-H ... no ... R-I-O. Excellent. Must use it myself. Good boy.*

"We think he was taken by someone," Troot was explaining. "I don't believe he would have gone off on his own. He likes his hooman very much and he has nice dinners and a basket."

"I'm sorry to hear he's missing," Moira said. "I didn't see anyone take him if that's what you're asking. I like to lie here and watch the market, but at times it can be busy. It's difficult to take everything in. Especially when it's hot. I get drowsy."

That made perfect sense to all the dogs. They too enjoyed a snooze while basking in the warmth of the sunshine. Or when there was no sunshine but it was warm. Or, in fact, at any time at all. There was never a wrong time to take a quick nap.

Toby nodded. "It was a long shot. I don't suppose you noticed anyone hanging around more than usual? Or behaving ... strangely?"

"Aren't most hoomans strange?" Moira asked.

Toby thought about Clarissa and her odd ability to buy food in a shop and not consume it straight away. Why, she even stored it either in the pantry or in the fridge! What self-respecting dog would do that?

Crazy lady.

"There is that," he said.

"But ..." Moira wrinkled her nose, thinking. "There was a car hanging around."

Toby glanced around. "A car?" Cars weren't allowed on the marketplace, but they were able to drive around the square.

"You see, there's no stopping here," Moira said. "My hooman complains about it constantly because he has to park in the road behind us, which means he can't keep an eye on his car. But this car I saw kept pulling over. In fact"—she nodded in the direction of a man in uniform who was standing at the corner surveying the traffic—"that chap moved it on a couple of times."

Toby examined the man. Dark blue uniform with bright yellow flashes; you'd be able to see him coming on a dark night. Some sort of dignitary or official, but not a police officer.

"Was there something special about the car?" asked Toby. "How did you know it was the same one?"

"Ha! That's an easy one. I remember it because it was small. One of those little bubble type cars. A Fiat, I think it was."

"Fiat 500?" Toby asked. Clarissa had been considering one of those to help her get around. Affording it was her main consideration. Her battered old Nissan was unlikely to make it through another MOT.

"Maybe." Moira sniffed. "Yeah. Sounds about right, now I think of it."

"That's something to go on." Toby nodded in satisfaction.

"And it was bright pink," Moira added, almost as an afterthought.

"Bright pink?" Toby's brain raced. You didn't see many bright pink cars on the road. One of those would be easy to trace, wouldn't it?

"Yep. And even better than that—"

Troot and Toby leaned close so that the wood at the bottom of the gate began to bite into the flesh on their noses. Even Pippin edged a little closer.

"Yes?" Toby asked.

"It was powered by faery dust!"

CHAPTER FIVE

"Powered by faery dust? What does that even mean?" Troot wanted to know.

Toby had thanked Moira effusively for all the information and, after promising to visit her from time to time, the dogs had headed across to the marketplace to seek out lunch. It transpired that Troot and Pippin were curiously adept at scavenging. Toby less so. He'd always relied on someone else serving his food on a platter, but he found it fun to seek out the scraps that market traders and their customers scattered all over the ground. Sandwich corners, hard pastry edges from pasties and pies, discarded crumbs in crisp packets—all of these provided rich pickings.

Best of all were the overflowing litter bins behind the burger and pizza vans on the edge of the square.

Gherkin slices, plastic cheese, lettuce and tomato, onions and ketchup—the paper plates the goodies were served on were awash with tasty treasures. While a surprising number of adults couldn't finish a whole burger, it was the children who provided the best bounty of all. The younger the child, the more likely the contents of a burger—or a hot dog, a sandwich, a cone of chips or even an ice cream cone, come to that—would end up on the paving stones and provide sustenance for needy dogs.

Needy? Or greedy? You decide.

The dogs had taken shelter underneath a wooden bench and table set, all the better to watch out for the next batch of lucrative snacks descending from above.

Toby licked a smudge of mustard from his beard. He wasn't sure about the taste, but mixed with tomato ketchup it wasn't too bad. Now he studied Troot and the look of confusion on his sweet face. "Sorry? What does *what* mean?" asked Toby. He'd been distracted by burgers.

Troot stamped a paw. "Powered by faery dust!"

"Ah, right." Toby wasn't one hundred per cent sure himself, but there was no way he would ever admit such a thing. "It means that when faeries ... erm ... die ..."

"This sounds jolly," said Pippin, tilting her head in surprise.

"They ... erm ..." Toby racked his brain for an explanation. Hadn't he heard Clarissa say that lots of witches and faeries didn't get on very well? She'd been covering some story for *The Celestine Times* that had involved reporting on a faery death, but the piece had been relegated to the inside pages because nobody cared about the demise of a faery. Not in the witchy press, anyway.

"Because there are lots of faeries ... there are lots of faery deaths," Toby decided. "And they cremate them all, so faery remains are a great way of powering cars." He felt slightly guilty for the lie. He had nothing against faeries, mainly because he'd never met one, and he presumed that Clarissa had nothing against them either, because Clarissa didn't have much against anyone.

Except The Pointy Woman.

Clarissa would hold that grudge forever.

"You add faery dust—granulated faery dust cremains—to your car instead of fuel. It's a form of green energy. Except it's not green precisely, more pink and sparkly."

"Right," said Pippin, evidently choking on her fish

bone again. "I suppose if you wanted properly *green* energy, you'd have to use dead leprechauns instead?"

"Exactly," Toby answered solemnly.

"I kind of feel sorry for the faeries," Troot piped up.

"You don't need to," Toby said. "Think of it as ... like ... donating your body to science. Those stickers on the back of cars are in lieu of a memorial."

"A memorial loo? What?" Troot blinked in confusion.

"I mean, instead of a headstone, the stickers on the car are ... a celebration of the faery's life."

"Ohhhh." That made sense. "Bless their little hearts. Such a wonderful thing to do."

The three dogs momentarily dipped their heads in recognition of the faery population's ultimate sacrifice for a sustainable future.

Pippin was the first to break the silence. "How are we going to track down this car?"

This was a good question and one that had been occupying space in Toby's brain ever since Moira had first mentioned it. The dogs had run several circuits of the market before seeking out their lunch and found no trace of a pink car at all. He'd spent a little time observing the traffic too, but hadn't spied a single car powered by faery dust, let alone a pink one. However, this fact alone suggested that if they *did* run across such a vehicle, it would be a rarity, and their chances of it being the right one were greatly improved.

"And even if we do find it, how do we know the driver was involved in the pupnapping?" Pippin continued.

Toby was on surer footing now. "One step at a time," he counselled. "We need to find the vehicle so we can eliminate it from our enquiries." This was a phrase often used on his favourite television shows.

"We could try and talk to the uniformed man Moira pointed out to us," suggested Troot.

"That won't work. Most hoomans don't speak dog," Toby reminded him. "He won't have the foggiest notion what we're on about."

Pippin was even more averse to that idea. "We should avoid anyone in a uniform! You never know. They might be a dog warden!"

The three dogs shuddered in unison.

"What next, then?" Troot asked. "We're not giving up yet?"

"Certainly not!" Toby said. "Our enquiries are in the tricky early stages, that's all." He considered their options. "We could go out to High Street, opposite the park, and watch the traffic going by." He could do with a bathroom break and that would be the best place to take one. "Or—" he faltered. "I have a friend in the police—"

Pippin sucked in her breath.

"He's alright, is DC Plum," Toby reassured her. "He might help me."

"Where would we find him?" Troot asked.

"At the police station if he's not out and about," Toby replied, a little doubtful. "It's not far from the park."

"We could kill a few birds with one stone," said Pippin, brightening at the idea. Even she enjoyed a jaunt around the park.

"Why would we want to do that?" Toby asked, aghast. "What have the birds done to us?"

Pippin tutted. "It's a figure of speech."

"Oh." Toby was relieved. "Hokay." He gazed longingly at the bin, but it hadn't yet been replenished with discarded treats. "Let's go."

On their bellies, the dogs slunk out from beneath the wooden bench and made their way back to the side of the market known as Draper's Row, in the direction of the shops, sniffing appreciatively at the array of lunchtime aromas. Coloured blinds sheltered the windows and displays here from the rays of the hot sun. Where possible, the dogs mooched along in the shade, hogging the inside of the pavement and causing more than one disability scooter to swerve out of the way to avoid them.

They were almost at the corner of Draper's Row when Toby pulled up short.

"What is it?" Troot asked, blinking back tears after being whipped in the eye by Toby's tail while trying to avoid walking into Toby's furry rump.

"Borlies!" Toby, instantly distracted, stared upwards at a large sack of balls. Some were the size of tennis balls, others the size of footballs.

"It's a pet shop," Pippin informed them.

"A pet shop? Where people sell pets?" Toby hadn't known that was a thing. Food shops, yes. And book shops. Clarissa liked those. Toy shops. He'd seen one of those on the high street. Oh, and a flower shop. But a *pet* shop? Were there shops for everything? Could you purchase new hoomans in a shop?

"Yes. Some small furries. Things you get in tanks. Snakes. That kind of thing. Oh, and things *for* pets." Pippin seemed to know a lot about the subject.

"Wow." Toby lifted the top half of his body and balanced his front paws on the narrow window ledge so he could gaze into the window. Pippin followed suit. Troot, despite his long, poky legs, still wasn't tall enough to see above the lintel.

"What are you looking at?" Troot hissed.

Toby wasn't sure. The inside of the shop was cluttered with cages of all shapes and sizes, tanks of fish, shelving piled high with pet food and accessories, and cat and dog baskets that would fit anyone from the tiniest kitten to the biggest Irish wolfhound.

"Have you ever expawed inside here?" Toby asked, flicking a glance down at Troot.

"Once. I didn't like the way the owner looked at me, so I left."

"Perhaps he was considering how much he'd get for you if he sold you on?" suggested Pippin.

Toby decided that warranted consideration. "Isn't there a law against selling puppies and kittens?" That had been another article Clarissa had been writing. Her angle had been about ethical ways to source familiars in an urban environment.

"Well, well, well. What have we here?" An older man in a long brown stained overall stood in the doorway staring down at the trio. He was slim and sallow, and not particularly attractive and Toby got a dose of the heebie-jeebies just being close to him.

Troot, standing closest to him, stumbled backwards in shock and fell into the road. Quick as a flash, Pippin dropped down onto all fours and jumped after him. Grabbing the puppy by the neck, she deposited him unceremoniously on the pavement between herself and Toby.

Toby, still balancing on his back legs, gazed at the man—the owner, he surmised, judging by the state of his clothing—with curiosity.

"You're a handsome boy, aren't you?" the owner asked.

"It has been mentioned," Toby replied modestly.

"Oh, and you talk!"

Toby perked up at that. If the man was a witch or a wizard, he'd be able to quiz him about Bourgie.

"That's so sweet," the man continued. "Woowoowoo!"

Ugh. That was the kind of thing people said when a dog made noises that they didn't understand. Perhaps the man didn't understand him after all. That seemed likely. Most people couldn't.

"Where are your owners, boys and girls?" the man asked.

Pippin made a low growling noise in her throat. A warning to the others that she wasn't happy with how the conversation was progressing.

"At home," Toby told the man. "Working."

The pet shop owner considered Toby carefully. "There's something special about you—"

"I think we should go," said Pippin.

"What she said," said Troot.

"Would you like a biscuit?" The pet shop owner dug around in his pocket and found a couple of gravy bones. Toby loved gravy bones, but they weren't his favourite favourite. If they'd been cheese, that would have been different.

"No thank you," he said politely. "We've only just finished lunch." Not that *that* would normally have prevented him from tucking in.

"Delicious gravy bones," the man said, stepping closer, attempted a smile. His lips curled at the edges although his mouth remained closed and the smile didn't travel any further than his nose.

Toby squared up to him. "I'm sure you don't mean to encroach on our boundaries," he said and wagged his tail, just to let the pet shop owner that he was still being polite. "As I said, we've just eaten and we were only browsing your window."

The pet shop owner reached out, his fingernails thick with grime and ingrained muck.

"Hey!" Toby jumped away in case the man grabbed his collar. "That's bad manners!" Behind him, Pippin and Troot scattered, heading for the corner of the road.

"Come on, Toby!" Pippin called. "Let's get out of here."

Toby turned to follow them but couldn't resist peering back over his shoulder to give the pet shop owner the benefit of some side-eye. Sniffing haughtily, he sent a little magick the owner's way. "Unravel," he ordered, and the uppermost loop of the string bag containing the balls suddenly unthreaded itself. The net sank lazily and, before the pet shop owner had a chance to react, yawned, opening a wide chasm through which every last ball could escape. They tumbled to the pavement, some of them bouncing high, others not so much, then, carried by their sudden velocity, they bounced off in different directions.

"Hey!" the man yelled, dodging first one way and then the other, reaching for balls that evaded his grasp. As they bobbed away, teasing him with their bright colours sparkling in the sunshine, he gave chase.

Toby, four paws planted firmly on the pavement, laughed fit to burst. The pet shop owner managed to grab one of the football-sized balls, probably because it was underinflated and therefore couldn't travel as far or as well as its companions. Hilariously, once he had a ball in his hand, catching any of the others became impossible.

Toby guffawed. "Great game! Great game!" He'd have loved to join in, jumping around, catching borlies and shooting off down the road, but Pippin was calling his name.

And so was nature.

He needed to get to the park and see to business.

Then he'd go in search of DC Ed Plum.

Wouldn't Ed be surprised to see him?

CHAPTER SIX

A little later, after discreetly attending to business in the park and drinking their body weights in pondwater—delicious!—the three dogs made their way into the car park to the rear of the police station. They sat beside each other in size order, Pippin to the left, Toby in the middle, Troot to the right, observing the comings and goings with interest.

Sunshine Valley Police Station wasn't the busiest branch of Her Majesty's Constabulary by any means—not that any of the dogs would have known that—but there did seem to be steady human traffic. A couple of officers in uniform, a couple who might have been plainclothes detectives. Some obvious local gangsters—Toby surmised this from the baseball caps, the gold chains and teeth and slouched walk—and numerous other seemingly ordinary men and women who may have been reporting crimes but could equally have been serial killers for all anyone looking on would know.

"What's the plan?" Pippin asked. Genuinely a patient dog, she didn't have much interest in humans.

"We need to venture inside and speak to DC Plum," Toby said.

"All of us?" Pippin evidently didn't like the idea of that.

"Well ... no." Toby wasn't sure about going alone. "But there *is* strength in numbers."

"What's to stop them arresting us all?" Pippin asked.

"They're going to arrest us?" Troot whined in alarm.

"Of course not, silly!" Toby cast a warning frown at Pippin. "Why would Ed do that? We're friends."

Troot wagged his tail. "Phew. That's alright then."

"Hmmm." Pippin pressed her lips together.

Toby looked from one to the other and then studied the entrance again. An older man with a flat cap and a cane was navigating the concrete ramp with some difficulty. Toby decided, based purely on the man's appearance, that he'd probably been involved in the Brink's-Mat robbery and had moved to Devon and turned full-time police informant. "Let's just wait for a lull before we go in, shall we?"

"This could take a while," Pippin muttered under her breath. To be fair, the old fella was taking his sweet time, clasping the rail with his free hand and sliding one foot tentatively forward before resting and following it up with his trailing leg.

In unison, the three dogs dropped down to their bellies. It wasn't an entirely unpleasant way to spend an afternoon. The sun was high but behind them, so the cars at their backs threw off a little shadow, allowing them to bask in the warm shade. They each flipped out their tongue, all the better to perspire.

Mr Brink's-Mat had conquered the ramp. He shuffled over to a beaten-up Rover Sterling in a fetching shade of silver and filth, yanked open the door and threw his cane onto the back seat. With that, seemingly unencumbered at last by his disability, he jumped behind the wheel and started the car. It roared into throaty life—the exhaust tentatively held on to the underside of the car by rubber bands—and, small stones scattering in all directions, ripped out of the car park at sixty miles an hour.

"That can't be legal," Toby remarked.

"Any of it," Pippin agreed.

With no-one else in sight, the dogs advanced on the

police station's entrance. The building was old, probably late nineteenth century, but the disabled ramp and sliding glass door were new additions. The original doorway at the front of the building had once opened out onto the street, but the proximity of the road hadn't left enough room to create an accessible entrance. In light of changing legislation, a new architect had flipped the inside of the building about and created this modern alternative. While the front entrance still looked the business with its smart, dark navy door and police light, these days it was a sham. That door didn't open anymore.

Toby led Pippin and Troot up to the sliding door. He'd seen how these things worked. You simply approached them and they would slide open, like Moses parting the Red Sea. You could walk inside without pausing. Unfortunately, it didn't work for Toby. He trotted towards the heavy door at a steady pace and, when it didn't open, bumped his nose on the glass, leaving a perfect outline of his snout.

"Ouch!" He bounced backwards and stared up at the door in surprise.

"Why didn't it work?" Troot asked.

"Lets' try it again," Toby said, and the dogs scampered back a few feet, lined up and walked forwards a little more slowly.

The door remained stubbornly closed.

"Do we have to press something?" Pippin asked, looking around for a button. There didn't appear to be one.

"Maybe we have to stand on something?" Toby suggested. At once, all three of them began investigating the concrete beneath their paws, searching for a hidden catch of some kind.

"I can't see anything," said Troot, turning in circles.

"Stop that, you're making me dizzy," Pippin complained.

"If there's no button on the wall and nothing below our feet, then the only alternative is ..." Toby lifted his head and stared upwards.

"Maybe it's magick," Troot whispered.

"Maybe it's a camera." Toby jerked his head at a small square device above the door. A red light glowed steadily down on them.

"Do you think there's a policeman in there who doesn't want to let us in?" Troot asked.

"I told you they don't like dogs," Pippin said. "We're *canina non grata*."

"Ed likes me," Toby replied firmly. "He'd let me in."

Pippin shrugged. "Well, it doesn't look like he's on duty then, does it?"

"Mmm." Toby frowned and turned about. To the right of the door was a sign. He stepped back to get a better angle, then read it aloud. "Sunshine Valley Police Station. Opening Times. Monday to Thursday, 8.30 to 6. Friday 8.30 to 4. Closed for lunch between 12.30 and 2. In the event of an emergency please call 999, state your location and ask for police."

"What time is it now?" Troot asked.

"Let me just check," Pippin replied, barely able to hide her sarcasm. "Darn it. Must have left my pocket watch at home."

"It seems reasonable to assume that it's after lunch," Toby said. "It's certainly after *our* lunch."

"So they should be reopening soon." Troot pressed his nose against the glass, adding his own snout imprint to Toby's. "I can't see any movement inside."

"Perhaps they're short-staffed," Pippin suggested.

"I dunno about that. Ed seems quite tall to me," Toby replied.

"All hoomans seem tall when you're only twelve inches high," Troot said. "Even the little ones."

"What do we do now?" Pippin asked. "Go back to the park?"

All three of the dogs liked that idea, but Toby had

a feeling that if they did that, the afternoon would be lost to them in a blur of playing, sunbathing, swimming and drinking. There was always a party going on somewhere in the park, with dogs arriving from all over town. That's why they all enjoyed going there so much.

"What about if I try some magick?" he suggested. "I've had some success with opening doors in the past."

Pippin waggled her eyebrows. "Go for it."

Troot barked in excitement. "Do it, Toby! Do it!"

Toby considered the red light above his head and the mechanics of the door. Had he a better understanding of how such things worked, this would probably have been an easier task. He understood that somehow, the light needed to stop being red. If it was anything like the traffic lights and crossings Clarissa insisted they use when crossing the road, that light needed to change from red to green and then the door would open.

Blind faith is a wonderful thing. The key to all magick you set loose in the universe is intent. The greater your intent, the stronger the result. It always helps to have a clear agenda, of course, and that's what Toby chose to focus on.

Red light to green. Door open!

What could be simpler?

Toby took a deep breath, grounded all four paws on the concrete ramp, just as Big Dom had shown him, stared up at the light and envisaged it turning to green. "*Viridis*!"

The red light fizzled and blinked rapidly.

"*Viridis*!" Toby barked.

"*Viridis*!" Troot echoed.

"Oh, hush!" Pippin scolded the puppy. "Don't you start."

The light blinked one more time, then glowed bright green.

"That's a start." Pippin stepped backwards then forwards, testing out whether the door would open.

"*Aperta*!" Toby ordered.

"*Aperta*! *Aperta*!" sang Troot.

Pippin performed her hokey-cokey dance once more, and this time the door slid open with a satisfying hiss.

"That's it! We're in!" Troot scampered through the open doors, with Toby and Pippin close behind him.

"'Allo, 'allo, 'allo!"

Troot applied his brakes and slid to a standstill; Toby and Pippin collided with him and each other. There was a commotion of squeals, whines and some fur flying before the three dogs had sorted themselves out enough to locate the disembodied voice.

A uniformed officer with a rotund belly and cheerful red cheeks had stood up and was now leaning over the reception desk to get a better look at them.

"What's all this then?"

"Good afternoon, officer," Toby said, sitting nicely and gazing up with a clear, earnest expression. Troot followed suit, wagging his tail a little. Pippin, however, rolled her eyes and skulked backwards towards the door.

"How did you three get in here?" The officer frowned at the door. "I could have sworn I locked that." He fiddled with something on his desk that the dogs couldn't see. "I did. We must have a malfunction."

"Sorry, it's not a malfunction," Toby told him. "It was me. We thought perhaps you'd forgotten to reopen after lunch. We were just helping you out."

The officer cast a wary eye over Toby. "You've got a lot to say for yourself, haven't you?" He picked up a receiver and began to punch a number into the phone.

"Just making pleasantries," said Toby. "We won't take up too much of your time—"

"Hi, ma'am, it's Ted here on reception. Sorry to bother you over lunch—what?—yes. Sorry. Erm ... Right. Sorry, ma'am."

He replaced the receiver, slightly redder in the

face than before, and glowered at the dogs. "Thanks for getting me into trouble with the boss. I don't know what she's complaining about. I'm supposed to be on a break too, you know?"

"If you could just ask DC Plum to come down and talk to us?" Toby butted in.

"Pipe down," the officer told Toby. "I can't hear myself think."

"Why would you want to hear yourself think?" Toby asked. "That doesn't even make sense. Thinking happens in your head. *Sounds* happen outside your head. If I were you—"

"Will you can it?" The police officer, looking increasingly flustered, slid the hatch cover up at the side of his desk. At that moment there was a whirr and a click, and a handsome young man, returning a card to his lanyard, stepped out of a side door into the waiting area clutching his sandwich box and a bag of crisps.

"Plum!" the reception officer cried in relief.

"I'm on my break, Ted," Ed said, still struggling to slide his card back in place.

"Aren't we all?" Ted chuckled, his good humour restored now that he had someone else to share his troubles with. "I appreciate that, but we have some unexpected visitors."

Only now did Ed glance up. He clocked the dogs

and raised an eyebrow. Taking a closer look, he frowned. "Toby?" he asked.

"Hi, Ed!" Toby wagged his tail in excitement. "Why haven't you been to see us lately?"

"I've missed you!" Ed enthused, leaning over to stroke Toby while taking in his companions in some confusion.

"Do you know these dogs?" Ted asked.

"I know this one." Ed indicated Toby.

"He's the mouthpiece. I swear he's been trying to talk to me."

"That doesn't surprise me." Ed stood and craned his head to peer through the glass doors. "Is Clarissa here?"

"No, it's just me," Toby said.

"Us," Pippin chimed in.

"Us," agreed Toby.

Ed frowned. "She doesn't seem to be out there. I hope she's alright."

"Who's that? The owner?" Ted held up the receiver of his desk phone. "Want to give her a call?"

"She owns this dog," Ed said, pointing at Toby. "Not the other two. Not as far as I know."

"She doesn't *own* me!" Toby protested. "We *belong* to each other!"

"Should I call the dog warden?" Ted asked.

"I knew it!" Pippin snarled. "You can't trust these people. Come on, Troot. Let's go!" She tossed her head and marched towards the door.

"Wait, Pippin!" Toby cried, then barked at the detective. "Ed! You can't—"

Pippin paused at the door, clearly annoyed.

"No, it's fine." Ed considered Toby and then the other two dogs, his face oddly blank. "I'll sort it." Then, making a tsk tsk noise, he jerked his head towards Toby. "Come on. Let's go outside and wait for Clarissa."

No matter how Toby tried, he couldn't make Ed understand him.

When The Pointy Woman had said, 'speak to none but me,' she'd inadvertently turned him into a talking dog. The problem was that only paranormal beings—meaning witches and wizards, as far as Toby knew—could understand him.

And sadly for all concerned, poor old Ed didn't have a magickal bone in his body.

"What are you doing here?" Ed asked again, peeling the beeswax wrap away from his sandwich and examining the contents.

"I *just* told you," Toby repeated, exasperated by Ed's lack of comprehension. Pippin and Troot looked on quietly, unsure where to place themselves but ready to make a dash for it at the slightest provocation. "One of Troot's friends has been pupnapped. We have a potential lead on the culprit, and we'd like you to look into it for us."

Ed blinked at Toby. "Ted's right. You are particularly vocal this afternoon." He waved half of his sandwich around. "I suppose you're asking for a piece of this?"

"I wasn't," Toby said. "But if you're offering—"

"Goodness, Toby. We're wasting our time here," Pippin remonstrated with her friend. "If he can't help us, let's get going—"

"Does he want a corner as well?" Ed asked.

"He's a she," Pippin snarled.

"Ooh. He's a feisty one." Ed angled his neck to get a better look. "No collar—"

"Grrr!" Pippin growled. "That's it, I'm done."

"Like a ... like a kipper!" said Troot. He at least seemed to be having fun. Puppies are easily distracted.

"Steady, boy," Ed said, and broke off three corners of the same sandwich half. He offered Toby the first corner and Toby, after considering whether he actually needed any more sustenance today, decided that it wouldn't go amiss and daintily extracted it from Ed's fingers. "Mmm. Chicken tikka," he told the other two. "My favourite sammich filling!"

Ed held out the next corner to Troot, who proceeded to take two steps forwards and, when Pippin yipped a warning, three steps back. Ed considered his options, then gently threw the sandwich scraps first to Troot and then to Pippin. Troot fell onto his share ravenously, as though he'd never seen food before, but Pippin only turned up her nose.

"Bread's a bit stale. Sorry about that," Ed continued.

"Can't you help us, Ed?" Toby asked, wondering if there was any way of making Ed spellbound, but only someone with incredible magickal prowess would be able to do that. Toby wasn't that advanced.

Yet.

"I guess I'd better give Clarissa a call," Ed said and, wiping his fingers on a tissue, fished inside the pocket of his smart trousers for his mobile. He placed his lunch box on the wall beside him and hit a single button.

Ooh, speed dial, Toby noticed.

It rang a couple of times, then Ed sat a little taller. "Hi. Cla—? Oh." He pulled the phone away from his ear. "Voicemail," he said, sounding most miserable. "Is she out of town?" he asked Toby.

"No, she's at home in the living room punching the keyboard. Well, she was earlier," Toby told him. Hopefully she hadn't come looking for him.

"Hi, Clarissa. It's ..." He faltered. "Ed. Erm ... Toby's just turned up here at the station and I wondered if you knew he was missing?"

"I'm not missing," Toby told him. "I'm right here."

"He has a couple of friends with him too. I don't know if you know anything about them or if Toby's started running with a pack or something?"

"A pack?" Pippin asked. "Are we a pack?"

"In any case, I'm not sure what to do with them. Probably not worth my while dropping Toby home if you're not there. Perhaps I could put them in the police kennel and you can give me a call back? They'll be moved to the rescue centre after five if I don't hear from you."

Ed thought for a moment. "It would be nice to hear from you anyway. Give us a call back, okay? Cheers."

He hung up.

"Did you two fall out?" Toby asked.

"He did sound a bit needy," Pippin agreed.

"Sheepish," Toby said.

"Sheeps? Where's sheeps?" Troot began some madcap scampering.

Ed watched him for a moment and laughed. "You're a real sweetheart."

Pippin curled her lip again. No-one had ever called her a real sweetheart, not even when she'd been young and sweet. Now, she wasn't exactly old, but she was street hardened. "Behave, Troot," she instructed the puppy, and Troot subsided, settling himself down on Ed's foot and rolling over to show his belly.

"You could do with a bath, mate," Ed said and resumed eating his sandwich, making quick work of it, offering Troot and Toby crust corners but missing out Pippin, who still hadn't scoffed the one he'd tossed her earlier. Finally he slapped his knees. "Right!"

That sounded final. Ed wiggled his foot to free himself from Troot's limp body and pushed himself off the wall. Snapping the lid of his lunch box closed, he straightened his shirt and checked his tie for chicken tikka leftovers. "Let's get you somewhere safe, shall we?" he asked, but as he turned he realised the dogs had disappeared.

Scanning the car park, he spotted Toby at the car park's side exit, staring back at him reproachfully. "Hey, boy?" Ed called. "Come on, don't be afraid."

"You only had to do one thing, Ed," Toby replied. "And that was to listen to me."

Ed whistled. "Here, boy!"

"But here we are." Toby's tail dropped. "You of all people must know that I have no plans to ever go back into a kennel again."

"Toby!" Ed raised his voice as Toby began to turn away.

"Not ever," Toby called back. "You're dead to me now, Ed!"

CHAPTER SEVEN

A*hoooooooooooobra*!

Toby heard the sound of an impressive car horn as Pippin and Troot bounded across the busy main road. He cringed. Pippin was streetwise but she certainly wasn't roadwise.

He decided not to follow them, although he would have used the zebra crossing if he had, and turned his nose for home. The problem with Ed—Dead-to-me Ed, as Toby now thought of him—phoning Clarissa was that at some stage she would pick that voicemail up and start to worry. By heading home, he could allay her fears and indulge himself in a little fuss and perhaps even have a post-lunch snack. Then, when she was lost in her world of words and research once more, he could hit the road, meet up with his friends and resume his Spellbound investigation.

"I'm a pawfectly perfick planner," he told himself, trotting gaily along the pavement, head high, tail wagging, oblivious to the curious looks of passers-by.

Leaping through his personal dog flap in the back door, the one Old Joe had thoughtfully fitted when Toby's constant need to be on the other side of the door he was standing in front of had begun to wear him down, he was surprised to find Clarissa in the kitchen frowning at her phone.

"I can explain," he said.

She looked up, her brow wrinkled. "What have you done now?"

"Nothing really." Didn't she know? And if she didn't, why had she been glowering at her phone?

"An interesting sentence there, Toby," said Clarissa. "Qualifying the word 'nothing' with 'really' means you've essentially done *something*."

Clarissa was too clever for her own good. He sat down nicely, like a good boy, and decided to come clean. "I went to see DC Plum," he told her.

"Ed?" Something complicated happened to her face. Her eyes lit up, then a cloud passed over them, then she frowned, and finally she looked annoyed. Toby had a feeling she was cross, but not with Toby.

"Yes."

"Hmpf."

"Have you two had a falling out?" Toby asked. Clarissa and Ed had been getting on rather well, he thought. Ed had been invited to a couple of picnics with them, and those were Toby's very favourite outings because the food was at floor level. Whoever had come up with that idea had to have been a dog, at least in a former life if not this one.

Toby often sent blessings to that person.

Ed and Clarissa had also gone out a few times in the evenings. Toby had not been invited along. He'd been put out by that, but Clarissa had left the television on for him and there had been snacks and fresh water available, so it could have been worse. If he got bored, he could always nip round to see Mrs Crouch.

"Not really."

Toby pondered on this. Did the word *really* qualify the word *not*? And in that case, did she actually mean yes? How confusing.

"It's complex," she added. "I don't want to talk about it."

Toby slunk closer to her and rubbed his muzzle against her leg. She reached down and scratched between his ears. "Who needs boyfriends when I have you, eh?"

"I'm a boy!"

"Well, yes, last time I checked you were." She giggled.

"And I'm your friend, aren't I?"

"You know you are." She crouched beside him and rubbed his ears between her palms.

Oh, man! *Heaven*!

"In that case," Toby drawled, "I'm your boyfriend."

"The only one I need." Clarissa finished the ear massage and dropped a kiss on the top of his head. "Look at the time! I'm running soooo late. I was just about to make myself some lunch. Are you hungry?"

"I might be persuaded—"

"Stupid question, I know!" Clarissa jumped up and opened the fridge. "Let's see what we have here. Cheese or cheese?"

"Cheese sounds good to me."

"Tomato?" Clarissa rummaged in the salad drawer. "A bit of ropy old lettuce? Hmm."

Ick. Toby stuck his tongue out. You might as well eat grass. It had far more flavour than a supermarket lettuce, with the added bonus that it aided digestion.

One way or the other.

"I'll have cheese and tomato please and thank you," said Toby. Tomatoes were okay at a push. Much better when they were mushed up and slathered over a pizza base.

Juggling half a dozen items, Clarissa hurried over to the counter with the bread bin. "You were telling me about DC Plum," she reminded Toby.

"Oh yes!" *Oh dear.* "About that. He doesn't understand a word I say—"

Clarissa laughed again. "You know that, darling. Why would you expect him to?"

"I need his help."

"You need Ed's help?" Clarissa wrinkled her nose and began rummaging in the cutlery drawer for the butter knife. "Why? Can't I help you instead?"

"You could help me talk to Ed," Toby said. Dead-to-me Ed. He narrowed his eyes. What had the detective been thinking? Threatening him and his friends with *the kennels* of all things.

"I'm not sure—"

Brrrrrrriiiiiiiinnnng!

The doorbell rang. Toby pricked up his ears. Clarissa froze. "Oh no," she said, in a voice so low that even Toby barely heard her.

"Are we expecting somebody?" Toby asked, marching out of the kitchen and into the hall. The glass in the door and the stained-glass side window illuminated the space with a beautiful soft golden glow. A dark silhouette could be seen on the other side.

Clarissa peered around the kitchen door, seemingly reluctant to join Toby in the hall. "I don't think I want to answer it," she whispered.

Toby tipped his head back to stare up at her. She had her lips pressed together in a tight line, her jaw tense. Who could provoke such a reaction in his beloved mistress, Toby wondered.

Brrrrrrrrrrrriiiiiiiiiiiiiiiiiiiinnnnnnnnnnnnng!

The person outside leaned against the bell, then, for good measure, rapped on the door with their knuckles as well. "Clarissa?" a male voice called.

For some reason that Toby couldn't explain, the voice and, perhaps, the aggressive nature of the knocking made his hackles rise. He dropped his head and growled.

"Ah-ah-ah!" Clarissa quickly intervened.

"Clarissa?" the voice called again, louder this time, slightly infuriated.

Clarissa sighed, reached down and grabbed Toby's collar and pulled him along to the front door. "I need you to behave," she warned him, then with her free hand, reached up and pulled open the door.

"Clar!" the young man bellowed and stepped into the house, wrapping Clarissa up in a bear hug.

Stupefied, not sure whether to wag or not, but favouring the no wag option, Toby stared up in surprise. *Clar? Who was Clar? And why, if thirty seconds ago Clarissa had not wanted to open the door, did this person think they could be so friendly towards her?*

"Babe! I've missed you."

Babe? Ewww! Clarissa wasn't old, but she wasn't a baby!

Toby sniffed the air. The faint tang of cigarettes and incense. Patchouli and musk. Leather and wood. Despite the hot weather that Devon had been basking in recently, the young man was wearing heavy black boots and a long green parka with a hood over worn jeans—not particularly clean ones—and a t-shirt. Here was a man who hadn't bathed for a few days. His hair, dyed black, was shoulder length and hooked behind his ears. He had a guitar case slung across his back and a piercing through one eyebrow.

Ouchie.

Clarissa pulled away from the man. "Gordon, I just said in my text—"

The young man, Gordon, rolled his head around dramatically. "That you're *working*. That you're *busy*. That you don't think it's a *good idea* to see me. Yada yada yada."

"All of those things are true—" Clarissa pointed out, and Toby prepared himself to bite into the fleshy part of Gordon's calf if it became necessary.

"I don't know why you're being such a—"

Toby barked once. A stiff rebuke. Nobody talked to his favourite hooman like that.

Gordon caught Toby's eye for the first time. Toby scowled at him.

"Gordon! Don't start, okay?" Clarissa folded her arms across her chest.

They glared at each other for a few seconds until Gordon breathed out noisily and visibly relaxed. "Sorry, babe. I just really wanted to see you. Look, I'll go, okay?" He stepped backwards as though he would leave. Behind him, a beaten-up Volkswagen was parked on the drive. It might once have been silver. Now it had patches of orange and navy where it had been rubbed down and coated with something else. "Could I just get a glass of water?" he asked. "Please?"

Clarissa hesitated, but she was too kind-hearted to say no to such a basic request. Still, Toby could sense her reluctance as she nodded once and stepped away from the door. Gordon stepped inside, closing the door behind him. "Don't want to let the dog escape, do we?"

"I'm not a prisoner," Toby pointed out. "I live here too. I can come and go as I want."

"Ha ha! Cute! He's talking to me, Clar!" Gordon followed Clarissa into the kitchen; Toby remained glued to his heels.

She stood at the sink, filling a glass with cold water. "He won't understand you, Toby," she said, without looking at him.

Interesting.

Toby examined the situation afresh. Here was someone from Clarissa's past, her relatively recent past by the sound of it, but pre-Toby. He wasn't a witch or wizard, but judging by Gordon's age and his style of dress, he and Clarissa had a few things in common. Clarissa favoured a gothic style too. However, unlike Gordon, she was no stranger to the shower and generally smelt of rose and rhubarb and bergamot.

"Sorry, what?" Gordon asked.

"Nothing." Clarissa handed him the glass. "I was talking to Toby." She pointed down. "My dog."

"Your dog? Wow. Things have changed. You never used to have a dog."

"I never used to have a home either, but here I am, with both." She reached down to stroke Toby's head. "Gordon, meet Toby. Toby, meet Gordon."

"Hey, mate! Alright?" Gordon enthused. He leaned over and patted Toby's back. There was no warmth to the touch. No curling of the fingers to stroke the contours of Toby's spine. Gordon quickly removed his hand, stood up again and drained his drink, peering around the kitchen. "Very nice. Bit dated maybe, but a lick of paint and some new cupboards and it would look great. Who did you have to kill to find this place? I'm surprised you can afford the rent on a whole house."

"I didn't kill anyone," Clarissa replied, her tone cold. "My grandfather died and left it to me."

Gordon whistled. "Nice one."

"A 'sorry for your loss' wouldn't go amiss," Toby said. Didn't this hoodlum have any manners?

"I didn't mean to interrupt your lunch," Gordon said. "Cheese, is it? I'm famished."

Clarissa nodded. "I'll make you one."

They sat at the dining table and ate their sandwiches in silence. Or rather Clarissa and Gordon joined Clarissa's laptop at the dining table while Toby sat between them, alternately taking bites out of his sammich and glaring at Gordon.

"How did you find out where I was?" Clarissa eventually spoke into the stillness.

"I called in at the *Sun Valley Tribune* where you

used to work and bumped into Jarvis. He told me you left—"

Clarissa grunted. Jarvis Winslow! She'd been *asked* to leave, but what's a little spin where it suits? "And he gave you my address?"

Gordon grinned. "He knew we're an item—"

"We *were*. Past tense."

Toby reeled. *An item? As in a boyfriend? Not a boy friend? No, Clarissa, no! Not with this chump!* How could she be annoyed with DC Plum when she'd had Gordon in her life? The two didn't compare. In comparison with Stranger-to-the-shower-cubicle Gordon, Dead-to-me Ed smelt like a fresh, salty breeze at the seaside.

"Right. *Were* an item." Gordon gestured vaguely. "And he knew I didn't mean any harm, so it wasn't that difficult to get an address out of him."

Clarissa shook her head. *So much for confidentiality.*

"Where are you working now? I asked Jarvis and he didn't know."

Because it's none of his business, thought Toby. *Just like it's none of yours.*

Clarissa must have thought the same because she shrugged. "I'm working remotely for a newspaper in

London." She changed the subject. "And what about you? Are you working?"

"Bit of this, bit of that. You know."

Bit of nothing, thought Toby.

"Freelance." Gordon sounded vague. "Been travelling. Went to Denmark for a bit—"

"As in a bit on the side," Clarissa spat.

Gordon shifted in his seat. The first time he'd had the decency to appear uncomfortable. "Ah, right. Yeah. You met Freja, didn't you?"

"I did. And how is your ice-blonde goddess these days?" Clarissa's voice dripped with sarcasm. "I take it it's going well?"

"Yeah. No." Gordon curled a lip. "We're not together anymore."

"Oh. Shame."

To Toby's ears, Clarissa didn't sound like she gave two hoots. He snickered quietly to himself.

Gordon leaned forward over the table without pushing his plate away. Crumbs of crusty bread and cheese shavings attached themselves to his t-shirt. "Listen, Clar. The reason I wanted to track you down was to apologise. All the time I was over in Denmark, I couldn't stop thinking about you. Freja was a mistake."

"A beautiful mistake," Clarissa said.

"Beautiful, sure. But she wasn't you," Gordon

cooed. "All the time I was with her, it was you I was thinking about." He reached for Clarissa's hand.

She sank back, picking up her sandwich, deftly avoiding his touch. "That boat has sailed, Gordon."

Gordon's hand remained where it was for a beat, then dropped to the table. He tapped the wood a couple of times. "Of course. I get it."

"Good." Clarissa finished off most of her sandwich then reached down with a corner for Toby.

"Can I ask a favour, Clar? For old times' sake?"

"Sounds to me like you used up all your favours, fren'!" Toby told him. "Time to hitch up your geetar and get the heck out of Dodge—"

"Ha ha! He's such a sweet dog, isn't he?" Gordon attempted to pat Toby's head but Toby squidged further under the table out of his reach.

"You don't touch my hooman and you don't touch me, pal!"

Gordon gasped and withdrew his hand. "Ow! He snapped at me!"

"I did not!" Toby gaped up at Gordon in surprise.

Clarissa hurriedly slid her chair back. "Did he get you?" she asked in alarm.

"Just shaved me, I think." Gordon waved his hand around, too quickly for anyone to see. "A bit dangerous, is he?"

"Not generally. I'm really sorry—"

"It's fine. Rescues can be a bit of a handful, can't they?"

"I'm not a rescue," Toby protested. "And I didn't bite—"

"Hush, Toby!" Clarissa growled.

Why was she taking that fibbing oaf's side? "But—"

Hands on hips, she glared at him. "Do you need a time out?" she asked.

Time out? What? "You can't put me on the naughty step because I won't stay there!" Toby argued.

"Go in the garden!" Clarissa ordered.

"Oh, fine." Toby crawled out from beneath the table. "Take his side, why don't you?" He started the long lonely march through to the kitchen and his escape hatch. "Fine. Fine. Fine!"

"I'm sorry about that. He's not normally bad-tempered," Clarissa was saying.

"Don't worry," Gordon laughed. "He's probably not used to strangers."

"Shall I put the kettle on?" Clarissa asked.

"That would be awesome. Let me help you clear up."

"Crikey, Gordon!" Clarissa guffawed. "That's a first."

Ugh.

Toby, unable to stand another minute in the same house as Greasy Gordon, dived through the flap and into the garden, startling a cat that was stalking the blackbirds in the rear hedge. Toby considered giving chase but, remembering Moriarty, decided to hold back.

At least I know how to be respectful, Toby thought, winding his way down the side of the house, past the tall ladder Old Joe had kept there, and out onto the drive. He took a good look at Gordon's Crapmobile. He had enough magick that he could let down one or all of the tyres, but if he did that it would take longer to get rid of the birdbrained blockhead. Instead, he resorted to an age-old revenge. He cocked a leg on each of the wheels in turn.

Just marking my territory.

"Strikes me that was overkill." A newly familiar voice from above stopped Toby mid flow. Moriarty had taken a perch on top of the garden wall.

"We've got a visitor," Toby grumbled.

"Ah." Moriarty stood and stretched, sheathing and unsheathing her claws. "Like that, is it?"

"Hopefully he's not stopping long," Toby grumbled.

"Well if he did, he wouldn't be a visitor," Moriarty pointed out.

"I'm going to make sure of that," Toby told her.

"Fighting words, my friend." Moriarty grinned, her green eyes glinting. "I do like a warrior."

Warrior? Toby recoiled. He tried to stay away from dog fights. "I'm not sure I'm a warrior. More of a worrier."

"Myself? I quite like a good scrap," Moriarty said. "I'm not above getting my claws out if I need to."

"I'll bear that in mind if I ever require backup," Toby told her.

Moriarty lifted a paw and daintily unsheathed her claws again. Tiny weapons of immense destruction. "Speaking of backup, your little friends came back."

"They did?" Toby hurried through the gate and stared down the road in the direction of the park.

"I think they were put off by the car in the drive."

"Did they say what they wanted?"

"Not to me," said Moriarty. "I mean, why would they? I'm a cat."

Forgetting Gordon for now, Toby bounced with excitement. "Maybe they have a lead."

"They most assuredly were not wearing leads. Or collars, come to that."

"No, I mean, I'm conducting an investigation into a missing puppy."

"Ah, I see! That does sound important," Moriarty agreed.

"I'd better go after them."

"Exhausting." Moriarty yawned. "It's all go with you dogs, isn't it?"

"Until it isn't," Toby agreed. He hadn't had enough naps so far today. Inevitably he'd have to catch up on those at some stage. "Thanks for the information, Moriarty."

"No problem," she purred. "Let me know if I can help in any way. I'm always up for a challenge, and I do love a good mystery."

"Me too!" Toby jumped up towards her and nudged her paw with his nose as a way of saying thanks. "I will do!"

"Ugh! Away with you," she said, but, as he scampered after his friends, she purred a little.

"He normally comes out for his walk any time now." Pippin lay on her belly in the dusty soil and stared out from beneath the hedge, scanning the immediate vicinity for the young dog in question. "When we spoke to him earlier, I told him we'd be back to get details."

"Maybe they're not coming." Toby kicked a leg, trying to get a little more comfortable. They'd been hiding under here for over an hour. It had been his idea and he thought it had been a good one at the time. He recalled that, when Clarissa had been waiting for Big Dom, she'd taken cover under the big weeping willow beside the park's boating lake. If that's what Clarissa thought being surreptitious meant, Toby intended to follow her lead. But it also had the added advantage of sheltering them from the sun. It had been a hot afternoon, but it was much cooler in the hedge.

No wonder his friend Mabel liked to live in one.

Beside him, Troot, curled snugly into a ball, whimpered in his sleep.

"They'll come. Dogs are creatures of habit, and most hoomans are easily persuaded," Pippin said.

Toby scanned the dogs he could see. A couple of Pekingese waded through the long grass not far from their hiding place. A German shepherd was being the bestest boy and walking to heel with his diminutive hooman. In the distance a golden retriever was bouncing towards the lake, his owner in hot pursuit. Too late. Three bounds and an impossibly long *boii-innnng* and the retriever belly-flopped into the water, ducks exploding into the air, quacking loudly in righteous protest, while children ran away screaming.

Such fun!

"There!"

Pippin pushed herself halfway up, jerking her nose in the direction of the tea hut. Toby followed her gaze. At first he couldn't work out what or who he should be looking at—there were far too many cyclists and joggers in the way—but then the crowd parted and he spotted a middle-aged woman in leggings and t-shirt walking in their direction, a phone clamped to her ear. Beside her, off the lead, a tiny corgi trotted at her heels.

"Is he going to be able to shake his hooman off?" Toby wondered aloud.

"She's just lost one dog—not sure she'll let this one out of her sight," Pippin said, and nudged Troot with a hard elbow.

"What? What?" Troot instantly awoke. Jumping to his paws, he cried, "Ready and able and reporting for action!"

"Pipe down, kid," Pippin hissed.

"Perhaps, rather than go in mob-handed, if his hooman is going to be jumpy, I should go alone," Toby suggested.

Troot pouted. "Aww. Why you? Me and him got on well when we met earlier. I could—"

"Out of the question," Toby replied, the tip of his tail wagging kindly. "*I'm* the senior investigator. I need to hear what happened directly from the horse's mouth!"

"Corgi's," Pippin pointed out.

"Right, yes. Agreed. Corgi." Toby shuffled out from beneath the hedge. "You two wait here," he whispered, not that anyone was close enough to hear what they were saying. "I'll be back shortly."

"It's true you're not a very tall dog," Pippin called after him, but Toby ignored the jibe. His legs were more schnauzer than whippet, that was for sure.

"Hey, hey!" He trotted towards the corgi and its owner, tail up and flapping, ears semaphoring at different angles. He'd practised how to be cute in the mirror and had perfected this adorable visage. The woman in leggings smiled down at him but didn't pause her conversation. The little corgi made as though to swerve away from Toby's advance, but Toby greeted him before he could do so.

"I'm Toby," he said. "Spellbound Investigative Services." The more he said this, the more he liked it. It could be the start of a whole new career.

The corgi wagged his tail but looked none the wiser. Of course, Pippin and Troot wouldn't have introduced him that way.

"Bryn," the young dog answered. He had a slight Welsh accent.

"You spoke to my friends this morning. A large fluffy white dog and a puppy about your age who smells of fresh swede and beetroots?"

"Oh, that's right!" The young corgi looked both relieved and concerned at the same time. He had ceased walking but craned his neck to check on his owner as she carried on without him. "I can't stop long."

"I appreciate that," Toby reassured him. "Your owner must be worried."

"She is. She's phoning everyone she can think of. Newspapers. Rescue centres. Vets. Lots of vets."

"Newspapers?" A little light went on in Toby's mind.

"To see if they'll run the story and raise awareness locally."

"Hmm. Good idea, that!" Toby wished he'd thought of it first. "Tell me what happened."

"It was my sister, see. Bron her name is. We were only playing out in the garden and someone stopped at the gate to talk to us. That's not unusual, like."

"So you saw them?"

"If it was this same man, yes. I mean, I don't know who else it could be because it all happened so fast, but I saw this chap ... I've tried to tell my hooman mum but she doesn't know what I'm saying.

She keeps telling me not to be upset and we'll find her."

"What happened?" Toby asked, wondering why Bron had been taken but not Bryn.

"He leaned over the gate to pet her. We were friendly, you know, because we corgis tend to be a friendly bunch, but he took advantage of that. He opened the gate and walked in! I decided that was a step too far and I ran back into the house—the door was open—and barked for my mum, but by the time she came out, Bron had gone."

Toby ran the scenario over in his mind. "You checked the immediate vicinity? Might she simply have run out of the open gate and gone exploring?"

"There's no way she'd have made it very far," Bryn objected. "There wasn't long enough. Besides, as we came out of the door and into the garden, we heard a car speeding away."

"Alright." Toby could only agree this sounded like too much of a coincidence. It seemed unlikely that Bron had run off of her own accord.

"Can you describe the man?"

"Old. Like Father Christmas."

Toby chuckled. "Is Father Christmas the oldest man you can think of?"

Bryn cocked his head, thinking. "He looked a bit like Father Christmas."

"Big belly?" Toby asked.

"No. Skinny as you like."

"Beard?" Toby guessed.

"Yes, a wispy beard. Not full like a cloud like Father Christmas, but straggly and thin. A bit rubbish, in fact. It had things in it." Bryn curled a lip. "Eww. But it was his hair. It was long, and a bit snowy."

"His hair was white?" Toby wanted to know.

"No. More grey. Grey and white but with brown and black."

Toby mulled this over. "Kind of a monochrome rainbow. Anything else?"

"He wore a long raincoat, which I thought was odd given how hot it is. He must have been sweltering in it. My hooman is always complaining about how damp her creases get. I tell her she should pant more."

"I say the same to my hooman." Toby nodded. "What colour was the raincoat?"

"Erm ..." Bryn had to think about this. "A kind of light colour. Might have been grey. Might have been beige. It was filthy though."

"Is there anything else you can tell me that might help? Tattoos? Accent?"

"No tattoos. Nothing unusual about his accent."

That meant he must be local, Toby decided. If the man had had any kind of accent, Bryn would have noticed it.

Bryn was still thinking hard. Suddenly his ears flipped up and his eyes widened. "He had a chip in his front tooth!"

"Excellent!" Toby wagged enthusiastically.

"Bryn? Bryn?" A woman's terrified shriek alerted them to Bryn's owner's sudden awareness of his absence.

"I'll be there now in a minute, mum!" the young corgi shouted. "I gotta go, butt," Bryn told Toby, casting a look up the path.

"Sure, just one more thing," Toby hurried to say. "The car. What did it look like?"

"I didn't see it, I only heard it," Bryn said.

Drat!

"Bryn!" The woman was calling for her puppy.

Bryn turned obediently and began to trot in her direction. Toby ran after him. "Did you notice any unusual vehicles in the vicinity before you saw the man for the first time?"

"No. I really gotta go." He scampered towards the woman, faster now. Toby followed him, but at a distance. He didn't want to be accused of leading the little corgi astray.

"Wait." The corgi slid to a halt. "That's not exactly true. I did see a car. I don't remember … it's all a blur. Just a flash of colour. So bright!"

"Pink?" Toby enquired.

"How did you know?" the corgi asked, ogling Toby with something akin to amazement.

"It's my job to know these things."

"Bryn! My goodness!" The woman had closed in on them. "You scared me to death! Come on."

"Where do you live?" Toby asked as Bryn's human crouched down to clip her lead to him.

"32 Meacham Street."

"I'll be in touch," Toby told the little dog as he was led away.

"Okay, boyo!" Bryn called back. "I hope you find her. She's my sister and she's a pain in the bum but I love her!"

"I'll do my best!" Toby barked as Pippin and Troot joined him. "We all will!"

"What did you find out?" Pippin asked. "Do you think there's a link between this disappearance and Troot's friend?"

"I do," Toby said. "I'm convinced of it!"

CHAPTER EIGHT

Toby jumped through the dog flap and skidded to a stop. So caught up in Bryn's plight and The Case of the Missing Puppies—as he had started to think of it—had he been, he'd completely wiped Gordon's miserable existence from his memory.

But here he was, larger than life and twice as ugly. Perhaps that was ungenerous of Toby, but the fact remained that Clarissa didn't seem that keen on him, and Toby trusted her judgement. Gordon was standing beside the washing machine wearing nothing but a pair of faded navy boxer shorts. Thank goodness for small mercies that he still had those on.

Devoid of clothes, Toby could see he was a slight man, although with well-defined musculature, like a climber. He had a decent tan and lots and lots of tattoos, mainly of Celtic squirls and knots and a few skulls, with the odd bleeding rose thrown in.

The washing machine was humming away, throwing its load this way and that, the suds inside a rather grim shade of off-white. *It's a funny time to do your washing,* Toby thought. Even with it being as warm as it was, there's no way you'd be able to dry it on the line overnight. It would be mid morning at the earliest—

Ugh! Did that mean Gruesome Gordon was staying overnight?

"Is that you, Toby?" Clarissa popped her head into the kitchen. "Must be nearly dinnertime." She winked at him.

"I need to talk to you—" Toby started.

"What are we having?" Gordon spoke over him.

Clarissa looked from Toby to Gordon. "Erm—"

"It's really important!" Toby intervened. Normally the evening's menu would have been top priority for him but for now at least—

"We could grab a takeaway?" Gordon suggested. "To celebrate our reunion."

"We're not reunited," Clarissa replied, sounding cross enough that Toby's ears whipped backwards. "I said you could do your washing and stay here tonight—"

"Reunion in a manner of speaking, is all I meant," Gordon replied testily.

"I've got enough stuff in to do a veggie pasta bake, if you like?" Clarissa offered.

"Not even any bacon or sausage?" Gordon grumbled. "Veggie pasta can be a bit bland."

"Not the way Clarissa makes it," Toby protested. "She makes it spicy! Makes my lips tingle."

"You shouldn't be eating it," Clarissa told him.

"Someone has to help you clean up." Toby smirked. "I doubt whether Gorgeous Gordon would."

"Why shouldn't I be eating it?" Gordon asked. "Just 'cos you don't—"

"Never mind." Clarissa winked at Toby. "I can pop to the shop and get some bacon when I take Toby out for his evening stroll if you don't mind waiting a bit?"

Gordon reached out to switch the kettle on. "Sure. I'll make us a cuppa, shall I?"

"I'm fine. I'll just have water," Clarissa said, watching as he rummaged in the overhead cupboard for yet another clean mug. They were beginning to pile up in the sink. Perhaps Gordon didn't realise that the kitchen was not equipped with a dishwasher, just as it didn't have a tumble drier. Old Joe hadn't been one for mod cons.

Toby nuzzled against Clarissa's leg. "Can we talk?"

"Come through," Clarissa said, pulling away.

"Won't be a minute," Gordon answered.

"I was talking to Toby," Clarissa pointed out.

"Are you really taking him out for a walk? He's been out all day. We could just get on with dinner—"

Toby fixed him with a cold glare. "We *always* go out for a walk in the evening. *Always*."

Gordon shifted uncomfortably. "It's almost like he's talking to me."

"Go figure," said Clarissa and disappeared into the living room to take a seat behind her laptop. "What's up, chuck?" she asked as Toby padded in behind her.

"What I was telling you about earlier? The lost puppy?"

"Oh yes." Clarissa reached down and stroked between his ears.

"Now there are two lost puppies—"

"Aw, that's so sad," Clarissa lamented.

"Perhaps not lost but stolen. I've been investigating."

"You've been investigating?" Clarissa stopped stroking and leaned over to get a better look at his face. "You're not getting into trouble, are you?"

"No!"

"Only we had that conversation earlier—"

"I know. No. I'm not getting into trouble. I'm just trying to find out who has stolen the puppies. I could really do with your help, Clarissa."

"Help, how?" Clarissa asked. "What do you want me to do?"

"Bryn—he's the brother of the latest puppy to be stolen—told me that his owner has been trying to get a piece written in the local paper about her puppy's disappearance."

Clarissa raised an eyebrow at this. "The *Sun Valley Tribune*?"

"I assume so."

Clarissa pulled her laptop towards her and quickly typed. "Have they run it?"

"I don't think she was having much luck getting them to bite."

"No ... I can't see anything on their website. Hmm." Clarissa pulled her notebook in front of her and flipped through to a blank page. "You know how much I'd enjoy getting one over on that publication."

Toby beamed. Just as he'd thought.

He nudged Clarissa's calf. "The other thing is, like I said earlier, I could do with picking DC Plum's brains. What he has there, at any rate."

"Ed?" Clarissa pulled a face.

Dead-to-me Ed, yes. "Please. I'm not asking you to have dinner with him." The goddess forbid. "Or even" —he cast a sly glance towards the kitchen—"make veggie pasta with bacon for him."

"Ha ha, clever clogs! Alright. We'll see if we can have a word with Ed. But first—" She reached for her mobile, tapped the screen, then scrolled through her list of contacts.

Holding her phone to her ear, she doodled on the blank page in front of her until someone picked up. "Hi, Rowena," Clarissa said. "Yes, thanks. You? Yes. Yes. Awesome. No. Right?" Toby listened to Clarissa making polite small talk. Remarkably polite and small because Rowena was her no-nonsense, high-powered, busy sub-editor of *The Celestine Times*. "Sure. No, the reason I rang is because there's something going down here that may be of interest, I'm not sure."

Clarissa nodded into the receiver as though her boss could see her. "Puppy theft," she announced. She nodded again. "I'm not sure if there's a paranormal angle—"

Clarissa bared her teeth at Toby as her boss rattled on. "No problem. Absolutely. Okay. Thank you. Take care. Bye. Bye." She slapped her mobile down on the table. "She'll give me a square column inch."

"Wow." Toby did a double take. "Just an inch? Can

you imagine the headlines if this were hooman babies going missing?"

"That would be quite the hoo-ha," Clarissa agreed. "The thing is, Tobes, this could be something or nothing, but at least now I can take a little look at it and we'll see what we can find out, eh?"

"You talk to that dog a lot." Gordon was leaning against the door jamb, mug in hand, looking less than impressed.

Clarissa smiled. "He's my best friend."

Toby wobbled his head, basking in the glow of Clarissa's love. "Right back atcha!" he said.

"All that woo-woo-wooing and arf-arf-arfing would drive me up the wall," Gordon said. "As a matter of fact, it already is."

"The front door's that way," Toby pointed out, perfectly courteously.

Clarissa put a hand on his shoulders. Part warning, part comfort.

"It's never a problem when it's just the two of us," she said quietly, and Toby understood the implicit meaning of her words. She didn't like Gordon being here any more than Toby did.

Gordon grunted. "About that bacon?"

CHAPTER NINE

"Tell me about Gormless Gordon," Toby said.

He had submitted to being on the lead because he knew Clarissa liked to feel as though she had control over his movements. She didn't, of course. Hooman power over their canines is an illusion. Clarissa was undoubtedly aware of this, but they kept up the pretence anyway.

It looked good for their mundane neighbours.

They were strolling in the direction of the park, as they did every night when Clarissa was at home. It was a beautiful evening, and the sunset promised to be magnificent. The sky was already turning gold and peach with that special shimmering light you only have when the day has been long and hot and glorious. The scent of mimosa and lavender, rose and jasmine fragranced their journey. Flies and bees and gnats and mosquitos—bless their little hearts—swarmed lazily around them as they walked, buzzing and zuzzing but tending to mind their own business. It was pleasant.

Except Toby was struggling to get Gordon out of his mind.

"You shouldn't be calling him names," Clarissa chided him. "That's not nice."

"I'm just saying what I see," Toby clarified. Recently, he'd been watching *Catchphrase* on catch-up telly in the mornings and that's what the presenter told the contestants to do. "Labelling parts, so to speak." And he'd been reading war poetry when he lay down in his basket at night.

He liked to keep his brain active, did Toby.

"Gordon's not 'a part', Toby." Clarissa trailed her hand against a lavender bush as they walked by, then inhaled the scent lingering on her fingers. "Mmm."

That's your opinion, thought Toby. He begged to differ. "Tell me about him, though."

"I met him at university. He was on my course in the first year. He dropped out after that but we began seeing each other. We were together on and off for about five years."

Ewww! He'd been Clarissa's special boyfriend? Yuck. And for ages! Double yuck!

"You had a lucky escape," Toby decided.

"We were living together until just before I met you."

"Did you kick him out?" Toby asked.

"You're incredibly nosy." Clarissa sounded a little annoyed. "No. He left."

Ah, the Fridge girl from Deutschmark. Or somewhere. "No great loss," Toby couldn't resist saying.

"Don't be mean."

Toby badly wanted to share his thoughts on Gordon but, given Clarissa's current level of angst, he decided that might not be the best idea. Not right now. He clamped his jaw closed and they carried on walking in silence.

It wasn't until they were waiting for the lights to change at the crossing opposite the park that Clarissa spoke up once more. "I was quite hurt when he left. I didn't expect it, and he didn't say anything about how he was feeling. I came home from work one day and there was a note on the table to tell me he'd decided to go travelling. It was only afterwards that I discovered he'd gone off with this ... this ..." Clarissa practically spat the words out, "Danish girl."

A girl made of Danish pastries? Toby licked his lips.

"I knew it wouldn't work. I kept expecting him to come home with his tail between his legs—"

Gordon had a tail? Whoa! That was news to Toby.

"And he didn't." Clarissa sniffed. Toby peeked up at her. Were those *tears*? "Eventually I gave up expecting him to and, I suppose, I realised it was all over and it was time to get on with my life. I thought I was alright. Finding you. Meeting ... Ed."

The lights changed and the green walk symbol lit up. Clarissa, lost in her thoughts, didn't make a move.

Toby wiggled his eyebrows in consternation. Should he mention the fact that the lights had changed and they had a mere thirty seconds to cross the road before the boy racers began to drive past them at the speed of sound once more? Or should he allow Clarissa to dwell on Dead-to-me Ed?

Toby tried some telepathy—not a skill he had thus far mastered. *If the world was ending and you could only save one other person—and one dog but that would be me, naturally—would you choose Dead-to-me Ed or Ghastly Gordon?*

"And look how that turned out!" Enraged, she stepped off the kerb and onto the crossing. Toby hurried to go with her. The amber light was flashing. Three seconds until they were squished into jam doughnut filling.

Both Clarissa and Toby jerked sideways in response to a loud and annoyed beep from their right. A black Mercedes had edged onto the crossing. Clarissa glared at the driver—a guy a little older than her, wearing a backwards baseball cap and a pair of mirrored sunglasses—and he beeped again in response, waving his hands as though that would move her on a little faster.

Ducking her head to get a better look at him, she yelled, "It's my right of way, numbnuts!"

As the traffic light turned green, Toby hurriedly yanked on his lead, pulling her to the other side. The driver, revving his engine hard, prepared to zoom away.

Clarissa flipped out a finger. "*Deflate*!"

Halfway over the crossing, all four of the Mercedes' tyres deflated at once.

"Oops," muttered Clarissa, and with a little toss of her head, stomped away. Toby remained where he was momentarily—watching the look of astonishment and fury on the driver's face—before the lead tightened and he was tugged after Clarissa. As he rushed to catch up, the car behind the Mercedes honked.

"Get that blasted thing off the road!" someone yelled.

What goes around, comes around, eh?

Safely in the park, Clarissa leaned over to unclip the lead. "Men! Meh!" She laughed softly. "Don't ever turn into one like that, darling."

"I won't!" promised Toby, and skipped off to check his pee-mails.

Pippin and Troot were waiting for him on the top of The Mountain.

It wasn't a real mountain; in fact, it hardly passed as a hill because it was only a slight rise in the ground, but it had become known by that name because during the winter, if there was even the merest hint of snow, the local kids liked to bring their sledges, or dustbin lids or mum's best baking tray, and slide down. Again and again and again.

Of course, for approximately 364 days of the year, this just wasn't possible. The south-west coast of England doesn't see much in the way of snow, and when it does, it doesn't hang around long.

Instead, kids occasionally used it for mountain biking, but the park authorities frowned on that activity and had instead provided trails they could tear around on. That left The Mountain pretty much free for Toby at this time of day. Tonight, he fully intended to utilise it for his own means.

With Clarissa over by the tea hut, drinking coffee and chatting with the lady who worked there, Toby was free to do as he wished. He lifted his snout into the air and began to bark.

You'll have heard of the Twilight Barking. Dodie Smith spilled that secret many, many years ago—and you'll have probably noticed the dogs in your own neighbourhood engaging in such activity. Of course, it's not merely relegated to twilight—it can be done at any time of the day—but most dogs like to do it once their owners are fed and drowsy, or otherwise engaged with evening activities that keep them occupied and out of the way. No dog wants to be in the middle of communication, only to be told to 'shut up and go and lie in your bed'.

"Hey there, friends!" Toby started. "Listen up! I need your help. Anybody there?"

Somewhere close by, from the direction of the pitch and putt section of the park, a dog quickly answered him. "I can hear you. I'm Buddy the dachshund."

"Hi, Buddy! Toby, the schnauzer-collie-whippet-terrier-thingie here. Please relay what I say. I need this to go viral!"

"I can hear you too!" The deeper bark of a big dog, sight unseen. "I'm Crispin! I'm in!"

"Listen up, good dogs of Sunshine Valley!" Buddy yapped. "Good buddies, come back!"

Crispin added his throaty bark to the mix.

From further afield, outside the park, more answering greetings. Toby cocked his head, listening. A ring of barking, yapping, howling and arfing could be heard, wave upon wave of dogs joining in, answering Buddy's greetings, then sending their own further afield. On they would go, relayed from dog to dog, an endless tsunami of canine communication, far beyond what Toby, even with his acute hearing, could discern.

"It's Toby here from Spellbound Investigative Services," Toby began. "Tonight I'm asking for your help. Two of our own—two puppies!—have been whisked away from their loving hoomans!"

"Puppynapping?" Crispin barked back. "Are you sure?"

"Shocking!" Buddy added.

"I'm absolutely sure. I'm investigating the case and I need everyone's help."

"Anything I can do, I will," barked Crispin.

"Anything!" Buddy agreed.

"Get this message out there!" Toby instructed

them. "Spread it far and wide. I need to know about any sightings of the puppies. They're called Bourgie and Bron. And, if anyone hears about any other puppies going missing, you need to let me know about them as well! If anyone can help in any way, get back to me. I'll be here again, same time tomorrow. Or you can find me on Chamberlain Drive. Just watch out for dog wardens!"

"Really, Toby," Clarissa was climbing The Mountain, a paper cup in her hand, his lead in the other. "Do you have to be so noisy?"

"Stay safe out there!" he barked.

"Stay safe? Who are you talking to?" Clarissa had reached the summit; now she inhaled deeply and swung about, simultaneously admiring the sunset and listening to the dogs barking in the distance. "Goodness me, it's busy out there tonight. Did you start all that?"

"I did," Toby told her. "I'm asking for more information on the missing puppies."

"That's a great idea," Clarissa smiled. "A kind of Facebook community page for dogs."

"I've been on the Sunshine Valley Facebook community page for dogs and it's full of dogs asking for recommendations for the best doggie ice cream, whinges about dogs not being allowed on the beach between the first of May and the end of September and complaints about the kennels in the area. It's a poopshow of negativity. I prefer not to demean myself by hanging out there." He gestured with his nose vaguely in the direction of the countryside beyond the town. "The old-fashioned ways are by far the best."

"I'll take your word for it," Clarissa said. "If you've finished your business for this evening, we'd better make a move. I need to buy some bacon before the Spar closes."

"You don't have to cater to Gauche Gordon's every whim—"

"Hush, Toby. He's our guest. Just for tonight. Let's get going, shall we?"

"If you insist." Toby wagged his tail like the obedient, good boy he tried so hard to be. As Clarissa started down the steep slope, Toby turned once more and barked his final address. "Toby out!"

Head high, ears cocked, all the better to hear the cacophony of conversations ongoing across Sunshine Valley, he trotted after her.

It had been a good night's work.

CHAPTER TEN

"Ed?" Clarissa, entering the living room from the hallway, a packet of bacon in her hand, stopped so suddenly that Toby ran into the back of her. Peering around her legs he realised that DC Plum was perched on the sofa, in the hallowed place where Toby liked to lounge and watch the television.

Greasy Gordon was sitting in Old Joe's armchair.

Toby growled.

Clarissa dropped her free hand and shushed him with a soft stroke.

"Hi!" Ed, flushing, leapt up. "I didn't mean to intrude. Your ..."—he gestured awkwardly at Gordon—"friend let me in."

"Boyfriend," Gordon volunteered.

Clarissa stared at him, totally aghast. "Gordon!"

"Oh, I'm sorry. Is it a secret?" Gordon smiled up at her from the sanctity of the armchair.

"That's not—" Clarissa began to say but Gordon jumped in again.

"Oh, brilliant. You brought home the bacon. Shall we get dinner started?"

Ed grimaced. "I'm so sorry. It *is* late. I didn't think—"

"It's absolutely fine!" Clarissa answered, and now her cheeks had turned red too.

Toby frowned. It wasn't fine. Not at all! Having Gordon in their house, telling Dead-to-me Ed that he and Clarissa were an item, was certainly not fine!

"I should have called ahead—" Ed made a move towards her, or rather the door, but Clarissa was still standing in the way.

"That's cosy," Gordon interrupted. "That the local constabulary have your number, Clar! You often in trouble?"

"Not at all!" Ed blustered, rushing to Clarissa's defence.

"Well don't you worry, officer," Gordon said, hanging his leg over the side of the armchair and lounging with an unwarranted familiarity. "I'm back now, and I'll make sure she stays on the straight and narrow."

Ed glanced uncertainly at Clarissa, then back at Gordon. "Right."

Clarissa glared at Gordon. "Why don't you go and get dinner started?" she asked, handing him the bacon.

"I don't know where to find anything," Gordon whined.

Clarissa shook her head. "Just open the cupboards. Everything you'll need is there somewhere."

Gordon remained where he was, staring at Clarissa. Toby found himself desperately wanting her to deflate Gordon's ego as easily as she had deflated the tyres on the Mercedes, but she simply took a sharp breath and turned back to Ed. "I'll see you out," she said.

Toby trotted to the front door with them, glancing up at Clarissa anxiously. "You have to ask him to find out about the puppies," he told her.

Clarissa shushed him with one of her 'looks'. Instead, she asked Ed, "Why did you come?"

Ed shrugged, looking bashful. "I wanted to see if you were alright," he answered.

"Why wouldn't I be?" Clarissa's response was sharp, unusually so. Toby had a feeling she was a bit miffed all round, what with Gordon behaving so rudely and Ed turning up when she didn't expect him.

"No reason." Ed lowered his voice. "It's just since I had to ..."

"Stand me up."

Wincing, Ed nodded. "Okay, it's just that you haven't been particularly communicative since I had to ... as you say, *stand you up* ..."

"Well, there you have it, Ed. I don't like being stood up. Show me a woman who does."

"I apologised, Clarissa! I was ... am ... really sorry. It's the job. Sometimes ... I just couldn't get away ... my DI ..."

"It's fine." Clarissa raised her palms. "Don't worry about it."

Ed nodded. Clearly he *was* worrying about it. His shoulders sank and his pained expression gave him away.

Clarissa opened the door and the three of them walked out onto the drive, where Gordon's Crapmobile was sitting. Ed studied it with the eye of someone who knows how to write fixed penalty notices.

"Ask him about pink Fiat 500s, Clarissa," Toby piped up.

Ed stared down at Toby, listening to the dog's noises. Shaking his head, he asked Clarissa, "Did you get my voicemail earlier?"

"Erm ..." Clarissa had completely forgotten to listen to it.

Ed interpreted that as a no. "Toby came to see me at lunchtime. With a couple of friends."

"Yes ...?" Clarissa hesitated.

"Ask him!" Toby barked.

"Shush," she said to Toby.

"He's pretty vocal today, isn't he?" Ed smiled. He was on safer ground discussing Toby rather than his relationship non-status with Clarissa, that much was clear.

"Clarissa?" Gordon's plaintive cry drifted out of the house.

"I didn't know you were seeing someone else," Ed said.

"I'm not," Clarissa told him, even though all indications were to the contrary. "And I wasn't. Haven't been. While we were ... are ... whatever." Her voice trailed away.

Toby stared up at two of his favourite hoomans. *Perhaps they should try a little Twilight Barking, enhance their communication skills*, he thought. *Does it really have to be so complicated*? Clarissa liked DC Plum. Dead-to-me Ed liked Clarissa.

There.

They could be special friends, and that would be smashing.

Fixed it!

Ed held Clarissa's gaze for a moment.

"Clar?" Gordon had raised his voice.

The spell was broken. Not that there had been a spell. Well, not one that Toby had cast. Or Clarissa, come to that. Toby pondered for a moment. *Do love spells cast themselves? Or is there a witch or wizard somewhere sprinkling magick love dust?*

"I should go," Ed said, although Toby suspected he didn't really have anywhere to go, apart from the pub or his empty house. That's why he needed Clarissa to be his friend.

Clarissa nodded and stepped away from the DC.

Toby whined and she dropped her gaze to him. "Please ask him," he reminded her.

"Toby wants to know if you've heard anything about someone stealing puppies?"

Ed frowned. "Puppies? I don't think so." His brow creased. "Oh. Wait. Yeah. There was something about a stolen dog on the bulletin this morning, but it's not my case. It might not be anybody's case."

"Even if there's more than one stolen puppy?" Clarissa, rightly, sounded outraged.

"I hadn't heard there was more than one," Ed said.

Clarissa indicated Toby. "There is. Toby knows there is."

Ed hesitated. "I know you love dogs and you're concerned, but ... it's not really my area of expertise." When Clarissa narrowed her eyes, he hastily added, "but I can certainly ask the desk sergeant tomorrow. Maybe find out who is investigating."

"Ask about the pink Fiat 500," Toby prompted.

"There might be a pink Fiat 500 involved somehow. Toby—we—were wondering if you could do a bit of digging into who owns a car like that?"

Ed glanced thoughtfully at Toby. "It's almost as if —nah." He shook his head. "How do you know about the car?"

"I'm doing my own research. Asking around," Clarissa told him. "I'm going to write a piece for *The Celestine Times*."

"It was seen in the vicinity—" Toby told her.

"Yes. It was seen in the vicinity of the puppynappings. Both times." Clarissa checked with Toby. He nodded, his face serious.

"I'm not sure—" Ed began, but one look at Clarissa's face and he backed down. "Of course. I'll look into that."

"Thanks, Ed." Clarissa favoured him with a smile, albeit only a fleeting one.

Ed nodded, glanced down at Toby again, opened his mouth to say something, closed it and started for the gate.

"Ed?" Clarissa stopped him.

The DC turned around. "Yes?"

Clarissa breathed. "About Toby—"

"Yes?" Ed repeated.

"Clar?" Gordon, inside, sounded annoyed now.

Clarissa stopped herself. "Nothing. Nothing. See you soon," she said and, turning her back, walked inside. "Come on, Toby."

Ed and Toby exchanged glances. "Don't worry," Toby told Dead-to-me Ed. "I'll get shot of Gormless Gordon for you."

You watch me.

CHAPTER ELEVEN

"Seriously?" Ed stared down at the dogs waiting at the rear entrance of the police station.

Pippin, Troot, Toby and Bryn stared right back at him.

"There appear to be more of you than before," Ed said, counting heads. "What? Are you multiplying or something? Like gremlins? Don't feed them after midnight—"

"You can feed us any time you like," said Toby. "We won't complain."

"What are you doing here, Toby?" Ed asked, his voice edged with exasperation. "You're aware you can't ... Wait! What am I even saying? Why am I asking you?" He fished in his pocket for his mobile phone.

"Clarissa must be aware that she can't allow you to run free all day. Surely!"

"Don't be difficult, Ed. I just need some information. You promised me—*us* if you include Clarissa—that you were going to find out about the Fiat." Toby sat at the DC's feet, gazing up at him. "I'm here to collect on that promise."

Pippin passed an admiring glance over the heads of Troot and Bryn. "You're beginning to sound like *The Godfather*."

"I'm gonna make him an offer he can't refuse," Toby growled in what he hoped was a Sicilian accent. "The Pointy Woman sleeps with the fishes. Hey! I could get into this role."

"Forgeddaboutit. You're far too cute," Pippin retorted. "And even your daft Italian accent sounds West Country. You're more Wurzel than mobster."

"Oh ar?" Toby poked his tongue out.

"Hi? Clarissa?" Ed said, and all four dogs craned their heads to watch him as he spoke into his phone. "I've got Toby here—"

Toby waggled his eyebrows and sighed dramatically. "She knows that, Ed," Toby told him.

"Oh, you know?" Ed asked in response to Clarissa's burbled tone.

Toby tapped Ed's shiny shoe. "She wants you to tell me what you've found out."

"I've only just arrived at the station—" Ed was explaining.

"How long? Erm ... I don't know. How long's a piece of string?" Ed jerked the phone away from his ear as Clarissa responded with some heat. "Sure. No. I know. You're a busy person too." He listened again. "Really?" He looked down at the four dogs waiting patiently in front of him. "But—" He moved the phone away from his ear again and grimaced. "Okay. Okay. If you say so. Bye."

Taking a deep breath, he clutched the phone to his heart. "Would you say Clarissa is under a lot of stress at the moment?" he asked Toby.

Toby shrugged. "Wouldn't you be if Grungy Gordon was sleeping in your spare room? He hadn't even woken up when I left this morning, let alone showered or had breakfast."

Oblivious to Toby's answer, Ed carried on. "She wants me to look into the puppy theft—"

"Thefts!" Toby reminded him. "Emphasis on the ssssss, Dead-to-me Ed!"

"—and tell *you* what I find out."

"What's wrong with that?" Toby asked. "Clarissa has a story to file for her paper before midday. She couldn't come down here herself to chase you. She asked me to do it because she was tired of me nagging."

"If that's not the most insane thing I've ever heard, I don't know what is." Ed took a few steps towards the sliding door. The dogs shuffled along with him, bunched together to avoid getting their tails caught when the door closed on them.

Ed halted. "You lot can't come in here," he told them.

"Why not?" Troot asked.

"He wants to see inside the police station," Toby told Ed. "He wants a grand tour. Cells and all."

The dogs tittered together. "I don't need to see the hooman cages. I've had more than enough of dog cages to last several lifetimes," said Troot.

"Amen to that," Pippin agreed.

"You'll have to wait outside in the car park," Ed continued.

There was a chorus of whines. Ed did a double take. "I swear you lot understand every word I say!"

Toby rolled his eyes. "Do you know hoomans have to go to school for a minimum of eleven years?"

"Eleven years?" Bryn squeaked. "I did eight weeks at puppy school!"

"And you're still quicker on the ball than this muppet," Pippin told him.

"I didn't go to school at all!" Troot announced, waiting for Pippin to praise him too.

"Least said, soonest mended in your case," she told him, and Toby and Bryn laughed.

"Go on. Outside with you noisy lot. Shoo, shoo!" Ed gestured them out of the way and the four dogs reluctantly did as they were told.

"I'm counting on you, Ed!" Toby called as the others retreated. "Don't let me down."

"I'll be as quick as I can," Ed told him, then shook his head and disappeared inside the station. "I don't know why I'm negotiating with a dog—"

"And don't forget the Fiat!" Toby barked after him. "Bright pink!"

Toby lay beneath the outstretched limbs of an enormous chestnut tree at the edge of the car park. The day was young and the air was relatively cool, but the sun had already started to climb and there wasn't a cloud in the brilliant blue sky. It was going to be another hot one, so it would pay to preserve the energy in his tank.

As Troot and Bryn began digging at the base of the tree—Troot claimed they would find treasure there and Bryn was easily swayed—Toby caught Pippin's eye. "You didn't hear anything on the Dawn Barking, did you?" he asked her.

"No," she answered, and began licking her feet. In between the gentle strokes of her tongue, she added, "The news is still getting out there. We might hear more this evening."

Toby blinked as he was showered in dry earth. "Oi!" he yapped. "I don't want a barf, thank you very much!"

"Sorry, Toby!" Bryn called back, instantly contrite.

Troot merely giggled. The little scamp.

"What does your hooman think of you being out without her?" Toby asked Bryn. This had suddenly occurred to him; he hadn't thought to ask before.

"She doesn't know," Bryn said sheepishly. "She's gone to work. I did a sneaky."

"Oh, crikey." Pippin covered her eyes with her—now clean—paws.

Toby couldn't quite believe what he was hearing. "Bryn! If she finds out you're missing so soon after Bron disappeared, she'll have kittens."

Bryn widened his eyes. "I don't want to live with cats!"

"Then you'll have to go home," Pippin told him. "What were you thinking?"

"But I want to find out about the tatty Father Christmas!" Bryn protested.

Toby and Pippin looked at each other, unsure what to suggest.

Sensing victory, Bryn demonstrated his best puppy dog eyes. "I'll go straight home afterwards, I promise."

"He shouldn't even be wandering the streets alone at his age," Pippin mused.

Toby indicated Troot, who had dug halfway to Australia. "He does."

"He's streetwise. I was too, at his age," Pippin answered. "I keep an eye on Troot. But Bryn has a proper home and hoomans who care for him. He shouldn't be out and about by himself."

"Straight home as soon as we hear the news," Toby agreed. "We'll walk him home."

Thrilled to have a respite, Bryn went back to helping Troot find treasure.

An hour passed. And then another. Cars came in and out of the car park. Humans walked in and out of the doors. The air began to heat up. Troot and Bryn abandoned their pursuit of treasure and lay on their bellies, tongues out, panting noisily.

"You're making me feel hot," Pippin complained.

Toby snapped at a couple of bluebottles that dared to land on his head. What were they insinuating about his smell and general level of cleanliness? He'd had a barf two weeks ago. He wouldn't need another one for ages!

"Whoop! Look!" Pippin jumped to her feet. Troot barked—at nothing—and followed suit. Toby, satisfied he'd put the fear of dog into the flies, lifted his head. Ed, clutching a bottle of water and his notepad, was making his way out of the police station, standing aside to let an elderly woman with a walking frame enter first. He pivoted, searching for the dogs. Pippin gave a sharp bark, alerting Ed to their position, and he strolled over.

"Hey, guys," he said, reaching down to fuss the puppies. "Nice and cool under the tree here, eh?" He checked the ground for any smelly surprises, then flopped himself down. Instantly, the puppies swarmed over him, licking his face and biting his ears. Laughing, Ed tried to fend them off. It took a while—they were overly excited to see him—before he could free his hands and pick up his notebook. Troot snuggled under his arm, looking at the page. "Are you reading what I've written?" Ed asked.

"I can't read," Troot volunteered.

"I can," said Toby, and moved into place beside Ed so he could see what the DC had scrawled there.

"I can't quite believe I'm going to discuss this with

you guys," Ed said, casting a covert glance back at the station as though he was worried someone might be watching them. "But here goes nothing." He sighed. "I've spoken to a colleague, and she confirms we've had reports of four potential puppy thefts. So there's that."

"14 Coronation Gardens," Toby read. "A Chihuahua cross poodle called Lucy. And 64 Valley Heights, a red setter named Fred."

"Red Fred? Must be a communist," said Pippin.

"I doubt a red setter in Sunshine Valley is a communist. Especially one living in Valley Heights!"

"You never know." Pippin tapped her nose with a paw. "Fur coat and no knickers. That's all I'm saying."

Ed took in the exchange between the two dogs and frowned. "What are you saying to each other?"

"Flip the page, Ed," Toby said, nudging his hand. "What else have you got?"

Ed, suddenly suspicious, clamped the notebook against his chest. "The reason it took me so long to get the information is that you have no idea how many Fiat 500s there are in the area. However, I must admit that pink ones are a rarity. I have found one. A young lady driver. I'll pay her a visit later."

"Can we come?" Toby asked.

"I doubt she's a puppy snatcher though," said Ed.

"He's not offering to take us," Pippin noted.

"And he's not showing us the address." Toby pawed at Ed. "Show me, please," he whined.

"That's all I have for you. I have no idea why Clarissa wanted me to tell you this, but ... I like her. A lot."

"That's sweet," Toby replied. "If you can persuade her to get rid of Grimy Gordon, maybe you can work your way back into her good books. You know what they say, Ed? You scratch my back and I'll scratch yours."

Pippin seemed doubtful. "Do you think he wants a back scratch?" she asked.

"I love a good back scratch," said Bryn. "And ears. And belly."

Ed popped open his water bottle and took a long swig. All four dogs stared at him. "What?" he asked. Pippin dribbled.

He grunted. "Are you lot thirsty? I suppose you must be, given the temperature already." Glancing around, he added, "I don't have anything I can use as a bowl." He tipped a little water onto the ground. The dry earth sucked it away instantly.

"Hmm." He offered the bottle to Toby first, tipped it and allowed Toby to drink from the opening. Toby lapped politely until Ed righted it once more.

"Next?" He offered it to Pippin, who backed away.

"Aren't you thirsty?" Toby asked.

"I'll visit the lake in the park," Pippin answered. "That meets my needs. Duck feathers and golden retriever fur and all."

Troot squirmed out from beneath Ed's arm. "I'd like some!"

Ed tipped the bottle once more, and Troot, little pink tongue darting in and out, showed Bryn what to do. Once Bryn had enjoyed his share, the dogs were ready to go.

"Thanks for your help, Ed," Toby called over his shoulder as he led his team away. *Maybe-Not-Quite-So-Dead-To-Me Ed, now?*

Ed remained where he was, sitting in the shade of the horse chestnut tree with his empty water bottle, staring after the dogs as they ambled towards the main road.

"How was your day, Ed?" he asked himself. "Surreal," he answered. "Totally surreal. And it's not even eleven o'clock yet."

After walking Bryn home and making sure he was safe and secure, the dogs strolled back to Chamberlain Drive. Toby wanted to update Clarissa on the information they had, and perhaps ask her to phone Ed and get the address of the bright pink Fiat owner.

And, of course, there was the question of snacks. So far this morning there had been a dire shortage, so it was time to collect from anyone who happened to be in the business of supplying them.

Like Mrs Crouch.

As they approached Mrs Crouch's gate, Toby spotted Moriarty sitting on the wall. "Good morning!" he greeted her.

She stared down at Troot and Pippin, her expression giving nothing away.

"Don't be scared," said Troot. "Any friend of Toby's is a friend of ours."

"I'm not scared of dogs," Moriarty scoffed. "Especially puppies."

"I'm not a puppy," Troot protested.

"You look like one from up here with your ridiculously oversized paws and silly ears."

Troot pouted. "That's not nice. I was just trying to be friendly."

Toby laughed. "Let's all try and be sociable, shall we?" he suggested. "How are you settling into the neighbourhood, Moriarty?"

"I'm making myself known," Moriarty said.

"If anyone gives you any trouble, let me know and I'll sort them," Toby offered.

Moriarty made a cute snuffly noise that might have been a snort. "What? Sort them out with your magick, you mean?"

Now it was Toby's turn to take umbrage. "If I have to."

"I'm sure I'll be fine without your intervention."

"She's catty," Pippin said, with a certain amount of grudging approval. Pippin appreciated sark. And she enjoyed the company of animals who could take care of themselves. Moriarty seemed like Pippin's kind of creature.

Even if she was a cat.

"Now we have the pleasantries over," Moriarty purred, "How is your investigation going?"

"Slowly," Toby answered. "It worries me. Every hour that passes is another hour when those puppies are away from their loved ones. I hate to think what might be happening to them."

"With any luck—and I use that term loosely—they'll simply have been passed onto another home. Equally caring and loving," Moriarty suggested.

"Chance would be a fine thing." Pippin couldn't help but disagree. Given her life experiences, she understood better than most that reality could be scarier than fiction. "Who takes in a puppy without wanting to know where it came from?"

Toby nodded. "Until we know better, it pays to assume the worst. And in that case, we really need to make some progress."

Moriarty hopped down from the wall so she could converse with the dogs at their level. "What do you know so far?"

"We know of at least three puppies who have been removed from their homes. We know that a man who looked like Father Christmas—"

"A tatty Father Christmas," Troot reminded him.

"Yeah, a tatty, *thin* Father Christmas was seen hanging around, and—"

"A pink Fiat 500—" Troot interjected, his eyes wide with excitement.

Toby shot him a look. "Who's briefing Moriarty? Me or you?"

"I'm helping!" Troot cried.

"Yelping, more like," muttered Pippin.

"A pink Fiat 500 was noticed on two occasions."

"That seems pretty damning to me," Moriarty agreed. "Not that I'm in any way, shape or form a mighty detective." She arched her fuzzy brow. Toby couldn't decide whether she was taking the mickey or not, so elected not to react. "Surely if we find the car, we'll find the culprit."

"That's our thought," Pippin agreed.

"Powered by faery dust," Troot remembered.

"That's right!" Toby had forgotten. "It's powered by faery dust!" He nodded at Troot. "Good work." To Pippin, he said, "We need to put out an APB—"

Moriarty, attempting to follow the turn the conversation had taken, asked, "APB?"

"All Pups' Bulletin! We need to let everyone know there's the possibility of real danger in our streets and lanes. We'll do that during this evening's Twilight Barking."

Pippin nodded. "Good idea. I'll start spreading the word in the market this afternoon. Hoomans and their dogs come from all over."

"I can spread it around too," Moriarty offered. "If you'd like me to?"

"We're grateful for any and all assistance," Toby said. Never let it be said he was too proud to accept the help of a cat.

"I'll pass it around the neighbourhood cats as and when I see them." Moriarty yawned and stretched and began to slink away. "On the Catvine."

"How long will that take?" Toby asked. Moriarty did not seem to be in any kind of hurry.

"It takes the time it takes," Moriarty replied without looking back. "You dogs are so impatient."

After agreeing to meet Pippin and Troot in the park later, Toby sprang through the dog flap and into the kitchen.

"I'm famished," he said, by way of reintroducing himself to all and sundry, and ready to bounce in and see how Clarissa was doing with her article. He stopped when he saw Grubby Gordon standing by the toaster wearing the same pair of undercrackers he'd been sporting the previous day. "Are you still here?" Toby asked in dismay. Obviously he was. The Crapmobile was still on the drive, and this wasn't Gordon's ghost.

Unfortunately.

"Whatever you want, you can't have it," Gordon told him. "Scram."

"Is that you, Toby?" Clarissa called.

"It is!"

She joined them in the kitchen. Smiling, she crouched to give Toby a hug. "There you are. It's been quiet this morning without you snapping at flies and nagging me for snacks."

"Peaceful, actually," sniffed Gordon.

"How would you know?" Clarissa asked. "You've only just climbed out of bed."

"Judgemental or what?" Gordon poked his knife into the toaster to extract his toast. "Isn't this thing working?"

"It was working fine this morning," said Toby. "I had Clarissa's corners."

"Pipe down, mutt," Gordon said.

"Gordon!" Clarissa glared at him.

"I don't know how you put up with all his noise. Dogs should be seen and not heard. Why don't you get a pet rat instead?"

"I don't want a pet rat."

"No. She wants me," said Toby.

"You never seemed keen on having a pet *at all* before."

"Things have changed. My grandfather left Toby to me for safekeeping," Clarissa explained.

Gordon threw his toast onto a plate. The last clean plate in the whole house. "Ah. That's what it is. You feel emotionally beholden to your grandfather's memory."

"No—" Clarissa frowned.

"Look, he's gone now. You don't have to keep the

dog or the house. You could give the dog away and sell the house. We could go travelling—"

"Toby," Clarissa said, her voice like ice.

"Huh?" Gordon asked.

"The dog's name is Toby, and he *belongs* here *with* me in *our* house."

"Ner ner ner ner ner," sang Toby. "You tell him, Clarissa."

Gordon tutted. "What happened to the old Clarissa? The Clarissa who loved excitement and challenges? You're not even thirty yet but here you are, ready to stay in this house until you die."

"That's not true—"

"Once upon a time you promised me we'd go out and see the world. Mexico! Costa Rica! Thailand! Japan! We wanted to visit all of those places together."

"I'd still love to see them all—"

"Yet you're cooped up here behind a laptop, tied to a dog. You're going nowhere, Clar. Nowhere at all."

"It's not forever," Clarissa tried to explain. Toby didn't like the sound of that. What did she mean?

"You used to be the one encouraging me to seize the day and make the most of every moment," Gordon argued. "Now you're wearing slippers and abiding by a routine designed to dull your senses."

"I don't have any slippers!" Clarissa's voice trembled.

Toby looked up at her in consternation. She genuinely seemed stung by Gordon's words. Did she *want* slippers? Should he have replaced the pair he'd chewed up? "Don't listen to him, Clarissa. He's trying to hurt you," Toby told her.

She glanced down, tears in her eyes, then twisted on her heel and stormed from the room.

Toby glared up at Gordon, ready to give him a proper tongue-lashing. But the triumphant expression on Gordon's face gave him pause.

"What do you make of that, furball?" Gordon asked, his lip curling as though the idea of speaking to Toby directly disgusted him. "I'm back. Get used to it. I'm going to remind Clarissa exactly what she's missing out on by staying here and playing at being a housewife and dog mummy. Mark my words, your days here are numbered."

CHAPTER TWELVE

"What's the long face for?" Moriarty must have taken up residence on the wall beside his gate, Toby reckoned, because she was becoming a permanent fixture up there.

"I'm a dog. Most dogs have long faces. We can't help it. We're born this way," Toby told her, checking out his friend's perfectly proportioned cat face. They were kind of ball shaped when you thought about it. No wonder so many dogs found them enticing.

Such silly little ears, though. What was that about?

It was early. The sun was an orange ball, silhouetted behind Moriarty. It was going to be another roasting hot day; far better to be out on the street this early. By ten, they'd both want to be in the shade somewhere.

Moriarty, not a hair out of place, stared down at him from her vantage point, her focus laser sharp. "I'm sensing below the sarcastic exterior there is a certain amount of pain and trouble in the floofy boy's head this morning."

"That's very witchy of you." Toby frowned. He wasn't sure he liked being referred to as *floofy*. Hard as nails. That's what he was!

"All cats have a little bit of magick in them, Toby; that's our nature. We don't all tap into those reserves. However, I do. On occasion."

"I didn't know that," Toby confessed, "but I've probably always suspected it." He could hear how flat his voice sounded, the slight huskiness to the tone. He'd woken up from a bad dream in which he'd been living beneath the vegetable stall on the marketplace with Troot and living off swedes and cauliflower stalks. Having tossed and turned most of the night, he didn't feel even remotely rested. He needed a nap and some treats.

But most of all, he needed Gruesome Gordon gone from his life.

And Clarissa's.

"You look like a dog with the weight of the world on your shoulders." Moriarty's soft voice suggested sympathy. "I have to confess there's nothing witchy about my concern. I couldn't help but overhear the exchange between your hoomans yesterday."

"Gordon is not my hooman," Toby snapped. "He's nothing to do with me."

Moriarty's reply was soft. "It sounds like you should be concerned though."

"I am." Toby sighed. Moriarty was right. He did feel heavy this morning, as though he were carrying a load of bricks on his back. His chest felt tight too. He couldn't imagine life without Clarissa. What if Gordon successfully persuaded her to sell their house and take off around the world? Where would that leave him?

Moriarty jumped from the wall, landing lightly beside him. Briefly, she touched her nose to his before backing away. "I have some news that might cheer you up."

"You do?" For the first time this morning, Toby wagged his tail.

"I heard back on the Catvine—"

"Yes? Yes?" Toby danced a little Irish jig, Gordon temporarily forgotten.

"A cat named Mittens on Gloucester Road has reported a neighbour with a bright pink car. She doesn't know what the make or model is because she doesn't much care, but it is a small car and it does have writing on the rear window."

"I take it she couldn't see what it said?" Toby asked. If it read *Powered by Faery Dust*, then they'd surely know it was the right one.

"No, she can't read, Toby. That's a bit advanced, even for cats."

"Fair enough. Great work!" Toby nodded with enthusiasm. "Where's Gloucester Road?"

"On the Dorset Rise estate, apparently."

"I have no idea where that is," Toby admitted.

"Me neither." Moriarty shrugged. "My excuse is that I'm new to the area, what's yours?"

"I'm neither a streetwalker nor a postman," Toby told her. "But that's not a problem. Pippin will know. Pippin knows everything."

Moriarty purred her approval. "Good luck."

"Thanks for your help, Moriarty! I mean it," Toby called as she began to slink away.

"Any time," she replied, her green eyes wide. "Happy to stay at base and take messages, if that's any use?"

"Definitely! Thanks!"

"Wonderful. I can leave all the rushing around to you, then. It's far too hot to be busy." Moriarty yawned and hunkered down. "Who'd be a dog in this weather?"

"I have a friend whose owners let him swim in a paddling pool in the garden," Troot was telling Pippin and Toby as he trailed them along the pavement leading out of town.

Pippin knew the Dorset Rise housing estate quite well as luck would have it. She'd been born there, along with half a dozen siblings. In fact, her first two homes had been within yapping distance of where her mother had lived.

And there had been a lot of yapping.

This estate was noisy!

Even now, relatively early in the day, the whole place was chaotic and loud. Dogs barking, lonely howling from dogs forced to live in gardens or back yards. This, added to car alarms and intruder alarms, children playing on the street and the older residents bawling and arguing back and forth within their own four walls and across fences, made the whole place a boiling cauldron of frayed tempers.

Pippin, after being passed from pillar to post as a

puppy, had enjoyed the peace and quiet of the rescue centres she'd ended up in over the next few years. Sure, she was a street dog living on her wiles, but at heart she craved a cosy sofa—however beaten up and broken down that might be—a log fire and a quiet home in the countryside. One owner, perhaps. Well away from other people, children—like the ones who had tied a firework to her tail—cars, dust and ... well, everything really.

But here she was, leading Toby and Troot back to her old stomping ground.

Dorset Rise was a large housing estate located on the outskirts of Sunshine Valley, just over a mile and a half away from the town's centre. Built in the aftermath of World War II, initially all of the houses had had at least three bedrooms with a decent sized garden and an upstairs bathroom, which improved on the houses they'd replaced that tended to be two up and two down with a toilet outside. Gradually, as the prefabricated buildings were torn down, many were replaced with smaller houses, making more use of the acreage available, but meaning tiny gardens and a lack of parking space. The cramped nature of the estate, with its peculiar mix of old and dilapidated but generous-sized houses and more modern but tiny cramped dwellings, where the less desirable members of

Sunshine Valley ended up, created a melting pot of both culture and tempers.

Toby stepped off the pavement to avoid an older woman wheeling a shopping trolley with a wonky wheel towards them, then instantly jumped back onto the pavement when a kid on a skateboard zoomed past him, nearly shaving the hairs from his shoulder.

"Jeepers," he muttered. This was a much busier residential area than his own, and while there was ample opportunity to locate dropped snacks on the ground, they had decided to press on without stopping. The temperature was rising and the trio didn't want to stay out all day.

The next sprinkler they came to, the three of them took shelter beneath it, tongues out, lapping at drops of water on the grass, enjoying the cool misting it afforded them.

"The thing about paddling pools"—Pippin belatedly acknowledged what Troot had told them—"is that you only need them for a few days per year. It doesn't stay hot enough or dry enough for them to be a permanent fixture."

"You certainly wouldn't want to be paddling in a plastic pool in January," Toby agreed, although secretly he had been wondering whether Clarissa would agree to him having a pool of his own. Hey! He could throw pool parties and invite all his friends. Troot would love it! What would Moriarty make of it?

And what about ... Gordon?

Urrrrrrrrrrgh. He growled softly. Troot and Pippin stared at him in surprise.

"What's up?" Pippin asked, scanning the area for hostiles she might have missed.

"Nothing." Toby straightened his back and forced a perky expression. Now was not the time to think about the Gormless One.

"See those street signs over there, Toby?" Troot lifted his nose, gesturing across the road to a T-junction. "What do they say?"

Toby gave himself a good shake, starting at the tip of his nose, working all the way down to the end of his tail and back again. The thing was, he was still underneath the sprinkler so it was a bit of a waste of time. It felt good though.

Trotting through the sprinkler spray, he made his way across the road, leaving damp paw prints in his stead, a dripping Pippin and Troot at his heels. "Her-e-ford Way," he read. "Wor-ces-ter Road—"

"Wooster," said Pippin.

"Wooster? Wor-cest-er?" Toby considered the spelling. "Right. Whatever. And ... what about this? Glow-cest-er? If you take out the cest, that's almost

Gloster. That's how you spell it, right?"

"That must be the one," Pippin agreed.

"This way." Toby led and the others followed, trotting together down Gloucester Road, one of the older streets on the estate, the white-painted stone-chipped exteriors of the semi-detached houses a little grey and worse for wear, many of the generous front gardens given over to be used as drives nowadays.

"Do we know what number we're looking for?" Pippin asked, but Toby shook his head.

"I didn't receive that level of detail from my spy on the ground," he answered. "All I know is that a cat named Mittens lives in close proximity to the car."

"Locate Mittens and we'll find what we're looking for!" Troot chirruped. Toby cast a wary eye over his small friend. He hoped Troot wasn't raising his hopes too high. Finding the lost puppies would be more difficult than finding the car.

But finding the car would, at least, be a start.

"Mmm. Cats," Pippin hissed.

Toby shoulder-barged her. "Could you try to drool a little less? Remember, they're on our side!"

"They're not really," Pippin argued. "Moriarty is blinding you with her feline charm, but mark my words, if she could out-manoeuvre you and have every dog on the planet exterminated, she most definitely would!"

"I'm not sure that's the case," Toby said, thinking back to Merrybutton, the cat who lived with Mad Mabel—the witch who lived in a hedge, whom he'd met earlier in the summer. Merrybutton was a wise old thing, and polite and friendly enough.

Pippin wasn't listening. Distracted, she suddenly darted away and began to bark at a gate post. Toby and Troot ran after her.

"Pippin! Don't!" Toby ordered. "We need to make friends, not enemies!"

Pippin stopped barking. "Too late now. That one's run inside the house."

Toby rolled his eyes. So much for a stealthy approach. Pippin was a good friend, and although generally the coolest dog Toby knew, she could be a little unpredictable at times, especially where cats were concerned. Perhaps he should have left her at home to look after the base with Moriarty.

On second thoughts, maybe that wouldn't have been a good idea either.

Gloucester Road was a long street that curved around the estate. The dogs walked up and down it twice, the pavement heating up beneath their paws. Of a bright pink car, there was no sign.

Toby mulled over their predicament. "Maybe Moriarty was yanking my chain."

"That's cats for you," Pippin replied, her voice laced with I-told-you-so satisfaction.

"Perhaps the car is out because the owner has driven it away somewhere?" Troot suggested, all wide-eyed innocence.

Toby tutted. Why hadn't he thought of that? *Dang and blast.* Of course! That's what hoomans did. They drove their cars around. Clarissa had taken him out in hers many times. He'd always enjoyed a drive. The car was unlikely to be here if the driver was using it for work or shopping or ... or ... puppy stealing!

"Maybe we've been wasting our time," Toby lamented. "Perhaps we should have considered setting up a stakeout."

"But ... Phew! There sure are a lot of houses and a lot of drives," Pippin said, arching a fuzzy eyebrow. "We have no clue which one we'd have to stake out."

"Yeah, but wouldn't we see a pink car coming a mile off?" Toby argued.

"Excuse me, mister?" A sweet musical voice, so quiet the dogs almost missed it, called out to them. "Excuse me? Mister?"

Toby spun around, looking left, right, up and finally down. There, to the side of the gate, cowered a small cat. Not a kitten, but a fully mature cat that hadn't grown very big. It had a slightly arched back, scoliosis perhaps, a stunted tail and one greyed-out eye. "Excuse me," she said again, her voice barely rising above a whisper.

Toby shot a warning glance at Pippin before dropping his head to meet the tiddly cat's one eye. "Hey, nipper," he cooed.

"Hi, mister." The cat inched closer, casting shy, frightened peeks up and down the street. "Did you say you were searching for a pink car?"

"That's correct. Have you seen one?"

The cat nodded, one eye wide, the other half-closed. "My name is Mittens. I heard on the Catvine that there was a bunch of dogs looking for a pink car. I sent a message."

"Thank you for your brave and honourable service," Toby said. It seemed like a nice thing to say, and he'd heard people on the television utter such things. "Where can we find the car?"

"I haven't seen it for a while—"

Pippin groaned.

"But it used to live in the drive three doors down."

Toby jerked upright, ears standing to attention. *They were so close*! "On this side of the road?"

"That's right," Mittens said in her serene, gentle

voice. "The one with the big grey car on the drive that has no wheels."

"No wheels?" Toby repeated. What was the point of a car without wheels? That wouldn't get very far. Unless ... Unless it was a flying car! *Magick*!

"That's right. The little pink car used to park half on the drive and half on the pavement. My owner would get annoyed."

"Thanks for the information, Mittens!" Toby said. "You've been a great help."

"Just one more thing," Mittens interrupted him, and Toby spotted the look of concern on her pretty ball-shaped face.

"Go on?"

"There's a Rottweiler." The tip of Mittens' tail flicked, an anxious tic. "I know you can't tar all dogs with the same brush—even if you want to—but that one ... he's not nice. A proper gangster. A mean, vicious, bitey, snarly Rottweiler. You need to watch out for him."

Toby swallowed. Pippin would be pretty handy—pawsy, perhaps—in a fight, but he and Troot? Well, they were built more for cuddles and snack times than street battles.

"That's erm ... useful ... information," Toby said. "Thanks again."

"Take care," Mittens said, retreating towards the hole in her fence. "It's a jungle out there."

"It certainly feels like it in this heat," Toby agreed as Mittens disappeared. "Bye!"

"A brave little cat," Pippin declared. "I'd have her on my team any day of the week."

Toby nodded down the road. "Come on. Let's have a look, shall we?"

They didn't venture all the way, pausing two doors down where the front garden had been given over to something akin to a desolate wilderness. Tall weeds grew up through piles of discarded waste, mostly children's toys and plastic; buckets, mops, bowls and pots and pans. Number 43—because that's what it was—seemed vacant. Net curtains hung at half-mast and the bedroom window upstairs had been broken.

Number 43 might be quiet, but number 45 certainly wasn't. Judging by the volume of the music that blasted out of the open windows—something grimy with a heavy bass that was so deep, the very earth they stood on seemed to vibrate—someone was home. The inhabitants must surely have been deafened by the row. No wonder number 43 had been vacated. Toby decided Clarissa, who hated noise when she was busy working, would probably have emigrated.

The fence that separated number 43 and number

45 had been repaired several times over, with odds and ends of wood, some painted, some bare. Even so, there were plenty of gaps to use as peepholes at varying heights, offering the three dogs a welcome opportunity to spy.

Spying was deemed necessary. Mitten's warning about the savage Rottweiler inhabiting their target property had not fallen on deaf ears. The front of number 45's drive was open to all and sundry, so theoretically they would have been able to stop in front of the property to take a better look. However, given that none of them had a death wish—at least not today—they'd decided on a stealthier approach.

Toby, peeking through his hole, had a good view of the grey car. Just as Mittens had described, the vehicle didn't have any wheels and had been raised on bricks. Both the bonnet and the front doors were wide open. The only place this car was going anytime soon was to a scrapyard on the back of a tow truck.

There didn't appear to be much possibility of it flying either. While Toby was somewhat disappointed by this, he needed to concentrate on the job in hand, because even though there was no sign of the pink car, if this was where it was usually parked, there was a possibility the puppy thief could live at this address.

Toby studied the inside of the grey car. The old-fashioned steering wheel, thin but wider than a normal steering wheel, was covered in worn green leather. The once-white seats were now a faded yellow and grimy grey in the front, and the same in the rear but with a hint of black and tan—

Toby shot backwards as the hint of black and tan suddenly lifted its head and stared straight at him.

Oops.

"Erm, guys?" Toby whispered as Troot and Pippin gawked through their own spyholes.

"I can't see much," Troot told him. "There's a great bush in the way or something."

"Guys?" Toby repeated.

"There's room for a small car to park here at the front," Pippin told them.

"Guys?" Toby raised his voice a little. "We're about to have company."

The three friends turned to face the pavement, ganging up as the Rottweiler slowly strolled into view, his thick chain collar jangling as he moved. "What's happenin', bros?" he asked.

"Erm ... not a lot," Toby replied. "We're erm ... just out for a walk. You know how it is?"

"Very companionable of you, I must say." The Rottweiler's massive head moved fractionally to size up first Toby, then Troot, and finally Pippin. "Do I know you?" he asked her.

Pippin shrugged. "Maybe you do, maybe you don't."

"You look kinda familiar."

"Given that there are so many fluffy white dogs around," Toby said blithely, "it's an easy mistake to make."

The Rottweiler grunted. "I don't make mistakes."

"Ha ha." Toby took a small step backwards as Troot pushed against him. "I'm sure that's true. I can't imagine that a fine upstanding gentleman like yourself has ever put a paw wrong."

The Rottweiler's eyes glinted. "You lookin' for summat?" he asked. "Or someone?"

Toby considered his options. So far, the bigger dog had not shown any inclination to attack them. Maybe there was strength in numbers, after all. Perhaps a frank discussion would be best. "Summat," Toby volunteered. "I mean ... something."

Pippin gave Toby a little side-eye, but Toby ignored her. "We're looking for a pink car."

The Rottweiler blinked. "What's your business with a pink car?"

"No business particularly," Toby drawled, offering up what he hoped was his most charming expression.

"We'd heard there was a pink car here and we ... erm ... we like pink cars." He winced. *What in dog's name have I just said? We like pink cars?* That was surely the most pathetic sentence he'd ever uttered.

"I've never seen a pink car," Troot piped up. "I wanted to see one. I asked my friends to track one down for me."

The Rottweiler said nothing, its face a mask of neutrality.

Toby held his breath, waiting for the Rottweiler to respond. When it finally did, its words disappointed them.

"You won't find a pink car here."

As if Toby would give up that easily. "Did there used to be a pink car here?" he asked.

"Whether there was or there wasn't is really no business of yours now, is it, sunshine?" The Rottweiler held Toby in his gaze, salivating a little.

Toby shivered at the thought of being clamped between those jaws. "I'm thinking, you know, if there used to be a car here, but maybe it was sold on ... then maybe ... possibly ... we could erm ... go and see it at its new owner's place." Toby trailed off.

The Rottweiler pulled its lips back, showing off a fine set of sharp pearly whites. "I'm not the keeper of pink cars."

"Not the registered keeper," Toby agreed.

"Are you being a smart arse, fella?" The Rottweiler took a step towards the trio of intrepid investigators. Now he was merely a nose length away.

Toby swallowed. "No. Just curious. That's all. Curious." He forced a laugh. Troot—and Pippin after a few moments' consideration—joined in.

"We just like pink cars," Toby reminded him. "Ha ha!"

"If I were you, I'd beat it," the Rottweiler told them. "We don't like snoops like you three on the Dorset Rise estate. Do you get me?"

Time to admit defeat. Toby sidestepped, pushing against Troot, who tumbled to the left. Pippin quickly picked him up and set him on his four paws again. Once he was righted, she ducked her head, suddenly distracted, staring at the rubble beneath her paws.

The Rottweiler growled. "Do you get me?" he repeated.

Toby nodded frantically. "Of course. We most certainly do 'get' you, sir. We'll be off. Thanks so much for your time." He sheepishly followed Pippin as she led the way, suddenly in a hurry, past the front of the marooned grey car and onwards down the road away from Mittens and the Rottweiler. At the bend in the road, he glanced over his shoulder. The Rottweiler was standing on the edge of his drive, his black coat shining in the sun, watching them, probably making sure Toby's word was good.

They carried on, heading back towards the sprinklers for some useful respite against the unremitting heat of the sun. While Troot scratched at his ears, Toby edged in close to the centre of the sprinkler so he could take a long drink of water. Once he'd emerged, he shook his head. "Sorry, you guys. That was a bit of a waste of time, wasn't it?"

Troot, tail between his legs, still trying to free something from his ears, nodded. "We didn't find out anything useful."

"What's wrong with your head?" Toby asked.

Troot whined. "I think I've got a flea in my ear."

Toby snorted. "In the end, that's all that Rottweiler gave any of us."

"Hold your horses, boys," Pippin said, her voice slightly muffled because she had something in her mouth. She dropped it onto the soggy grass and nudged it with her nose. A filthy piece of rag on a rope.

"Ewww, Pippin. If you want a toy, I've got a few at home you can have." Toby stared at it in disgust. "Clarissa washed all of mine the other day." He didn't admit to having conniptions once he'd recognised them all hanging on the line well out of his reach.

"It's not a toy, silly," Pippin remonstrated with him. "Not a dog toy anyway. Look closely. What do you notice?"

Toby pawed at the material. Some kind of imitation fur. Teddy bear skin, as he tended to think of it. On one side there were several panels; the central one had five dots and was flanked by four dots on the right and three dots on the left. There might have been more, but they had been savaged.

Undoubtedly by the Rottweiler.

The layout of the dots seemed familiar, but he couldn't quite place them.

"It's a dice," Pippin explained, tapping at the arrangements of dots. "See?"

Of course! A die, Clarissa would have corrected them, but what's a suh sound between pals?

"And if you look closely at the other end of the string, you'll see that there would have been another one. A pair of furry dice!" Pippin crowed triumphantly.

"That's all well and good, but what does it prove?" Toby asked. What was he missing?

"There. Look." Pippin scratched at the matted, furry material, scraping some of the grime away.

Toby gaped at what was revealed. Once upon a

time, the sad forlorn dice had been pink. Bright candy pink.

Not a dog toy at all, but a dangling toy that you'd hang over the rear-view mirror of a car.

Didn't it stand to reason that a pink car would have pink dice?

Toby thought so.

CHAPTER THIRTEEN

"Clarissa!" Toby called as he leapt through his dog flap. It clattered noisily behind him, but Clarissa didn't complain as she usually would. The kitchen was devoid of hoomans, but even from his position close to the tiled floor, Toby could see the pile of washing up in the sink. There was a strange smell in the room too. A kind of cooped-up-with-stale-food smell.

Toby wrinkled his nose. Clarissa wasn't obsessed with cleaning, but she did tend to stay on top of the housework—and if she was falling behind, a little cleaning spell took care of the worst of it.

From the direction of the living room came the sound of roaring and cheering. Toby tilted his head, listening. What could be going on in there? Was there a party?

Toby crept out of the kitchen and poked his head into the living room. Gobby Gordon was lying on the couch, feet up, wearing only his boxers and a pair of grey socks that might once have been white, watching football on the television. Clarissa was sitting in her regular place at the dining table behind her laptop, small earbuds in her ears, her forehead creased as she struggled to concentrate.

How selfish, thought Toby, sidling up to Clarissa and nudging her knee with his nose. She glanced down and the frown disappeared. "Hey!" She pulled out her earbuds and stroked the top of his head. "You're warm. What have you been up to?"

"I had to go and see a dog about a car," Toby started to explain.

"Could you pipe down?" Gordon asked, without turning around.

Clarissa shifted uncomfortably in her seat. "Sorry, Toby. Gordon's watching the match."

What the actual fluff? Toby could feel his hackles prickling. *So whatty what! It's* our *television in* our *living room in* our *house! Tell him we can talk if we want to!* But he thought better of vocalising his internal rant. Instead, he tapped Clarissa's foot. "Would you mind filling my bowl for me, please? I'm awfully thirsty."

"Sure." Clarissa slid her chair back and followed Toby into the kitchen. His bowl was full of clean water but she picked it up anyway, rinsed it out and filled it with cold water.

"I need your help," Toby told her as she leaned over to return the bowl to its place on his easy-clean meal mat. "We—"

"We?" Clarissa looked around. Toby had left Pippin and Troot outside.

"My investigative team and I—"

"Oh yes?" Clarissa smothered a grin.

"*We* have an address for where we think the puppynappermobile has been parked, but there's a Rottweiler living there and he wouldn't answer our questions."

Clarissa was struggling to keep up. "Puppynappermobile?"

"The pink car!"

"Oh yes. And you spoke to a Rottweiler?"

Toby shrugged. "There was no way of getting past him to speak to the residents of the house. Not in one piece, anyway."

"I see."

"He sent us packing, but we desperately want to find out who owns the car and where it is now—"

"Hmmm." Clarissa glanced at the kitchen clock. "And you want me to go and ask the owner?"

Toby drew in a breath. "Clarissa! I would never put you in such danger. Who's to say you'll get past that Rottweiler any better than we were able to!"

"Any dog has to be kept under control." Clarissa held up a hand. "There are laws against them attacking humans, Toby. I'm sure I'll cope."

"Oh. Well, if you insist," Toby said. Of course, he'd known that, but he was pleased she'd taken the bait. He trotted towards the dog flap. "Shall we go? The others are waiting."

As Toby, Pippin and Troot hid in the bushes observing proceedings, Clarissa paused at the opening of number 45 Gloucester Road's driveway. Toby could see her checking out the grey car and its lack of wheels, and he'd prewarned her about the Rottweiler sleeping in the back, but she still jumped in surprise when it launched itself out of the car and blocked her way.

"Whoa," she said. "Steady on there, Fido."

"My name's not Fido!" the Rottweiler snarled at her. "I'm a killer. I've got a serial killer's name."

Toby grimaced, somewhat relieved that Clarissa couldn't understand what the dog was saying. She seemed to get the gist though.

"Not Fido? Is it Tiddles then?"

The Rottweiler was incensed. "I'm going to tear out your throat and drink it down with a nice bottle of Chianti! *Fuh-fuh-fuh-fuh.*"

"Jeepers," said Troot, and hid his eyes behind his paws.

"That boy needs therapy," Pippin whispered.

"You're a handsome lad," Clarissa cooed. "I'm sure you have a handsome name—"

"Hannibal!" A young woman had opened the front door of the house. She stomped out onto the top step, she bellowed at the dog. "Hannibal! Cut it out! Oi!"

"Hannibal the Cannibal!" Troot whispered.

"If ever a name suited someone," Toby said, but he found himself distracted by the woman's pastel pink hair, caught up in a messy bun, and her long fingernails, like ice lolly sticks glued to the end of her fingers, similarly painted pink, but this shade more neon.

Clarissa smiled and held up her notebook and phone. "Hi there!"

Hannibal barked a couple more times, but the

woman screeched his name again, and he slunk away, climbing into the back of the car and settling down on his rug. As Clarissa inched past him, he afforded her a grumble then plonked his head down on the seat.

Toby watched Clarissa's relieved skip as she passed the car and navigated her way through mounds of sand and bags of soil towards the young woman waiting for her.

"Hi," she said again, reaching for her press credentials. "My name's Clarissa Page and I'm a reporter. I was wondering if you could spare me a few minutes of your time?"

"Reporter? What sort of reporter? BBC?" The young woman sniffed, suspicion making her eyes hard.

"BBC? No. Sorry. I'm a newspaper reporter," Clarissa clarified. "*The Celestine Times*?"

"Celery Times?" The woman flipped strands of hair from her eyes. How she managed not to pierce her eyeballs with her talons, Toby wasn't quite sure.

"Celestine," Clarissa repeated.

The woman shrugged. "Never heard of it."

"And the *Sun Valley Tribune*," Clarissa added hurriedly. Everyone around here had heard of that.

"Oh, right, yeah. What can I do for you?" The woman folded her arms across her ample chest and lifted her chin in defiance. "I'm no snitch, so whatever it is you're looking for, I'm probably not going to be much use."

"It's nothing like that, I promise!" Clarissa flipped open her notebook. "I'm writing an article about how cars reflect their owners' personalities."

Toby chortled. *Perfect*! Super-fast thinking by Clarissa. He couldn't be more proud of her.

The young woman frowned, clearly not understanding. "You what?"

Clarissa maintained her poise and her relaxed, cheerful voice. "I'm writing an article about how cars can be an extension of the owner's personality. So, you know—" Clarissa swept one hand down her body. She had donned black jeans and a plain black t-shirt this morning which she was wearing with thick-soled Doctor Marten sandals. Add in the black hair, heavy eyeliner and silver jewellery, and it was quite obvious what her musical affiliations were. "I'm a little gothic—"

"Yeah. Bit warm for you today, isn't it?"

"I don't really feel it," Clarissa lied. Truth was, like most witches, she hated being out in the sun for too long. "Anyway, my car is a black beetle." This was a lie. Clarissa's car was almost as much of a Crapmobile as Gordon's was. "I have black seat covers, red cushions on the back seat and a bat mobile hanging from the mirror."

"Cool!" The young woman had become more engaged. "Have you got it with you?"

"Sorry." Clarissa pulled a face. "I walked here today."

"Oh, that's a shame."

"Anyway, my editor suggested I write about other people who decorate their cars to match their personalities, and a friend of mine gave me your name—"

"A friend?" The young woman was instantly suspicious again. "Who was that then?"

"Sorry, I can't reveal my sources. You know how it is." Clarissa appealed to the young woman's ego. "It's the same as if you asked me for total confidence, I would have to respect that. It's your right."

The woman gave this some thought and nodded. "Yeah. I suppose that's important because you don't want the wrong kind of people taking an interest in your vehicle and tracking you down."

"Exactly!" Clarissa agreed. "I take your security and wellbeing incredibly seriously."

"That's good to know." The young woman was definitely thawing.

"Is my information correct, Miss ... Ms ... erm ...?"

"Madeley. Nikki Madeley."

"Ms Madeley." Clarissa wrote that down. "May I call you Nikki?"

"Sure."

"Tell me about your car." Clever, thought Toby. Clarissa hadn't even asked whether she had a car. The assumption between them was that she did and that it was noteworthy.

"It's a Fiat 500. Four years old. My grandad bought it for me for my eighteenth birthday."

"That was generous of him," Clarissa acknowledged. "Grandads are the best."

"Better than my good-for-nothing father at any rate," Nikki agreed.

Don't go down that route, Toby thought. We'll be here all day, and it's too hot!

As though Clarissa could hear his thoughts, she quickly prompted Nikki to move on. "And you did some work to it?"

"Yeah, yeah, I did. That's probably why your 'friend' noticed it. You see, I adore the colour pink."

"No kidding," whispered Pippin in Toby's ear.

"Have done ever since I was little. I dreamed of being a Disney princess, and after that I wanted everything in pink. Pink dresses. Pink bedclothes. Pink pyjamas. You name it. It had to be pink."

"I see." Clarissa was making notes. Toby could

only imagine that they would read something like, *Lost the plot. Pink. Pink. PINK.*

"When Grandad gave me the car, I saved up the money until I could afford a respray and then I had it sprayed pink."

"Pastel?" Clarissa asked, pen poised.

"Bright flamingo pink," Nikki confirmed proudly. "I had a pink steering wheel cover, pink covers on the seats and a replacement knob for the gear stick. In pink, of course."

"Of course."

"I even had a furry dice air freshener for the mirror, but Hannibal chewed it up—"

"He probably has an aversion to pink," Pippin murmured.

"A na-na-navershun?" Troot asked.

"Meaning he doesn't like pink," Pippin explained in simple terms.

"Oh, right, gotcha." Face serious, Troot nodded. "I'd chew the dice up too."

"You'd chew anything up," Pippin told him. "You're a puppy. That's what puppies do."

"It sounds phenomenal!" Clarissa said. "Is there any chance I can take a photo of it?" She glanced around as though expecting it to be there, when quite clearly if it had been, she would have spotted it from the other side of the county.

"No," Nikki replied, her voice sharp.

"Oh, erm ..." Clarissa pretended to be flustered.

"Who is it?" An older woman's voice drifted out of the house. Clarissa edged sideways, perhaps hoping to see who it belonged to.

"It's a reporter, mum," Nikki called over her shoulder.

"A reporter?" A diminutive round woman with short bleached hair appeared behind Nikki, her dark eyes raking over Clarissa standing before them. "What does she want?" she asked, as though Clarissa wasn't there.

"She's writing an article about cars and how they mirror the owner's personality. She wants to include mine."

"Does she think your car's a crackpot like you, Nikki?" the older woman tittered.

"Ha ha."

Clarissa smiled politely.

"Is there any money in it?" the older woman asked.

"I never thought of that," Nikki said. "There should be, shouldn't there. You hear of people being paid a fortune for their stories!"

Clarissa chuckled. "That can be the case in

national magazines, but I'm afraid it doesn't work like that for a local newspaper."

"Oh." Nikki's face fell.

"I might be able to get you a fee if we can include a photo—" Clarissa wheedled.

Toby, even from his hidden place behind the neighbour's hedge, spotted the look that passed between the two women. Mum shook her head ever so slightly.

"I can't," Nikki replied, her voice flat.

"That's a shame," Clarissa commiserated. "In the garage, is it? Having work done?"

Mum's eyes narrowed.

Nikki shrugged. "Stolen," she said.

Why hadn't she said that before? Toby wondered. Why bang on about how pink it was if she wasn't actually the owner anymore?

"I'm really sorry to hear that. The police don't have any leads?"

"No," Nikki's mum replied. "They don't. Useless."

"That's a rotten shame," Clarissa said.

And a rotten lie, thought Toby. This pair of women couldn't have been any shiftier if they'd been found wearing balaclavas and crouching in the corner of a bank vault with duffel bags stuffed full of gold bullion.

Clarissa stepped backwards. "I guess that's that then. Thanks so much for your time."

"You can't use it in the article?" Nikki traipsed after her. Perhaps she'd fancied the idea of being semi-famous.

"I can certainly add some of your comments if they fit and if you're happy for me to do so?" Clarissa smiled.

Nikki glanced at her mother, who thought for a moment, pulled a face and then shrugged. "That would be fine," Nikki announced.

"I'll do that. Thanks again." Clarissa waved a hand. "Take care." Walking away, she paused when she reached the grey car up on its bricks. "Just one other thing. Did you incorporate any ..."—she bit her lip, pretending to think—"graphics on it, or writing or other personalisation?"

Before Nikki's mum could intervene, Nikki nodded, full of enthusiasm. "Yes! I had graphics printed for the rear window. They said, *Powered by Faery Dust*."

"That's so cute." Clarissa grinned. "Thanks again. Hope you get it back." She turned her back and kept walking, past Hannibal who indulged in a quick growl, and past the hedge where Toby, Pippin and Troot were hiding.

"Powered by faery dust," she scoffed. "Ugh. You'd be better off on a broomstick."

"Now what?" Pippin asked.

After conferring with Clarissa, the three dogs had retreated beneath the sprinklers to discuss a plan. Clarissa had agreed that she would try and talk to DC Plum about the missing car, although she wasn't optimistic that he would share any information with her.

For now, they found themselves temporarily stumped.

"Good question," Toby replied, stalling for time.

"We should get your kitty friend to ask for more information on the Catvine," Troot suggested.

"We can do that," Toby agreed. "I'm sure she'll be happy to assist. There's also the Twilight Barking."

Pippin tilted her head. "Agreed. We should put out an APB for information about the stolen car."

"It could be anywhere," Troot said. "It might be on the other side of the country."

"There's no better way of finding that out than by asking our friends and country dogs," Pippin told him. "They can share far and wide."

"I'll do that this evening," Toby said. "Is there anything we can be getting on with this afternoon?"

"My vote is to get our heads down somewhere cool," Pippin said. "I need a nap and to get out of this sun."

"I'm famished," said Toby. "I need snacks."

"Me too," said Troot, thinking of his cool spot beneath the vegetable stall and the odds and ends of fruit and vegetables he could have tucked into, not to mention the discarded burger buns.

"Let's head back into town," suggested Toby. "Naps and snacks for all!"

They slipped out from beneath the sprinklers, each having a good shake as soon as they were clear, then trotted along the road and, eventually, towards the edge of the housing estate, where the meanly built houses were located. They hurried along, seeking shade where possible, but with the sun directly above their heads, that proved difficult most of the time.

"Hello." A Jack Russell had meandered towards them from the opposite end of the road. He wagged his tail in a friendly way, and the four dogs exchanged polite butt sniffs. "How's it going?"

"Fine, thanks. Bit warm for us," Toby replied. "What about you?"

"I don't mind the heat so much," the little dog said.

"Feeling a bit fraught though, because I've lost my friend. I've been searching all over the estate and I just can't find him."

Toby pricked his ears up. "You've lost your friend?"

"He's not a puppy, is he?" Troot asked.

"Yes. He's called Alphonse and he's a Jack Russell just like me." The little dog scanned the others' faces. "Do you have news? Have you seen him?"

Toby shook his head. "Sorry, no. But we're already looking for some missing puppies—"

"Ooh!" The Jack Russell pricked up his ears. "Are you Toby from Spellbound Investigative Services by any chance?"

"I am, as it happens." Toby fought to maintain a modest and serious air, although what he really wanted to do was preen. "These are my co-investigators, Pippin and Troot."

Pippin rolled her eyes, but Troot, oblivious of the fact that he had the appearance of a drowned rat, sat up very straight, trying to look more alert than he felt.

"I'm Jack," said Jack. "I know it's not very original but my hoomans like the name. Alphonse only came to live with us a couple of weeks ago, but he disappeared this morning."

Toby's feeling of self-importance deflated at the

little dog's words. "This morning?" How horrific. They'd been on the estate at that time! So close! What if the pink Fiat had been here? They could have caught it red-pawed.

"It may not be linked to what we're looking into," Pippin said, seeming to understand Toby's silent thought process.

"It's quite a coincidence though," Toby argued. "Especially this close to where the pink car lives."

"Or used to live," Pippin reasoned.

"Meh." Toby was convinced Nikki and her mother had been hiding something, but he couldn't prove it without running the gauntlet of one rabid Rottweiler.

"If Alphonse has been puppynapped, that makes ..." Troot's eyes rolled upwards as he tried to count. "Two ... six ... four ... no." He gave up. "*Lots* of puppies missing."

"Bourgie, Bron, Alphonse, Lucy, Red Fred. Maybe more. What would someone do with that many puppies?" Toby pondered.

"They might love them," suggested Jack.

Troot and Pippin gave him a hard stare.

Jack changed his mind. "Or not."

"We can only hope." Toby nodded at Jack. "Leave it with us. We'll let you know what we find out."

He turned to leave but Jack scampered around him

and blocked the path, although using the word 'blocked' when the object blocking it is no bigger than a box of cereal is probably an overstatement. "No," Jack said, squaring his shoulders.

Toby regarded him doubtfully. "No?"

"No, I won't leave it with you." Jack sniffed in defiance. "I want to work with you to find Alphonse. I owe it to my hoomans."

"The disappearances may not even be—" Pippin started to say, but Toby intervened.

"It's fine," he said. "Welcome to the gang."

"Attention, dogs and puppies everywhere! Attention, friends and allies!" Toby stood on top of The Mountain and barked into the sunset. "It's Toby from Spellbound Investigative Services here! I'm seeking your assistance once more. Is there anybody out there?"

Toby cocked his head listening. Answering barks from the dogs in the park. Several in the streets surrounding the park, and a few in town towards the market. That was good. It was busy tonight. When the answering yelps and barks had died down, Toby raised his head once more. "This is an All Pups' Bulletin. Firstly I want to thank everyone for their kind assistance. We believe there is a puppynapper on the loose."

"Repeat, over?" Someone, relatively close by and with a deep bark, responded.

"Puppynapper. Confirmed!" Toby called and, hiding not far away, Pippin reinforced his message.

When she'd finished, Toby continued, "First and foremost, we should prompt our canine friends to remain safe at all times. Never willingly go with strangers, no matter what kind of snacks they're offering." Toby sent a mental apology to Mrs Crouch. "If you have any suspicions of who is doing this or who the puppynapper might be, we would ask you to contact us either via the Twilight or Dawn Barking system or through the Catvine."

There was some consternation about this: howls of derision and some general amusement, but Toby pressed on. "This is too important for us to become factional." He nodded, listening as a number of approving barks drowned out the snider ones.

"In tonight's appeal, we're asking you all to look out for the vehicle we believe may be involved in the pupnappings. If we can locate this vehicle, we will be well on our way to finding the person who stole our babies."

Toby performed a little jig, gearing himself up for

the most important information. "It's a small car. A Fiat 500, for those of you who know what that is. It's kind of bubble shaped. Most importantly, it's bright pink. Even if you don't know what a Fiat is, if you see a bright pink car, spread the word. Get that information back to me. Understood?"

Those listening close by sent their confirmations. Toby, satisfied, lifted his head one more time. "Stay safe out there! Toby out!"

"How was that?" he asked Pippin as she slunk out from beneath the bush where she'd been hiding. There had been rumours that the dog warden was patrolling Sunshine Valley because of an increasing number of dogs prowling the streets during the hot weather. Humans had a tendency to leave doors and windows open, not to mention gates, and that was a red rag to a bull for dogs who fancied an exciting few hours exploring.

Until they became hungry, thirsty or tired.

"Perfect." Pippin gave herself a shake, dislodging leafy detritus and a number of ants who had been foraging in her fur. "I guess I'll call that it for the night."

"I'll walk you to the exit," Toby offered, falling in beside her. They trotted companionably side by side, both keeping their eyes peeled for a man in uniform.

All around them, dogs were barking, sending Toby's message or relaying one of their own. The air was heavy with canine communication.

"Wait!" Pippin, voice breathless, pulled up.

Alarmed, Toby scooted round, peering into the distance. "What?"

"Ssh! Listen," Pippin replied.

Toby clamped his jaws shut. It was a hot night and he'd been panting. He could hardly hear himself think. But ... there ... a dog barking from quite some distance away.

"I've seen a pink car," it was saying. "I've seen a pink car. Can someone get my message to Toby on The Mountain? Can someone contact him urgently?"

CHAPTER FOURTEEN

"Good morning, Toby!" Clarissa, freshly showered and fully dressed, breezed into the kitchen and reached for the kettle. Once it had been filled and set to boil, she bent down to stroke his ears.

"Morning, Clarissa. Oooh yeah. Just there. That's lovely." Toby wiggled under her expert touch. He'd read somewhere that it takes four thousand hours to become an expert at something. Four thousand hours of ear massage sounded like his idea of heaven. He was willing to be a tester for anyone intent on passing their grade one competency badge in Dog Fussing.

"Are you hungry?" Clarissa asked, and abandoned him in order to see to her own breakfast.

Toby gazed up at her. Was that a trick question? "I'm always hungry."

"Even if you weren't, you'd still eat."

"There is that," Toby agreed. "What are we having?"

"I'm having toast. You're having ..." Clarissa opened the base cupboard and peered inside. "Oh, imagine that. Looks like you're having dog food again."

"Phooey." Toby jumped, placing his front paws on the counter. "Someone should definitely research into manufacturing toast and jam dog snacks. They'd make a fortune."

"You can have my corners if you're a good boy."

"I'm always a good boy." How could Clarissa forget? "By the way—" He dropped the words casually, hoping she wouldn't notice he was about to change the subject.

"Mmm?" Clarissa was checking out her jam supply. Raspberry, blackberry, strawberry or lime marmalade. Toby would have chosen strawberry, but it wasn't his decision to make, and Clarissa currently had a thing for blackberry.

"It's going to be such a lovely day again—" Toby said.

"Glorious," Clarissa agreed. "I'm happy to be staying indoors."

"I was thinking ... why don't we... we could ... couldn't we ..."

Clarissa took down the jar of blackberry jam and turned to study him. "Spit it out."

"How about a picnic?" Toby stared up at her with his soft brown eyes, trying to hide the eagerness but wagging his tail with enthusiasm.

"That sounds nice ... apart from the bit about being outside in the sun," Clarissa said, pulling a face.

"We could find a nice shady spot ... by a river or something." Toby had no idea whether there was a river where he needed to go, but surely there would be trees and shade and maybe some rancid pool of rain-water somewhere.

If not a cattle trough. Would that do?

"I don't know." Clarissa sounded reluctant. "I should be working."

"You're *always* working," Toby reminded her. "You're entitled to have a day off. It's good for you."

Clarissa smiled at him. "You're such a love, worrying about me the way you do."

"You work too hard."

"It's because I want to prove myself to my editor at the newspaper. I'd like her to give me some bigger stories, that's all." She reached out to stroke his soft head. "Do you think I'm neglecting you?"

"Maybe a little," Toby sniffed, hamming it up. He didn't mind Clarissa being busy. They still went out for a walk together twice a day, and he knew it wasn't forever. He enjoyed just lying in his basket half listening, half dozing as she tapped away on her laptop or made phone calls to all and sundry.

"One of my friends recommended Bushy Leaze for picnics," Toby said, insinuating the idea even further into Clarissa's mind. "Fresh air, green trees, space to run ..."

"I do fancy getting out—"

"Getting out where?" Gordon was at the door, listening to Clarissa.

"I was just thinking it would be a nice day for a picnic," she told him. "Get out and enjoy the weather while we've still got it."

"Sounds good." Gordon nodded, reaching for the piece of toast that had just been ejected from the toaster. "Is this mine?"

"Help yourself," Clarissa said, adding another couple of slices to the toaster.

Toby glared at Gordon. Why did he want to come? Wasn't he supposed to be heading off to wherever he belonged? Why was he still in this house? What had he missed while he'd been out with his friends yesterday? Had Clarissa agreed that Gordon could stay longer?

"Any butter?" Gordon asked.

"In the butter dish, right in front of you," Clarissa told him.

Gordon plucked the lid off the base. "Nothing in here. Only dregs."

"What?" Clarissa yanked the dish away from him to look inside herself. "I filled it up a couple of days ago! A pat of butter normally lasts me a week."

"Pffft!" Toby couldn't help himself. "Houseguests."

"There's some more in the fridge. I'll have to microwave it." Clarissa hated doing that because she had a tendency to overbake it, and it ended up like an oily yellow soup. Butter was expensive and she didn't like to waste money.

"Grand." Gordon folded his arms, waiting for Clarissa to attend to the butter crisis for him.

"Your turn to wash up this morning," Clarissa told Gordon, and belatedly Toby realised that the kitchen had been cleaned. It must have taken Clarissa hours.

"How about you make the picnic and wash up, and I'll drive us to wherever we're going?"

"Bushy Leaze," Clarissa said.

Gordon curled his lip. "Do we have to take the dog?"

"Yes, we have to take Toby. He'll love it!"

"It'll be more romantic if it's just me and you."

Gordon flashed what he probably assumed was a winning smile. "If you catch my drift."

Toby bristled. "It was *my* idea, Faceache!"

"It's an excellent opportunity to give Toby somewhere new to run," Clarissa told him. "You go through to the dining table. I'll bring more toast through in a second."

And don't trip over a rug and break your neck in the process, thought Toby. But then he remembered Old Joe and his heart ached. It wasn't right to wish ill on people.

Even gormless idiots like Gordon.

"Hurry up, Toby," Clarissa urged him. "Why are you hanging back?"

Toby exchanged a glance with Moriarty, perched on the garden wall, observing proceedings. From her vantage point she could see Pippin, Troot, Jack and Bryn hiding beneath the buddleia bush in Clarissa's front garden. Thank goodness Clarissa had neglected to trim it back this spring. Not only did it attract countless numbers of pretty butterflies, but it smelled wonderful and could shield up to a dozen small dogs.

Or perhaps a Pippin and eight small dogs.

Gordon's Crapmobile had been packed up with the picnic basket and a rug, a flask of tea, some bottles of water and a plastic drinking bowl for Toby. The problem was that Toby needed to sneak his friends along too. He had assumed he would be travelling with Clarissa and had been certain he'd be able to persuade her that his friends joining them would make excellent sense. In fact, he'd probably have come clean about the excursion if it had just been him and her.

Unfortunately, Gordon's insistence on driving them—and even coming along—had put paid to that.

The added complication was that whereas Clarissa's grotty old car was a hatchback with room in the boot, Gordon's car was a saloon with a closed boot. To make matters worse, because he'd been practically living in his car, his back seat was covered in ... stuff. Belongings, Toby supposed. Musty, dust-caked belongings.

"There's no room," Toby pointed out. *Not for me* and *my four friends*!

Clarissa yanked open the side door and peered inside. "Yeah, it is a bit cramped in there." She began to collect together some of Gordon's things. "Can we move these into the boot?" she asked.

"How about we move them into the house?" Gordon asked. He was wearing a sleeveless stripy t-shirt and a pair of gaudy knee-length shorts that showed off his slim, sporty physique and impressive tan, in stark contrast to Clarissa, who was as milky pale as the ghost of Old Joe.

"How about we don't?" Clarissa replied without looking at him, still gathering up an armful of items.

"Then how about we leave the mutt at home?" Gordon pulled a pair of dark sunglasses out of the side pocket of the driver's door and slipped them on.

Clarissa flashed a look of annoyance at him. "Oh, alright," she sighed, and headed towards the front door to dump everything just inside. "But can you at least put the paddle board or whatever it is, and the oars, down by the side of the house? They'll be fine there."

Huffing, Gordon did as he was told. That left just a few items remaining in the Crapmobile—some throws or blankets, a couple of jumpers and a raincoat —but space behind the seats. It was workable.

Toby nodded at Moriarty. Quick as you like, the cat leapt gracefully through the air and landed on the car's bonnet right beside Gordon, who, amusingly, nearly jumped out of his skin.

"Where the blazes did you come from?" he asked.

"Literally five feet away," she told him, but all Gordon heard was *meowowowow*.

"Scoot," he said. "Bloomin' furry creatures left, right and centre. Doing my nut in! Bog off. Go on."

Moriarty dug her claws into the Crapmobile's paintwork.

Gordon reeled, gasping in surprise. "You did *not* just do that! Get off!" He swung for the cat and she danced backwards. "Get away! Shoo!"

Sending a silent blessing to Moriarty, Toby hissed into the buddleia bush. "Quick!"

Jack shot out first and dived into the back of the car, dropping into the well behind the passenger seat; Bryn followed him but struggled with his short legs to make it up. Pippin hoisted him upwards and buried him next to Jack. That left Troot—whose legs were long enough to jump inside—and Pippin. Toby brought up the rear. Pippin seemed to take up an enormous amount of room.

"Lie down!" Toby ordered, and when she did so, he uttered a little spell. "*Blanket*!" he said, and one of the throws rearranged itself to cover her up. It was a spell he employed on himself regularly whenever he was cold.

Not that he'd be cold today. Poor Pippin; she was liable to swelter if they didn't get going soon.

"I'm ready!" he called to Clarissa.

This also acted as a signal to Moriarty. Finally,

much to Gordon's relief, she jumped from the car bonnet back to the wall. "Good luck!" she called as she fled from there and Gordon's wrath, across the road and into the safety of her own garden.

"Blasted thing." Gordon threw himself into the driver's seat and slammed his door. "Hurry up, Clar!"

"I'm coming, I'm coming," Clarissa said, clambering in beside him. "Okay, Toby?" she asked.

"I'm good," Toby said, and finally Gordon started the engine.

The Crapmobile didn't have air conditioning, but fortunately for everyone—particularly the stowaways—Gordon preferred to drive with the windows down anyway, so there was a welcome breeze.

More like a hurricane when he put his foot down, but that wasn't possible when he was driving up the steep hills that led out of Sunshine Valley.

Toby settled in a sitting position on top of the raincoat and what turned out to be a sleeping bag. It offered him a bird's-eye view of Chamberlain Drive as they cruised away. Not that the Crapmobile 'cruised' particularly. It had an engine like a tractor. Rumbling and noisy with a tendency to clank. To Toby it sounded as though pieces were missing that shouldn't have been.

He crossed his paws that they would get where they were going without incident.

Sunshine Valley was a small town and they quickly left the houses behind, driving past Dorset Rise and then Somerset Downs—the brand-spanking-new housing estate with its teeny-weeny houses that all looked identical—and out into the lush countryside. The trees were wearing their full glorious summer foliage; the hedges were bursting with birds and wildlife; there were pretty summer flowers nestling on the verges and chocolate box cottages with thatched roofs dotted here and there. The fields were full of sheep and donkeys, cows ... and was that a llama?

Toby twisted around to get a better look. Really? A llama? But Gordon had his foot down now and the fluffy thing—resembling Pippin but with a longer neck—disappeared behind them.

"It stinks of dog in this car," Gordon grumbled. "Don't you ever give him a bath?"

Clarissa sniffed the air. "Toby doesn't smell. And yes, I bathe him every now and again. When he needs it."

"No-one ever needs a barf," Toby muttered, although to be fair, both Pippin and Troot could have done with one, but given that they'd spent a significant amount of time the previous day taking shelter beneath the sprinklers it couldn't be them who were a bit stinky.

That left Bryn and Jack. Toby's money was on Jack. Bryn smelt of incense and herbs. A proper sweet puppy smell.

Gordon sneezed. "Ugh. I think I have an allergy to dogs."

Clarissa pointed at the yellow field they were passing. "It's probably hay fever. That rape blossom gets everyone. It even makes my eyes itch."

"I've never had hay fever before," Gordon argued. "It's the dog hair, I'm telling you."

"Toby doesn't have hair, he has fur."

"I'm hypoallergenic," Toby agreed.

Gordon tutted, directing a glare in the rear-view mirror at Toby. "Sit back, will you," he demanded.

Clarissa half turned. "Relax, Tobes," she smiled. "We'll soon be there."

Having consulted one of Old Joe's maps, Toby knew they didn't have far to go. He kept a partial eye on the direction Gordon was taking because he didn't trust him, but as long as they ended up within a stone's throwing distance of Bushy Leaze, he'd be happy.

Once they reached the village, Misty, the dog who'd alerted them to the pink car the previous evening, would be guiding them towards where she lived.

Gordon took a right. The road, already narrow, became a lane, and not even one that was properly tarmacked. This was East Devon all over. Tiny roads and paths that led deep into the countryside, following ancient tracks shrouded by mystical trees.

They didn't go much further. A white on brown road sign alerted Clarissa to the existence of a picnic spot with a car park. She pointed it out to Gordon, who, driving much too fast for the condition of the road, had to swerve hard left, almost taking out an old gatepost and sending Toby flying sideways.

"Ooh! Tobes! Are you alright, darling?" Clarissa cried, turning and reaching for him.

"I'm fine. Fine!" Toby said, willing her to turn back, but too late, she spotted the wriggling bump that was Pippin.

"What–" she began to ask. But Toby decided offence was the best form of defence in this situation and lifted his nose to howl.

"*Ooowooowooowoow!*" he sang. "I think I wrenched my neck!"

Clarissa's eyes widened. "Whiplash?"

"Can't you shut him up?" Gordon demanded.

"He's hurt!" Clarissa snapped back.

"He's a woos. A noisy nuisance!" Gordon wrenched the handbrake on and everyone shot forwards then backwards. Troot groaned.

Clarissa glared at Gordon. "It's your driving!"

"Feel free to walk home," Gordon sneered. "And take your furry monster in the back there with you."

"What's the matter with you?" Clarissa grumbled. "I don't understand why you don't like him!"

Clarissa might not understand, but Toby did. Gordon didn't want to share Clarissa with anyone. That seemed obvious.

"I thought you were an animal lover," Clarissa said. "That's what you always used to tell me."

Gordon didn't seem to have an answer to that, but Toby was willing to bet that Gordon told his girlfriends whatever they wanted to hear just to remain in their good books.

The car was beginning to heat up now that they were stationary and there was no breeze to keep everyone cool. As the humans bickered, Toby considered his options. Getting everydoggy in the car had been no mean feat, but now they had no Moriarty to cause a distraction so he could get everyone out.

The answer came to him like a shot out of the blue. The same spell Clarissa had used on the Mercedes a few days ago. "*Deflate*!" he whispered, nodding at the front passenger side. Clarissa looked back over her shoulder at him and frowned. Almost immediately, the front left-hand side of the car slumped gently downwards.

"What the blazes?" Gordon sat in stunned silence for a second before throwing open his door and jumping out.

Toby heard him cursing as he discovered his flat tyre.

"What's going on, Toby?" Clarissa narrowed her eyes. "What are you up to?"

Toby scratched at the blanket next to him, revealing a rapidly overheating Pippin.

"Toby!" Clarissa scolded. "Gordon will be furious if he finds out—"

"Let's not let him find out then," Toby suggested. "We just need an hour or so. Have your picnic and reinflate the tyre. We'll be back before you know it."

Clarissa considered her options, then, blowing air out of her lungs in a hard sigh, she clicked her seatbelt free and opened her door. Ignoring Gordon, who was crouched next to the flat tyre trying to ascertain the issue—there wasn't one except a lack of air in it—Clarissa hurried around to Toby's side of the car and opened the rear door. He hopped down, quickly followed by Pippin, and then before Clarissa could close the door, Troot, Jack and finally Bryn bringing up the rear.

Clarissa shook her head as the stowaway dogs darted for the cover of the nearest thicket.

Only Toby hung back, taking a moment to cock his leg against the driver's side rear wheel.

"Honestly, Toby," she remonstrated, but quietly. Gordon was only feet away. "You'll be the death of me."

"I hope not!" Toby winked at her. "Cheers, Clarissa! See you in a bit!"

The dogs gathered behind a fallen tree for a swift powwow. There wasn't a plan as such, but Pippin had been acting as a mediator earlier this morning and Misty would be expecting them anytime now.

"Should we split up?" Jack asked. He'd turned out to be amazingly gung-ho for such a small fellow, but Toby was wise enough to realise that they needed all personality types on their team. Bryn was a little cutie who liked tummy tickles, and Troot, while doing his best to be fierce and brave, could at times be a worrier.

"I don't think that will be necessary," Toby told his wayward band of furry followers. "Once we're clear of the car and hoomans, we'll let Misty know we've arrived."

Pippin nodded. "That's the most sensible option. We really don't want to alert anyone else to our presence if we can help it."

Bryn shivered. "Especially the puppynapper."

"Exactly," Toby replied seriously. "This is a dangerous mission so we need to stay together." He glanced around, nodding at each dog in turn. "No going off-piste."

Troot and Bryn exchanged looks, Troot's face aghast. "You mean—"

"We're not allowed to pee?" Bryn finished for him. "But ... but ... I can't hold it in for very long. I've only got a small bladder."

Toby's brows knitted together. What were they on about?

"It's fine," Pippin intervened. "All calls of nature are permitted."

"Of course they are!" Toby jerked his head. "Let's get going."

Sneaking a peep over his shoulder to check on Gordon, Toby nodded in satisfaction. Clarissa was effectively body-blocking Gordon's view. The boot was open, suggesting they'd been searching for a jack—of the mechanical kind. It would take them a while to sort out the issue that wasn't actually an issue, *but* it wouldn't take all day. He needed to get a move on.

The dogs followed Toby through a gap in the fence separating the car park from the lane that Gordon had driven down. They made their way back towards the main road—although it wasn't that much wider than a country lane itself. They took the right turning and trotted along the grass verge, the soil dry and crumbling between their paws, ants and small beetles going about their business beneath the cool clover and dandelion coverage. A little further along, they spotted a small, crooked cottage with an enormous barn beside it. Toby nodded at Pippin.

Lifting her head, Pippin barked. A series of three short yips, clear and loud. "Yip. Yip. Yip."

Almost instantaneously, she received an answer—a loud "Yip, yip, yip," in return.

A microsecond later, a Border collie vaulted over the closed gate and ran to meet them. She was a young dog, two or three years old, part house dog and part working dog by the look of her.

"Which one of you is Toby?" she asked, examining all of the dogs with wide, sparkling eyes. She spoke loudly, and Toby couldn't help worrying that she might alert her humans to his presence.

"That would be me," Toby replied, with just the right amount of gravitas. Or so he thought.

"I'm so thrilled to meet you!" Misty gushed.

"The pleasure is all mine, I can assure you." Toby smiled. "May I introduce you to Pippin," he said, gesturing to his fluffy white friend, "Jack"—he nodded at the Jack Russell—"and these two rapscallions are Troot and Bryn."

"Pleased to meet you all," Misty barked, staring intently at each in turn. "Can I interest you in some water? I know a great little stream. The water is as cool and clear as you like."

"Pipe down, Misty!" a woman's voice called, but Misty took no notice.

Toby would have preferred to get straight down to business given the time restraints, but he had a duty of care to the puppies so, reluctantly, he nodded and fell into step beside Misty as she led them past her crooked cottage and down to a wooded copse behind the barn. The countryside fell away here, and they could hear the stream before they saw it. It bubbled quietly over flinty terrain, carving its path down the hill where eventually it would meet the river and join forces on its way to the sea, not so very far away.

While the puppies lapped at the water, Pippin and Misty exchanged polite—but loud—conversation. Yes, she occasionally worked with her hooman, who was employed on the neighbouring farm, but most of the time she kept her hooman mummy company in the barn. "She has a kitchen in there," said Misty.

"A kitchen?" Toby looked back up the hill at the gigantic structure they'd passed. *Must be an industrial size kitchen*!

"Yes. She bakes cakes for garden centres so she has a special unit in there."

"Ohmygollygosh!" Toby could hardly believe it. "And you get to spend time in there with her?"

"I'm confined to a corner, to be fair. Health and safety and all that—"

"But even so! It sounds heavenly!"

Troot, water dripping from his little baby beard, piped up, "Do you get to lick the bowls?"

"Beg your pardon, young man?" Misty asked, coming close to peer down at the puppy.

"I said, do you get to lick the bowls?" Troot repeated.

"Absolutely not," Misty replied firmly. "But I do get plenty of leftovers, the semi-burned bits."

"Ohhhhh." Troot pretended to faint. Bryn giggled and jumped on top of him. Together the two of them rolled into the water with a splash.

"Stop messing around, you two," Pippin barked. "It's my turn to have a drink."

"And then we *really* need to crack on," Toby agreed.

"Beg pardon?" Misty asked.

"We should get moving," Toby said, enunciating every word. He had a feeling Misty was as deaf as a post.

"We don't need to go up to the road; we can approach it from the back," Misty told them.

The hill became steeper as they followed Misty down. Not far from the edge of her property—the barn was set in an unused paddock—was a tall fence concocted from old doors, chicken wire of various vintages—some of it badly rusted and some of it almost sparklingly new—and fence posts and panels that had long seen better days.

Beyond the fence were several low, ramshackle and decaying buildings reminiscent of the old Anderson air raid shelters, but taller, longer and sturdier. Judging by the domed shape of them, they'd first been utilised during the Second World War. The white stucco of the concrete had long since turned grey; the single-paned windows were taped or covered in faded newspaper. Tall weeds grew out of the rocky, unkempt ground surrounding each of the buildings. Old wire crates, water barrels on their sides, a wheelbarrow, discarded tyres, a child's bicycle, an old tin bath and half a dozen faded buckets and washing bowls lay abandoned. Black bin liners full of rubbish had been piled against the wall of one of the buildings, and plastic and tin cans had spilled out of some of them where the neighbourhood's foxes had managed to get at them.

Toby pressed his nose against the rusted wire and took it all in. Cocking his head, he listened.

"Do you hear that?" he whispered to Pippin, who had sidled up next to him to get a better look.

"Hear what?" she whispered back. "I can't hear anything at all."

"Exactly." Toby stood silently. Behind him he could hear the faint rustle of the leaves on the fully loaded trees and the twittering of the birds who sheltered there. He could still hear the stream as it slipped away from them, enjoying its meander over rocks and pebbles. He could hear the breath of the puppies and the jangle of Bryn's collar. But from the buildings in front of them? There wasn't the slightest sound.

There was no pink car either.

"Can we get in to have a look?" Toby asked.

Misty nodded. "I can get you in to wander around the compound, but there's no way into the buildings."

I could get in if I wanted to, Toby thought to himself. He gestured at the others to stay where they were. "Don't follow me," he told them. "Pippin is in charge. I'll be back shortly."

Misty had found a concealed entrance that had been missed by whoever had repaired the mish-mash of fences. The wire had peeled away from the corner of a post, and by crawling on his belly, Toby was able to get through. The little rat run had been well used and stank of fox with a hint of badger and undertones of weasel.

Clarissa would be pleased. Once through to the other side, Toby padded up to the first structure. The old wooden door at the front, painted a rather dismal shade of green, had been chained and padlocked.

Toby paused there, tipped his head and sniffed.

The air smelt ... of nothing.

That really wasn't possible.

He hurriedly sniffed himself, his chest, his paws, his armpits. Yes. A bit of fox. A bit of badger. A bit of rat. A lot of his own smell.

Elsewhere?

No sounds.

No smell.

Magick, he decided. *But why*?

He trotted across to the next building. Nothing

interesting to see. Nothing to hear. Still nothing to smell.

Disappointed, he wandered back towards Misty waiting at the gap in the fence, but stopped before he made it halfway, turned about and sniffed the ground some more. In the wide space between the two buildings was evidence of oil, as though a car had been parked here recently and had been leaking. Not much. Just a little.

"Yep," Misty hissed. She probably thought she was being quiet, but chances were every dog within a mile radius could hear her. "That's where I've seen that pink car."

Toby turned in a circle. The buildings were secure and yet there was no fence to the front. The property opened out onto a dirt track. The same track that ran down the side of Misty's crooked house. Toby could tell by the amount of vegetation growing up through the mud ruts in what passed as a road that very little traffic ever came this way.

Toby, out of ideas, slowly returned to where Misty waited for him. On the way, he couldn't resist investigating the pile of black rubbish bags. They called out to him and probably every other four legged creature in the vicinity. They had to be worth examining. He sniffed all around them first, but could discern absolutely nothing. Not a hint of food or clothing or anything that might give off a scent.

And yet the foxes had dragged out a number of items and dispersed them around the general area. Old rags. Blankets. Curtains. Books. Newspapers. General household rubbish. None of it had a scent. How could that be?

Toby scraped at one of the bags himself, slitting the plastic. He recoiled, staring down at what had been revealed.

A pair of tiny collars.

Puppy collars.

The kind puppies grow out of very quickly.

CHAPTER FIFTEEN

"What now?" Pippin asked as they took their leave of Misty and hurried back towards the car park, following the scent trail they'd left earlier—not that they wouldn't have been able to find it, but every little sniff helps.

Toby knitted his impressive eyebrows together. "I don't know, really. There's no hard evidence of the car there, just the oil, but that could belong to any car." Clarissa's Nissan leaked like the proverbial sieve. "And no evidence of dogs—"

"But the puppy collars," Jack interrupted. "That's evidence, surely?"

Neither Bryn nor Jack had been able to positively identify the collars, which meant they probably didn't belong to Bron or Alphonse. "If I was DC Plum, I'd almost certainly say a pair of discarded puppy collars doesn't have to mean anything." Toby sighed. "And would a police officer have justifiable cause to gain entrance to those buildings? Again, I think not." Toby knew from watching all his favourite television shows there was a thing called a warrant, and they were stupidly hard to get. He couldn't understand why, if a crime was suspected, a police officer couldn't just break down the door and let him or herself in.

But apart from the collars, what did Toby have?

A possible sighting of a pink car which might or might not be the one they were trying to find and which might or might not be involved in the puppy-nappings ...

It wasn't much to go on.

Feeling a little down in the dumps, Toby led the dogs into the car park. Gordon's car was up on a jack, doors open, and Gordon was half under it, tinkering. How long had the dogs been gone? Not quite forty minutes.

So preoccupied was he, that Toby momentarily forgot about all the subterfuge. "Hop in, team," he told the others, and one by one they all jumped into the back. The addition of weight to the back seat caused the car to overbalance on the jack and it began to wobble.

Quick as a flash, Clarissa grabbed hold of Gordon's shoulders, and with a little magickal surge of strength and a quick spell, yanked him clear.

"Oopsie." Toby wandered around to their side of the car to check on Gordon.

"What the blazes?" Gordon sat up, slightly dazed.

Clarissa widened her eyes at Toby.

"Soz," he said, then nodded at the tyre. He couldn't be bothered to wait any longer and he'd run out of imagination. The afternoon was too hot. He wanted to head home and give himself space to think. "*Inflate*!" he ordered, and the tyre began to fill up by itself, hissing as the air sucked in.

Gordon glared at Clarissa. "Did you do that?"

"No." She shot Toby a warning glance.

"You and your witchy, wily ways—"

"Gordon!" Clarissa glowered back at him. "You know who I am and what I am, and you always have."

"I find it unnerving." Gordon shuddered. "And if you were going to do that all along, couldn't you have done it two hours ago?"

"We haven't been here for two hours," Clarissa pointed out. "I didn't make the tyre flat, and I didn't reinflate it."

That much was the truth.

"Shall we get going?" Toby asked, scratching at the ground impatiently.

"Where's he been?" Gordon asked. "I was hoping he'd run off somewhere."

"Bad luck, sucker," Toby sniped back at him. "It's a shame *you* don't."

"Toby," Clarissa warned him. "Get in the back of the car."

"Okay! Okay!"

"What about the picnic?" Gordon asked. "I thought that's what we came all the way out here for?"

"To be fair, it's not all the way out, is it?" Clarissa asked, leaning down to start collecting Gordon's tools together. "We're not that far from home."

Gordon picked up the jack. "I really don't understand what's going on."

"Let's just go home. Get out of the sun. We can have our lunch in the back garden," Clarissa suggested.

"If you insist." Gordon threw the tools and the jack into the boot, slammed it so hard the whole car vibrated, then clambered into the driver's seat. The dogs settled themselves beneath the throws and in the footwells ...

Gordon, in a temper, sneezed violently all the way home.

Moriarty was waiting for Toby on the wall as their car pulled in. Clarissa was quick to hop out of the car first and open the rear passenger door so that the dogs could make a rapid escape. Pippin dived out, followed by Jack and Troot. Bryn tumbled nose first and face-planted on the asphalt. "Ow!" he yelped.

"Ooochy!" Clarissa straightened him up and rubbed his face better, sliding his mouth open to check on his tiny little shark teeth. "You'll live," she murmured, "now scat!" The dogs shot off in different directions, hurtling past Gordon at the speed of light. Distracted by movement, he turned his head, but the dogs were fast and he didn't catch sight of them.

He did spot Moriarty, however.

"Stay away from my car," he warned her. "If I catch you damaging my paintwork again, I swear I'll turn you into a bagpipe."

"That's not very nice," Moriarty told him. *Meow meowow.*

"Ignore the crotchety old tyrant," Toby told her. "We'll turn *him* into a sporran."

Moriarty cackled. "I like it."

"I'll set up the table and chairs out the back, shall

I?" Clarissa offered, grabbing her things from the car and fumbling for her phone.

"I s'pose," said Gordon, less than graciously. "I'm bloomin' starving!"

"Won't be long—" As Clarissa uttered the words, her phone signal suddenly tapped into the house Wi-Fi and sprang into action. *Beedley beep*! it sang.

Beedley beep!

And again. *Beedley beep!*

And again! *Beedley beep!*

And over and over for what seemed like an eternity.

Moriarty and Toby simultaneously turned to cock heads. "She's popular," Moriarty remarked.

"She doesn't get a signal on that thing when we're out. It's useless. It must be catching up."

"Oh."

Clarissa dropped her bags and belongings to paw at her screen. "Crikey," she said. "I'm besieged with emails. Look at this—"

Beedley beep!

Beedley beep!

"They're still coming in!"

Gordon sidled up to her to take a look over her shoulder. "What is it? Spam?"

Beedley beep!

Beedley beep!

"Let me see." Clarissa thumbed open a message. "Dear Miss Page," she read. "I saw your piece in *The Celestine Times* this morning—Oh!" Clarissa gasped. "Of course. My puppy piece has probably been released today. I didn't get a date for it but—wait—let me ... oh yes. Look!" She waved her phone. "This woman had a puppy stolen in Somerset two weeks ago!"

"Big deal," Gordon grumbled. "Can't you read them after lunch?"

"Hang about." Clarissa began to scroll through the other emails. "Yep. There's another stolen puppy here. Torbay. That's not far away. And one here in the Blackdown Hills—"

Toby pricked his ears up. That's where his squizzel friends lived.

Beedley beep!

Beedley beep!

"Oh my goodness. I think the world is blowing up!" Clarissa grabbed her bags and made a rush for the side of the house, intending to go in through the back door. "Sorry, guys. Could you set up lunch for me? I really must have a proper look at these and contact my editor. This is a much bigger story than I imagined. Than anyone imagined!"

Toby listened to the excitement in her voice. Finally! A story she could get her teeth into, so to speak. With the added advantage that the more people who heard about it, the more likely it was that he'd have some more tip-offs and would be able to rescue the puppies.

"That's good news, kind of," Toby said. "Not good news for the puppies and their owners maybe, but people will start to take it serious—"

From down the side of the house came a sudden rumble, a clatter, a thud and a long, drawn-out shriek that turned Toby's blood cold. Quick as a flash he abandoned Moriarty and dashed around the front of the house and up the side. Clarissa, her face as white as a sheet, lay on the ground, partially covered by the long ladder that was usually secured into place there.

Beneath her was a paddle board and a pile of Gordon's other belongings: stuff he'd removed from the car earlier to make room for the picnic items. And Toby.

Toby jumped over the tangle of debris. "Clarissa? Clarissa?" he wailed.

She pushed herself up on one arm, reaching with the other hand to touch her leg. "Oh, oh, oh!" she cried, tears streaming down her face. "I've hurt myself. I've hurt myself badly."

Gordon appeared next to them. "Clar?"

"Call an ambulance, Gordon," she sobbed. "I think I've broken my leg!"

"Stand back, please, let us through!" The first paramedic on the scene hurried down the narrow passageway between the house and the fence to next door's property.

Gordon, twisting his hands, backed away, his face ashen. "Thank heavens! I didn't know what to do. I thought you were never going to get here."

The paramedic merely nodded in his direction, but set down her case and knelt beside Clarissa. "Alright, love?" she asked. "We're here now. Can someone take the dog?"

"Take me?" Toby began to shiver. That was exactly what had happened when the police had come to the house after Old Joe had died. He'd been incarcerated in the Sunshine Valley Pet Sanctuary and had come a smidgen too close to being terminated.

"No," Clarissa said. "No-one's taking him anywhere. He's staying with me."

"He won't be able to come to the hospital with you," the paramedic replied.

"I don't need to go to the hospital," Clarissa told her. Toby stared down at the strange angle of her ankle. Quite clearly she did. He would be separated from his beloved hooman, and he would need to be brave.

"I'll be okay," he told her, dying slightly inside.

"You stay here with me!" Clarissa hugged him close, the tears beginning to roll down her face once more. "I promised you—"

"What's your name, my lovely?" the paramedic asked. Another one was rushing up the path now; presumably he'd been parking the ambulance.

"It's Clarissa," said Gordon. He hovered awkwardly close by, not sure where to put himself.

"Clarissa Page," whispered Clarissa, her face contorted in agony.

"Alright, Clarissa. I'm Abi and this is Mark. I'm going to take a look at you and Mark is going to give you some air."

"What sort of air?" Toby asked. He felt a responsibility, like he needed to check everything they were doing.

"Magick air," Clarissa told him.

"Can you tell me what happened, Clarissa?" Mark asked, reaching over to attach a mask to Clarissa's face before clipping something to her finger.

"I wasn't looking where I was going." Clarissa gestured at her mobile phone. It had been launched out of her hand as she'd tumbled and ended up in a flower bed about eight feet away.

Gordon offered his two penn'orth worth. "She's so clumsy."

Clarissa didn't have the energy to cover for him. "I tripped over his paddle board and landed awkwardly. The ladder fell on top of me."

"Did you bang your head at all?" Abi wanted to know. She was shining a wand—or a pen or something —into Clarissa's eyes.

"No." Clarissa shook her head.

"And you didn't lose consciousness at all?"

"No."

"Okay. Great." Abi fiddled with the mask. "Take big gulps of that for me. That's it. Excellent. I'm going to take a look at your leg."

Clarissa shrieked so loudly that Toby's hair stood on end. He barked, partly in empathy with Clarissa, partly because he was afraid, and partly because Clarissa was squeezing him so tightly, he was worried that his insides were going to pop out.

"Please take the dog," Abi told Gordon.

"Noooo!" Clarissa growled, clutching Toby's collar.

Gordon took a step back. "He's nothing to do with me."

"I'll take him." Mrs Crouch's calm, quiet voice reached them from the front end of the narrow passageway.

"Oh, Mrs Crouch!" howled Toby. "Clarissa is hurt and they want to take me away."

"Come on," she cooed softly. "Come to me and let them look after Clarissa properly."

"No, it's okay." Gordon suddenly intervened. He stepped closer to Clarissa and grabbed Toby by the collar. "Come on, scruffbag."

"Ow!" Toby tried to twist out of his grasp.

"Behave!" Gordon glowered.

"Gordon!" Clarissa protested.

"Settle down, my love," Abi soothed. "It's for the best if we remove the dog just in case he turns nasty."

"But he's never nasty—"

Gordon dragged Toby around the corner, opened the kitchen door and almost flung the poor dog inside. From outside, Toby could hear Clarissa calling for him. Shaking with indignation, he threw himself back at the exit. Gordon was too quick. Stretching out his leg, he effectively blocked Toby's progress. Then, reaching down, he snapped the locks into place on the dog flap. Before Toby could respond,

Gordon backed outside and slammed the door shut after him.

"*Reperio*!" Toby barked, and the locks worked their way free. From outside, he heard the clanking of the ladders and the grinding sound as they were dragged around the corner. "You can't keep a good dog down," he said and launched himself at the dog flap. It rattled but remained closed. Toby pushed his nose against the flap. It opened an inch or two, but that was all. Gordon had barricaded it shut with the errant ladder.

Furious, Toby chased to the front of the house, ready to unlock the door there and make his way back to Clarissa from that direction. He pelted down the hallway but skidded to a halt when he realised that a pair of eyes were staring in at him through the letterbox.

"Toby?" Mrs Crouch's soft, urgent whisper. "Are you alright?"

"Stand back, Mrs Crouch. I'm coming through!" he told her.

"Noooo," Mrs Crouch hissed back at him. "I wouldn't do that."

Toby faltered. "You wouldn't?"

"No. Let the ambulance folk do their work in peace. Don't give them an excuse to set the authorities on you."

That's what had happened before.

"The sooner they get Clarissa sorted, the sooner she'll be home with you," Mrs Crouch continued.

Toby's lip wobbled. "You promise?"

"I do. Cross my heart."

"Okay." Toby sat on the cool floor, shaking with shock and fear.

"Good boy," Mrs Crouch said. "Just be patient. It will be alright."

What choice did he have? "Alright."

"And Toby?"

"Yes, Mrs Crouch?"

"I'm only next door if you need me."

That made him feel a little better. Tail firmly between his legs, he slunk into the living room, avoiding the mess of belongings Gordon had littered everywhere, then jumped up onto the armchair beside the television. It was the one Clarissa—and Old Joe in his time—liked to proffer to guests. It also provided Toby—not the guests because they would be facing the wrong way—a great view of the front garden, the Crap-mobile and the ambulance.

Toby watched as Mark, the second paramedic, entered the ambulance to collect some things. He disappeared out of sight back up the passageway. A crowd had gathered to watch what was going on, heads craning to see whatever disaster had befallen the hapless inhabitants of number 13 Chamberlain Drive.

Toby remained there, stock still, only his eyes flickering left and right, for another fifteen minutes until the spectators began to shuffle backwards, making a little room out of respect. Clarissa was carried out on a stretcher, the mask clamped to her face. She did appear to be a little more relaxed now, so Toby assumed they had given her more magick air. Lucky Clarissa! He needed some magick air to take away the pain in his heart.

He slapped a paw against the window, wanting to make contact with his beloved hooman. Perhaps she felt the weight of his need and his love, because she wriggled upright and lifted her hands. As she disappeared inside the back of the ambulance, she formed the shape of a heart with her fingers.

Mark had a quick word with Gordon. Toby couldn't hear what was being said, but Gordon shook his head and gestured at the house and then the Crapmobile. Mark nodded and slammed the ambulance door, walked around to the driver's side, and spoke into a radio.

That was it. A few moments later, he was indicating and pulling away from the front of the house, Abi in the back of the vehicle with Clarissa.

Toby lifted his head and howled.

"You can stop that bleedin' nonsense," Gordon said. He'd let himself in the front using Clarissa's house keys. "I'm in charge now, so things are going to be a whole lot different." He gestured at the front door. "I'm going to start by setting you free."

Toby sniffed sadly. "You can't set something free that's already free," he pointed out.

Of course, all Gordon could hear was *woowoowooowoooowooo*!

"Go on. Get out, you blasted noisy bogger! When Clarissa comes back I'll tell her you ran off."

"Tell her what you like," said Toby. "She won't believe you." Pulling together every ounce of dignity he possessed, he tossed his furry head and jumped down to the floor. "This is as much my house as Clarissa's. I'll go, but I can assure you ... I'll be back."

"And don't go whinging to that nosy old battle-axe next door, either," Gordon spat.

"You have no control over me, Greedy, Grubby, Gruesome, Gormless Gordon." Toby lifted his tail and trotted past him. "You'll get what's coming to you, I promise."

CHAPTER SIXTEEN

"So now what?" Moriarty asked.

Effectively homeless thanks to Grubby Gordon, Toby hadn't ventured very far. He and Moriarty were sitting together in front of Toby's garden wall. Moriarty had been watching events unfold from a safe distance, and now Toby had filled her in on how the morning's venture up to Bushy Leaze had gone.

"That's a very good question," Toby answered. "On all fronts."

He sighed. *Poor Clarissa. Poor me. Who knows where my next sammich will come from.*

"I suppose you could go and hang out with your *friends*." Toby kind of had the feeling that Moriarty didn't much approve of Pippin, perhaps because

Pippin was also distrustful of Moriarty. Cat and dog wars. What can you do?

Toby had considered heading over to the market but quickly dismissed it out of hand. "I don't think that will be necessary. I know Mrs Crouch will let me stay with her." He sniffed. *And there's no danger that I'll starve with dear old Mrs Crouch. The last thing I want to do is eat cauliflower stalks and beetroot ends off the ground in the marketplace.*

"That's cool. I'd offer to put you up but ... you know." Moriarty stretched.

"Sure." Toby didn't know, but he decided to assume that Moriarty's hoomans wouldn't like it.

"And what about your *case*?" Moriarty asked. "What are you going to do about that?"

The pain of recent events had *almost* knocked Toby's investigative impetus out of his mind, but now that he'd stopped shaking and had warmed up, and the shock of what had happened had begun to ease, he realised that he needed to refocus.

"Before the accident, Clarissa had just found out that there are lots of other hoomans—some local, some a little further afield—who have also had their puppies stolen. This is much bigger than we initially thought. Whatever happens to me—" he replied stoically, not that he was in *any* impending danger, thanks to Mrs

Crouch, "I have to press on. For the sake of the puppies."

"Is the case too big, do you reckon?" Moriarty asked. "Perhaps you'll have to leave it to Clarissa and some other hoomans?"

"Like DC Plum?" Toby mused. The problem was, he couldn't communicate with DC Plum without Clarissa's help.

But that wasn't strictly true, was it? If push came to shove he could talk to Mrs Crouch, and she would talk to Ed for him.

"I think you have to go back," Moriarty was saying.

Toby blinked. He'd been lost deep in thought. Would it be right and proper to involve the elderly Mrs Crouch? He didn't want to get her into any kind of trouble or put her in danger. "Go back?"

"Back to the place you visited this morning."

"There was nothing there," Toby reminded Moriarty, but without much conviction. There had been something remarkably odd about that place. The silence and the memory of the puppy collars were weighing on him. It was too coincidental.

"Check it out again," Moriarty urged him. "Maybe at a different time of the day. Maybe at night."

That made a lot of sense. If the pink car had often been parked there of late, as Misty had suggested it had been, the chances were he'd simply missed it this morning. Maybe this pink car *was* the car they were looking for, and maybe the driver was both a car thief and a puppynapper. The possibility was that the puppynapper had a regular job too; lots of hoomans did. Toby couldn't afford to leave any stone unturned.

And in the absence of any other leads, what else did he have to go on?

But now he had one glaringly obvious problem.

How would he get there?

"I understand the problem, Toby." Mrs Crouch returned her delicate teacup to its saucer. She, Toby and Moriarty were sitting in Mrs Crouch's front room. Moriarty had chosen the armchair, and if Mrs Crouch minded having black cat hair shed all over her otherwise pristine three-piece suite, she didn't say so.

As always, she'd been the perfect hostess. Toby had had a clean bowl of fresh water, and Moriarty a saucer full of cream milk. They'd both enjoyed fresh tuna biscuits, not long out of the oven, almost as though Mrs Crouch had been expecting them to turn up.

Toby had the sofa to himself and was stretched out,

resting his head on the arm. It had been a long, trying day and he was exhausted.

"Truly I do," Mrs Crouch continued. "I agree with you both that you need to get back out there and take another look."

Moriarty nodded, elegantly washing her face. "That's what I said."

"And I want to help you, but there's a major issue, of course."

Toby waited, but he knew exactly what it was.

"I don't drive. I mean, I do. Or I did. But I haven't had a car for a long, long time now."

Toby nodded, trying not to look miserable. Is this where he had to try and get Mrs Crouch to talk to Dead-to-me Ed? Ed had a car. But even if he managed to get Mrs Crouch to convey the problem to Ed, surely Ed would think Mrs Crouch was being eccentric and refuse to give her the time of day?

Mrs Crouch was one step ahead of Toby though. "Of course, there is one possible way of doing this?"

Toby sat upright. Moriarty stopped washing her face.

"I vaguely know Bushy Leaze. I had a friend who used to live there—many years ago." Mrs Crouch's slightly dull eyes slipped sideways as she remembered the past. "The thing is, there used to be a regular bus service up there." She smiled at Toby. "I wonder if there still is?"

"Squidge up, Troot!" Bryn was complaining.

"I can't!" Troot hissed. "That lady's bottom is taking up all the room!"

'That lady' happened to be Mrs Crouch. She hadn't so much as blinked when Toby had told her he would have to bring along his whole investigative team. It wasn't so much that he *needed* them—although there was strength in numbers—but rather he felt that, given everyone had so much at stake, they all had a right to be part of the investigation.

Mrs Crouch had pulled out an archaic paper timetable from her bookshelf—probably from the 1960s—and with a little twist of her forefinger, had magickally updated it and been able to check on bus times to Bushy Leaze. As luck would have it, one of the few services that ran from Sunshine Valley towards Lyme Regis passed through Bushy Leaze.

The next one would be along at 4.03 pm.

Perfect timing.

Toby, with a little help from Moriarty and the Catvine, had summonsed his friends back to Chamberlain Drive. They'd all turned up together—Pippin made a marvellous sheepdog—and after they'd all gathered in Mrs Crouch's warm, welcoming kitchen for last-minute drinks and snacks, and careful supervision of the packing of emergency supplies and more drinks and snacks, they had said their farewells to Moriarty, leaving her up on the wall to bask in the glorious afternoon sunshine, and set off for the bus stop.

It must have looked comical. Mrs Crouch leaned heavily on a stick. Since her attack, she'd struggled to walk far, and so the dogs shuffled along with her, nose to backside, trying not to trip over their paws or bite each other's tails, blinking if the dog in front wagged and accidentally hit them in the eye. Toby walked beside the old lady, helping to set the pace, and Pippin brought up the rear, usefully keeping the puppies in order—particularly Bryn, who twice had to be rescued when he mis-stepped and rolled off the narrow pavement and into the gutter.

They had then joined the short queue of hoomans and one other dog waiting for the bus. It turned up bang on time, looming into view like some huge mechanical Jurassic monster. Tony stared up at it, wondering at the laws of physics, and where the centre of gravity might be on such an enormous machine. As it reached the stop, it pulled into the kerb with a hiss and a squeal of brakes. "Whoa, Nelly!" Toby whimpered, while the puppies shook and shot backwards.

Mrs Crouch grabbed hold of the handle on the door to haul herself up the high step. Pippin thoughtfully buried her snout under Mrs Crouch's ample and beautifully soft bottom to give her a hand, and Mrs Crouch giggled. "Good girl!"

Jack jumped straight up behind her, but Toby could see that Troot and Bryn needed a little more persuasion.

"Come on, boys and girls," Mrs Crouch cooed. "This is ours."

"Last one on the bus has to kiss Gordon," Toby sang and leapt up beside Mrs Crouch, pressing himself against the driver's cab to avoid the resulting frenzy of legs, tails and snouts as the others fought to get on board.

"Settle down, guys," Toby said, peering anxiously upwards.

No-one in the bus queue had batted an eyelid at the sight of the eccentric old lady with all the dogs, but the driver was an entirely different beastie. He cocked an eyebrow and leaned over to get a better look. "I dunno about this ..."

"Is there a limit to the number of dogs you can

have on board?" Mrs Crouch's polite voice rang out around the bus.

"Well ... no, but ..."

"And is there a limit to the number of dogs one person can escort?"

The bus driver sighed. "No. But—"

"Then I really don't see a problem." Mrs Crouch smiled. "Which is nice, isn't it? See how quickly we've managed to banish negativity!"

"I'm not a dog transport," the bus driver grumbled. Toby began to worry that any moment now he would refuse outright to take them.

"Don't be such a stick-in-the-mud," someone from a nearby seat called. "Look at how good they're all being."

It was true. Pippin had managed to get the puppies to sit. They had engaged 'puppy eyes' and were staring up at the poor besieged bus driver with their adorable pools of shining chocolate love.

"As good as gold," another passenger said.

"Alright." The driver caved to passenger pressure. "But they're not allowed on the seats."

Not allowed on the seats? Toby pouted. How else would he see out of the window? Wasn't that the whole point of travelling on a double-decker?

"That's fine," said Mrs Crouch.

"It really isn't," Toby grumbled.

"And you'll have to pay for them," the bus driver said and began ringing through the tickets. *Clickety-click. Clickety-click. Clickety-click.*

Mrs Crouch had her purse in her hand, but now it was her turn to arch a well-plucked eyebrow. "*Pay* for them?"

Wait, what? Toby pricked up his ears. All this time he could have been travelling on the bus *for free*? Think of the places he could have visited! Why hadn't Clarissa let him in on this marvellous secret?

"Half fare," the bus driver said.

"If I'm paying half fare for five dogs, believe me, they're getting a seat," Mrs Crouch said, dropping a handful of coins into the driver's tray and snatching the ribbon of tickets he was holding out. "Come on, ladies and gentlemen," she said to the dogs, and they trooped after her towards the rear of the bus. Toby would have liked to go up to the top deck but Mrs Crouch, relying as she did on her stick, probably wouldn't have been able to navigate the stairs. The bus lurched as they reached their seats. Mrs Crouch scooped Bryn and Troot onto the seat next to her, while Toby took the one in front, with Pippin and Jack on the one in front of that.

It was a fabulous antiquated old bus: A big green

double-decker with a diesel engine at the front and the old-fashioned leather and carpet-style livery covering the seats. It could probably have made more money in a museum than shuffling from village to village in the East Devon countryside, but Toby, thrilled to be aboard, couldn't hide his excitement at his first bus journey.

Given how warm the weather was, every window on the bus had been slid open to allow the air to pass through, and now the dogs nearest the windows, much to the merriment of the other passengers, hung out, enjoying the wind as it whistled past them. There was plenty of nudging, a couple of snarls, one or two occasions when the puppies overbalanced—causing hilarity among the observing passengers—but, as the bus rattled on, with a top speed of about twenty miles an hour as it climbed the steep hills out of Sunshine Valley, every dog had its moment in the sun.

And breeze.

They snapped at flies and other wee beasties that had the audacity to fly anywhere near them and played at being bi-plane pilots while humming the theme tune from The Dambusters or making zooming noises.

Ack-ack-ack-ack-ack went Toby's rifle as they passed a caravan park—populated by enemy soldiers, naturally.

Pee-own! *Pee-own*! went Bryn's cowboy gun.

Puhtoom! *Puhtoom*! Pippin preferred to let off enormous bombs, entirely indiscriminately.

And so it was that the hounds who alighted from the bus at the Bushy Leaze village stop—in front of a cute, thatched pub—were a merry band indeed. Even Toby, who had been thinking and worrying about Clarissa. How would he find out how she was? Gormless Gordon wouldn't let him know.

Mrs Crouch turned to thank the driver.

"Yes, thank you," called Toby, and the other dogs added their gratitude.

"You're welcome," the driver replied sheepishly. "They really are a well-behaved bunch," he told Mrs Crouch. "And they've cheered the other passengers up no end. Have a lovely outing!"

"Isn't that nice," remarked Mrs Crouch as they watched the bus trundle away. "Now, little ones." She turned to address Toby specifically. "What's the plan? Do you know where you are?"

Toby lifted his head, inhaled deeply, then peered up and down the road. If he wasn't mistaken, the little crooked cottage was up ahead, on the very outskirts of the village.

"We're going to stake out the compound we found this morning," Toby told her, "so we might be some time. What about you?" They hadn't thought this through. He couldn't ask Mrs Crouch to walk to the crooked cottage and then trek down the hill to the place behind the paddock. She'd never manage it.

Mrs Crouch grinned. "I'm going to wait for you here." She indicated the pub. "I can't think of anything better, can you? A country pub on a warm evening."

"I'd hate for you to be bored," Toby said.

"Don't worry, I brought my latest crochet project with me, and I'm sure the pub has a good supply of gin and tonic." Her eyes twinkled. "I'll be perfectly happy."

"Alright, if you're sure." Toby was relieved. This solution would give him one less thing to worry about.

"I have a little something for you," Mrs Crouch said and led them into the pub's garden. She deposited her carpet bag on a table and flipped it open before rummaging inside among the treats she'd packed. "Oh, what did I do with it? Hold on." She pulled out her bag of wool, then a book, her purse and a shawl. "There it is!" She held a small trinket aloft. It caught the sun and sparkled a bright lime green. "I'm going to clip this to your collar, Toby, but first–" She placed the jewel, about the size of a pebble, on the palm of her hand, waved her other hand across the top of it, whispered something unintelligible, blew on the jewel then held it up again. It had turned a darker green, more of an emerald shade than before.

Leaning over, she twisted Toby's collar so she could get at the buckle and clipped the jewel to his existing tag. "This will enable you to communicate with me if you need to," she told him, "just speak low. It will activate and I will hear you."

She nodded at each of the other dogs in turn. "If anything happens to Toby, you can use it to reach me too. Do not be afraid. You are not alone."

The dogs exchanged looks, feeling important and cared for. Pippin cleared her throat, suddenly a little emotional.

"I'll stay right here," Mrs Crouch promised, indicating a wooden table covered by a large bright sun umbrella. "Take care. See you later!"

Toby and his cheery band took their leave of Mrs Crouch and trotted away. They were quiet, but Toby could feel the excitement. They hadn't managed to get very far—just a few doors down from the pub—when they were apprehended by an elderly Yorkie with floppy ears and a pretty face. "Hey!" he called. "Hey!"

"Hey yourself." Toby stopped to exchange butt sniffs.

"Are you the dogs Misty was telling us about?" the Yorkie wanted to know.

"Probably," Toby said. How could he possibly know, given that he hadn't been party to their conversation?

"She's been telling the whole neighbourhood about you. Said you'd come to see the man in the pink car."

"You've seen him?" Toby asked. The others drew closer.

"I've seen the car for sure. It drives up and down this road regularly."

"And it's definitely a man driving it?" Toby asked, thinking about the young woman they'd met. This was the first clear sighting they'd had.

"Sure is." The Yorkie thought about this for a second. "Unless it's a bearded lady, which I guess is possible, right? You can never tell with these hoomans. Man buns. Tattoos. Hair extensions. There's always a new craze and they jump on the bandwagon and—"

"That's true." Toby cut the Yorkie off. He had a feeling that this dog would chat until his batteries ran out.

"Can I come with you?" the Yorkie asked.

Toby regarded the pretty cottage next to them. "Would your hoomans mind?"

"I doubt they'll notice." The Yorkie wagged his tail. "My dad will be napping. Please say yes! I've always wanted to be in an adventure!"

Toby shrugged. "Why not? Fall in, Mr—?"

"Spark," the Yorkie told him. "Sparky Spark!"

"Fall in, Sparky!"

They trotted happily onward, but again didn't get very far before Sparky pulled up. "Hey, guys? My friend Kimmy lives here. Can we invite her along?"

Toby scanned the faces looking back at him. Was this a good idea? It would be hard to keep everyone quiet. Bad enough with the puppies. "Erm ..."

"Honestly, I really think you need this girl on your side." Without waiting for Toby to agree, Sparky woofed gently. Moments later a large bumbling Labrador-cross-something-furry ambled out of the side door of her owner's house.

"S'up?" she asked. Toby couldn't help noticing that her claws had been painted bright gold to match the shaggy gold of her coat.

"This is Toby, the Spellbound Hound that Misty was telling us about earlier. Do you remember?"

"Yo. There's nothing wrong with my memory, Sparky," the Labrador-furry-thingie said. "Pleased to meet you, babe."

"And you," Toby smiled.

"Sparky's been telling youz all about the car, huh?" Kimmy asked. "We see it a lot. It drives backwards and forwards a few times a day. You can't miss it, the colour of it, y' get me, babe?" Kimmy wobbled her head gently from side to side, listening to a tune that only she could hear.

"We're hoping this is the person we've been looking for in relation to the missing puppies," Toby told Kimmy. "I don't suppose you've seen any unusual activity hereabouts?"

"I haven't seen nuffin," Kimmy said, "but y'all can ask any dog who lives around here, any cat ... in fact, you can ask any animal that lives within a half-mile radius of that compound, some mighty strange noises come from there at times."

"Misty didn't mention that," Pippin said.

"She wouldn't hear it," Sparky informed them. "She's a rescue. Got battered when she was a pup. She doesn't hear much. That's why she barks so loud."

"She's a good egg, though," Kimmy acknowledged. "Won't have a bad word said about her."

"We liked her," Toby agreed. "Tell me about the noises?"

"Barking," Sparky said. "Sometimes. Gets shut off very quickly."

"Mid bark sometimes." Kimmy pulled a face. "We don't like that. Not at all."

"Yeah," Sparky agreed. "That sudden silence." He gave an exaggerated shiver.

"And weird mechanical sounds. Never heard anything like it." Kimmy shuddered. "Whining, squeaking, a clinking noise ... I can't explain it. It's eerie—"

"And it only happens in the middle of the night," Sparky said.

"I didn't find any evidence of what that might be when I looked around there earlier," Toby mused. "In fact, I didn't hear anything."

Kimmy dropped her head so she could look directly into his eyes. "And you won't. That's the thing. The place looks derelict. But still that pink car drives in and out. In and out."

"So what's there?" Pippin asked.

Toby took a breath and inflated his chest. To his mind, all he needed was a cape and he could have passed as a superhero. "Let's go and find out, shall we?"

CHAPTER SEVENTEEN

It seemed only polite to include Misty in their foray, so the growing pack of dogs stopped off at the little crooked cottage to call on her. Given that Misty was unlikely to hear their approach, Kimmy took it upon herself to stand outside the gate and woof in her deep, low bark. Misty, evidently not able to tell one woof from another, launched herself out of the cottage with a raging snarl, drooling and spitting and ready to take on an army or whichever foolhardy hound had dared to encroach on her personal space. The second she realised who had come a-calling, however, she transformed into the cutest and sweetest of pupsters.

"Toby!" she shouted, jigging a greeting. "I didn't expect to see you again!"

"They couldn't stay away from your irresistible charm, Misty," Kimmy said and winked.

"We want to take a closer look at the compound," Toby told Misty. He noticed for the first time just how closely she watched his mouth. Presumably she could lip-read what he was saying.

"I'll take you down there," Misty agreed, and led everyone through her gate, into the paddock, around the barn and down through the thicket of trees towards the cheerful little stream, where everyone took a moment to drink deeply of the cold, fresh water. Bus travel had clearly made everyone thirsty!

When they were done, Toby gathered everyone together.

"Listen up!" he called, casting a sympathetic look at Misty. "My apologies."

She waggled her ears and leaned in closer.

"Whatever happens in the next hour or so, I want everyone to remain focused and calm. Chances are we won't discover anything, but at this stage we can't tell. There's a possibility that there'll be something untoward that we need to watch out for."

The dogs grew serious and still, shoulders rubbing against their neighbours, water dripping from beards and chins.

"First and foremost, we need to look out for each

other. I don't want anyone coming to any harm on my watch—"

"Amen, brother." Kimmy waggled her head.

"Secondly, no barking or noise if you can help it." Toby nodded at Bryn and Troot. "None at all, okay?"

Troot pressed his lips together and stole a quick look at Bryn. The puppies dissolved into nervous giggles.

"Perhaps we should leave them here?" Pippin suggested.

Bryn was quick to protest. "No. I have to find Bron, mun!"

"And I want to rescue Bourgie!" Troot echoed, stamping his paw.

"Then *listen* to what I'm telling you," Toby replied, his eyes stern. "This mission depends on stealth. Do you understand?"

Troot and Bryn individually considered their options. The worst thing that could happen would be to be left alone in the thicket, listening to strange countryside noises while waiting for the others to come back.

"Yes, Toby," Troot agreed.

Bryn, eyes wide, nodded hastily, keeping his mouth closed.

Single file, the dogs followed Misty down the hill

to where the paddock ended and the compound began. The sun was a huge orange ball in an otherwise gloriously blue sky. Full dark was still hours away, but the light would begin to dim in an hour or so. All the better to stake out the joint.

Toby sensed a slight jangling on his collar, one that hadn't been caused by his own movement. Mrs Crouch checking in on him, perhaps. "All is well," he whispered, and the crystal became still.

The dogs moved slowly and quietly, eyes and ears and noses fully alert, all crouching low to avoid detection. This was easier for Bryn as his belly almost scraped along the ground anyway, but for Kimmy, with her long chubby legs and thick coat, it was almost an impossibility. On several occasions, Sparky had to help untangle her from prickles.

"Yo! This is why I never come down here," she hissed. "Takes forever and a day to get these burrs out of my fur. You get me?"

"I'll have a go later," Sparky whispered, eager to be a good neighbour. "I'm good at detangling."

"Shhh!" Troot, glancing over his shoulder, gave them a baleful stare. Now that he'd cottoned on to the need to be clandestine, he had turned into a proper little sergeant major.

At the boundary, Misty came to a halt. Toby lifted

a paw as a signal to the others. Like canine commandoes, they sank further into the grass. Toby, panting slightly now that he was out in the open and under the baking sun, stole forwards. Nothing appeared to have changed.

Returning to Misty, he indicated she should wait where she was, before signalling to Pippin who moved forward to join him.

"Tell the troops to spread out along the fence," Toby whispered. "They should scout around for anything unusual or any sign that there have been dogs in the compound. Or"—he cocked his head—"other entrances and exits that we may have missed. It's always a good idea to have plenty of escape routes."

"Right-o," said Pippin.

"And tell them to keep an eye out for any movement whatsoever," Toby added.

"Okay."

"And no barking!" Toby hissed fiercely.

Pippin's fuzzy eyebrows twitched. "On it," she said.

She relayed the information to each dog in turn, then, one by one, each slipped past Toby to take a section of the fence. Eventually even Pippin slunk past him, leaving Toby alone with Misty. She offered a little smile, saying nothing. Her work was done.

Toby took the barely worn track through the long grass to the gap in the fence and slid through on his belly. He made it halfway through but froze when he heard Pippin's soft yap.

She only did it once, then fell silent.

Behind him, Toby could sense seven pairs of eyes straining to see. The compound was deadly still, but yes, there in the distance came the quiet hum of a car engine. It grew louder as it navigated the narrow lane, and Toby began to pick out the sound of tyres scattering small stones and rubber crunching over flint rocks.

He inched backwards until he was behind the chicken wire fence. This offered him a deluded sense of security. The car drew closer and slowed, the engine gradually becoming less shrill, but as it quietened it became obvious that it wasn't alone. From a little further away, but approaching rapidly, came the roar of a different vehicle. This one was louder and angrier and driving altogether faster, spraying gravel like machine gun bullets and showing no signs of decelerating.

A small pink car—a shockingly bright, candy pink bubble-gum milkshake of a car—lurched into the compound. The driver, oblivious to everyone and everything else, yanked the handbrake on and opened his door. As he stepped out, the second vehicle, a larger estate in a fetching shade of dog-sick beige, performed a handbrake turn at the end of the lane and skidded into the compound, only narrowly avoiding taking off the Fiat's door and taking out the driver at the same time.

"Oi!" The man who had been behind the wheel of the Fiat bellowed at the newcomer. "What in the giddy goddess's name—" He ducked his head to stare through the estate's windscreen. "Oh, Gawd." He tutted, shook his head and turned his back, reaching into the little Fiat.

Toby's eyes widened and his heart began to speed up. Who was this peculiar chap? Why did he seem familiar? This was the Father Christmas Bryn had told him about. Long hair, ash and snow, salt and pepper, a thin and singularly unimpressive beard.

And he'd said 'goddess'. Didn't that make him one of ... well ... one of his *own* tribe?

The feelings Toby had experienced when exploring earlier today, the sense of something not quite right, not entirely natural, of magick ... if this odd fellow was indeed a witch or wizard, he'd been right!

Toby held his breath, waiting to see what the funny little man would draw out of the car. A weapon? A wand? But when he did extract his hand, all he was clutching was a large bunch of keys: an old-fashioned ring with dozens of keys hanging from it, some rusty, some bronze, some silver.

"Are you following me?" he yelled without turning round. "Leave me alone!"

Toby waited for the driver of the estate to get out of the car, but it wasn't the driver's door that opened. It was the passenger side. A young woman threw herself out to confront the man. A short young woman with a large chest, pastel pink hair hanging free and razor straight, and much neater than the last time he'd seen it.

Nikki Madeley.

"Uncle Larch!" she screamed at him, even though he was merely feet away from her. "You bleedin' well told me you were only borrowin' my bleedin' car for three bleedin' days!"

"Oh Gawd, is that what yer 'ere for, Nikki? To nag me 'alf to death?"

"I'll nag you all the way to death, you crazy old loon. I want my car back!"

"I told you you'd get it back—"

"In three bleedin' days, you said. It's been seven bleedin' weeks!"

"I've been busy!"

"We're all busy, Uncle Larch! I've gotta get to and from me job and I can't do that without me car!"

"Take a bus," the man snarled.

"You take a bleedin' bus!" Nikki screeched back at him.

"They don't run up 'ere!" Larch grumbled, making a beeline for the strange little bunker-type building closest to him.

"They bleedin' do! I've been stuck behind one for the past twenty minutes!" She jabbed a neon pink fingernail back towards the estate. "Jordan there threatened to put me out on the side of the road and go home without me." She chewed frantically on her chewing gum. "You've gotta let me have me car back."

Jordan wound down his window and threw his arm out, a cigarette dangling from his fingers. He jerked his head backwards and forwards, mouthing words to a song that Toby couldn't hear. Maybe he had those little ear doofah-ma-jiggimmies in. Clarissa liked to wear those.

Ears buds. Buds for ears. Something like that.

"I need it for the shop, Nikki, I told ya. Making deliveries and stuff!"

Toby, watching the exchange carefully, frowned. Now he thought about it, he could place Larch with a shop ... but which shop? Not the Spar that Clarissa liked to use, so where?

It wouldn't come to him.

"You're not in the shop now, are ya?" Nikki asked. "What is this place anyway?"

"It's mine." Larch hunched his shoulders, his nose turned up. "My private place."

"Well, what are you doing here?" Nikki's bravado had disappeared. She stared around at the buildings, at the fence, then shivered and crossed her arms across her chest. "'Ere. Are you up to no good?"

"Is that what you think of me? You and your mother? Up to no good all the time? Sneering at me?"

"Leave my mum out of this, Uncle Larch. You know she'd go to the ends of the world for you. Why, I don't know." Nikki had quietened considerably. She shifted her weight uneasily from one foot to the other and back again. "You're not a serial killer, are you?" she asked.

Jordan stopped jerking his head and scrunched down in his seat to get a better look at Nikki and Larch. He might be wearing ear doofah-ma-jjigammies, but he'd heard that alright.

Larch laughed. It was the friendliest noise he'd made since Nikki had arrived. He threw back his head and bared his teeth. One of the front teeth had a corner knocked off it. "Don't be daft, Nikki my love. You're going soft in the 'ead. I just keep my supplies up 'ere. You know, things that won't fit out the back of the shop?"

"Right." Nikki stepped backwards, edging towards the car.

"That's why I need the car, innit?" Larch nodded. "To transport goods from here to the market."

The market? Of course! The pet shop! The one on the marketplace.

Toby exhaled. That's where he'd seen Larch before. At the pet shop. This was the guy who ran the pet shop!

"Right." Nikki had opened the passenger door now. "Well, just so you know, I need it back. And"—she hesitated—"people have been asking about it."

"What do you mean asking about it?" Larch's voice had turned icy.

Nikki shrugged. "A journalist."

"A journalist has been asking questions about your car?"

"Yeah." Nikki slid inside the estate. "And a police officer."

"The police?"

"I saw him off, don't worry." Nikki nodded at Jordan. "Let's go, babe."

"Flippity flip," Larch grumbled.

"I want it back!" Nikki yelled as Jordan started up his engine.

"Alright, alright. You can have it back tomorrow!" Larch hopped around. "Gawd," he muttered. "Gawd."

"Right, thanks!" Nikki shot her uncle the bird as Jordan slammed into reverse. The gears protested, the engine whined, and he reversed hard out of the compound, sending more stones and grit skittering in all directions and a cloud of dust billowing towards Toby.

"I'll have no more use for it," Larch mumbled. "Need something a little more incognito. Dang it."

Toby blinked as the cloud of dust enveloped him. Tiny shards of grit and glass showered his face and he closed his eyes. Too late. He breathed in, the dust tickled his adenoids, and without thinking, he sneezed loudly. A snotty dog sneeze that caused his whole head to shake.

Larch lifted his head, staring directly at Toby.

Oops.

"What have we 'ere?" Larch asked and tottered forwards, peering down into the long grass. "Ooh, it's a doggie." Toby blinked his eyes clear. "A very handsome doggie by the look of it." He crouched and held out his hand. Toby caught the scent of chicken treats.

"Would you like to come and play with old Mr Larch?"

This was quite possibly the creepiest thing anyone had ever said to Toby. "Not really," he replied.

The man's eyes lit up. "I knew it. You are a magickal dog!"

Double oops.

Toby wormed his way backwards through the gap. Larch was faster than he looked, however. He grabbed Toby's collar and hung onto him. Toby dug his paws into the ground and fought to drive himself backwards with all his might, but Larch was strong and equally as wily.

"Owwoooowwooow!" Toby howled.

His friends took that as their cue. They rushed from their hiding places, most of them on the paddock side of the fence, and began barking at Larch, showing their teeth, snapping and snarling. Larch let go of Toby's collar and backed away. Pippin took a tight hold of Toby's tail and pulled him through the gap.

Larch scowled and turned away, the chicken wire fence blocking his progress, only to be confronted by Troot standing mid shin, his head tipped back, giving Larch a darn good telling off.

Pippin let go of Toby's rump. "Troot!" she barked. "Get away!"

With Toby looking on in horror, Pippin tried to dive through the gap in the fence, but she was too big. The cruel barbs of wire caught her and held her tight. She twisted and wriggled, stuck fast.

Triple oops.

Larch didn't think twice. Entirely unphased by the young dog's angst and Pippin's panic, he leaned over and calmly scooped the puppy up. Holding Troot at arm's length, he cooed and chuckled. "What a find! And right on my doorstep!" Without so much as a backward glance, Larch tucked the puppy under one arm and, clamping Troot's jaw shut with his free hand, he stalked towards the first building, let himself in and slammed the door closed.

The remaining dogs stood at the fence, staring through, silenced by the abrupt turn of events.

Quadruple oops.

CHAPTER EIGHTEEN

"Troot?" Pippin whispered. If it is possible for a white dog to have a pallid face, then Toby could have sworn that's what he was seeing.

She'd stopped wriggling and sunk onto her belly. "What have we done?" she asked and, lifting her head, howled.

From the inside of the odd dome-shaped bunker, there was no response.

The others broke cover and came over to help Toby rescue Pippin. Now that she wasn't thrashing around so much, the job was far easier. Toby stood back and allowed Sparky and Jack, the two smallest dogs with the sharpest adult teeth, to work on extracting Pippin's woolly fur from the spiky barbs.

"I'm sorry," Toby told her, as Kimmy utilised her strength to pull Pippin backwards.

Pippin shook herself off. "It's not your fault," she said, her voice trembling.

"I shouldn't have allowed the puppies to come with us."

Bryn planted his little bod firmly on the grass between Pippin and Toby. "But we wanted to come," he argued in his soft Welsh lilt, his eyes shining with defiant tears. "We have as much right to be here as anyone else."

The dogs remained hushed, each gazing through the fence at the bunker, but the quiet of the early evening was disturbed once more by the rattling of locks.

"He's coming back!" Sparky hissed.

"Everyone hide!" Toby ordered, and they all did so. Except for Pippin. She refused point-blank. Instead, she stood at the fence and growled, long, low and menacing.

"Pippin!" Toby whispered, sinking into the long grass beside her.

"He knows we're out here," Pippin said. "Hiding won't change that fact!"

Larch appeared at the side of the building. He'd

altered his appearance, donning a tall crooked hat in navy felt and a matching smock with silver embroidery. *He quite fancies himself as a witch*, thought Toby. But no witch worth his salt would harm a puppy.

Not a decent one, anyway.

Larch's head hung low as he peered towards the fence. "Hello, my pretty," he sang. "Hello."

Pippin snarled. Throwing herself against the chicken wire, she shouted, "Where's Troot? What have you done with my friend?"

"You're an angry one, aren't you?" Larch edged a little closer, warily checking that Pippin wouldn't be able to come any closer. "You're a bit old for me, otherwise ... we could be friends."

He squinted into the grass. "But there are more of you, aren't there?" Reaching inside the pocket of his smock, he extracted a handful of treats and threw them over the fence. They plopped softly into the tall grass, scattered around the hiding dogs.

"Hold fast, troops!" Toby, a dog who had never knowingly turned down a snack in his life, sniffed at the lump of indeterminate brown cereal that had landed closest to him. "They're cheap and nasty. We don't need them in our lives."

"They might be poisoned!" Sparky added. "My

dad told me to always be careful about things left on the ground."

"Sensible advice," agreed Kimmy. She was having trouble getting comfortable, squidged into a hollow in the ground surrounded by thistles. As she wriggled, Larch trained his beady eye on her.

"Ugh. No. Too big. Too big," he muttered. "Where's that schnauzery-thingie gone? The one with the teddy bear face. He's perfect. And any more puppies? Come out, come out, wherever you are!"

Toby, from his hiding place behind a mound of compost, bared his teeth. "Nobody moves," he whispered, but his mind whirred. Now was the time to gain access to the inside of the bunker. If he broke cover, could he get through the fence without Larch seeing?

Probably not.

He would need to create a diversion. Set a trap. A trap that could lure Larch away just long enough to allow Toby to sneak inside.

He glanced around at the other dogs. From his vantage, he could see Jack behind an upturned wheelbarrow, Sparky underneath a gorse bush and Bryn behind an old water trough.

Any of them would make for an enticing piece of cheese, figuratively speaking, with which to set Toby's mousetrap. He couldn't risk putting Bryn in danger, surely? Not that the puppy would refuse. But Sparky? With his soft eyes and kooky ears, his long waggly tail. He might be getting on but he looked like a puppy.

And he had the heart of a lion.

Mind made up, Toby called out to the others. "I have a plan."

Half a dozen heads turned to look at him.

"Sparky," Toby called, "front and centre and listen up!"

"I really don't think this is a good idea—" Pippin cautioned Toby as he slid into position next to the track beneath the wire. Jack and Bryn had broken cover and diverted Larch's attention for the time being by running around the other side of the paddock.

So far, this strategy had worked. Larch had followed them over and was currently attempting to pry the chicken wire from the wooden struts it had been nailed into, in order to make a hole big enough for him to squeeze through.

Kimmy and Misty had been sent up to the crooked cottage and out onto the track that led past the cottage and back down towards the dead end where the compound was situated. They would take cover there and only become involved if required.

Pippin was designated lookout and chief comms officer, leaving Toby free to attend to the main business of rescue.

Sparky was the small piece of cute tasty 'puppy' cheese in the Larch trap.

"Trust me," Toby reassured Pippin now. "We can do this. I can get Troot out of there." *I have to,* he thought. *It's my fault he's in there in the first place.*

He nodded at Sparky. "Ready?"

Sparky straightened his back and his tail. "Yes, sir!"

Sinking to his belly so as not to draw attention to himself, he crawled forwards commando style. "Give my love to my hooman," he called back over his shoulder as he disappeared along the track and below the chicken wire. Sparky was so small, there was room to spare and then some.

Toby quickly followed him. "You'll see him in a few minutes," he whispered, bolstering the older dog's confidence. *Maybe not a few minutes, but soon enough.* "We're all getting out of this in one piece, I promise."

Sparky had been well briefed. Once out of the gap,

he stuck to the overgrowth that lined the front of the boundary on the compound side, weaving in and out of the weeds and nettles and the tall wavering plants shedding fluffy seeds, guaranteed to make most dogs sneeze. Sparky held his breath, blinking rapidly, not wanting to give himself away until the right moment.

When he drew level with the second bunker, he paused. Turning, he checked for Toby.

Toby, eyes trained on Larch, waited for Pippin's signal.

Pippin, head cocked, held her breath, anticipating Misty's excited yip. Kimmy had been tasked with ensuring poor Misty knew what they were up to once the dogs were out of hearing range at the crooked cottage. Toby felt that Larch would probably have become accustomed to Misty's loud bellowing bark over the time he'd inhabited the compound. He was counting on Larch's desensitisation to Misty's communication so that the dogs could alert Pippin to their proximity to the compound without alarming Larch.

From the other side of the compound, in the distance, Misty barked once.

They were all where they needed to be.

Pippin sat up in the long grass and howled.

Larch glanced at her and dismissed her. He

already knew of her existence, and he was way more interested in the puppies frolicking in the grass in front of him. He yanked hard at the chicken wire, trying to free it from the posts.

Brute force and ignorance. It was only a matter of time before he gained access to the paddock.

Jack and Bryn, understanding Pippin's howled instruction, danced a little closer to Larch, rolling and tumbling, enticing him to venture nearer ...

Pippin howled again, and Sparky streaked like lightning past the bunker towards the entrance of the compound and the mud track road beyond. Larch, who apparently had eyes in the back of his head—at least where small dogs were concerned—spun about. "Oooh! Puppy! Puppy!" he cooed, Bryn and Jack instantly forgotten. He scampered after Sparky, chortling with delight as Sparky wagged his tail and jigged in place, giving the impression he was thrilled to meet the dastardly witch. Once Sparky knew Larch was committed to chasing him, he trotted—tantalisingly out of reach—a little way up the lane towards the crooked cottage.

Now it was a case of tease and release. Reel Larch in, then run. Tease, make him follow, reel him in and release. Over and over in order to gain Toby time.

With Larch's attention well and truly diverted

from the first bunker, Toby sprinted for the door, his paws barely touching the ground.

His luck was in.

A chink of artificial light glinted between the wooden door and the door jamb.

Larch had left the bunker open.

CHAPTER NINETEEN

Toby cautiously shouldered the door open a little more so he could squeeze his fluffy backside through. He remained in place momentarily, allowing his senses to take over. He found himself in a cold passageway with bare concrete walls. The walls had been heavily graffitied at some stage—whether that had been by Larch or someone else, Toby couldn't tell. There were words, 'tags' Toby believed they were called, painted by Sunshine Valley 'yoof' at some stage before the buildings had been secured, and obscene images. Nothing much of interest and nothing that gave him a clue about what this place had been. Or indeed now was.

The first door to his left opened into some kind of living area. There was a camp bed in the corner, a rickety old armchair with the cushion missing, a television and a table. In the other corner was some kind of orange kitchenette with a water heater that looked like something straight out of the 1950s with an enormous cistern and a long wiggly silver tap. The sink hung from the wall, dripping water.

Plink. Plink. Plink.

There were bags-for-life from three or four popular supermarkets scattered around, full of clothes or blankets or other textiles, numerous bowls and plates and mugs, but nothing that spoke of this being a place where Larch kept puppies.

Troot had to be somewhere in the bunker. Toby had seen him carried inside.

Returning to the passageway, Toby poked his head into the first room on the right. He could already smell what it was: a lavatory, complete with a number of closed stalls and vintage urinals. He crinkled his nose at the acrid twang.

The room was empty and, given that the floor was sodden thanks to the water leaking from a rusty faucet, Toby backed slowly away. He didn't want to leave pawprints on the floor and, as interesting as these smells were, he didn't have much time. How long could Sparky hold off Larch until Kimmy and Misty had to get involved? Once they made themselves known to Larch, his instinct would be to run back here to the compound and shut the door on them.

Back in the passage, Toby's ears twitched. Ahead of him, a door blocked his way. Beyond that, he could hear the muted whirr and clickity-clack of machinery.

"Here goes nothing," Toby whispered, keeping himself company in the absence of his friends. He crept up to the plain door and pushed against it. It opened easily. Perhaps Larch had been in here before he came back outside with the treats to try and entice more dogs inside.

The door swung wide. Toby did a double take. Over half of the building was taken up by this long room with its low ceiling and murky atmosphere. The windows had been covered up with collapsed cardboard boxes and parcel tape, and the overhead lights were on, bulbs swinging from thick electric cables surrounded by silver domes, rather like the light the vet liked to angle at him when taking a close look at something.

Cages were piled high. Floor to ceiling. Larger ones at the bottom, smaller ones at the top. Brightly coloured plastic tubes dropped from some enormous flying saucer type contraption bolted to the ceiling. Not that it was particularly well attached. Small pieces of plaster had crumbled away and now, as Toby slipped further into the room, they crunched beneath his paws.

A large, utilitarian-style wooden desk stood in the middle of the room. There were piles of paper on top of it, a copious number of glass jars and an old black telephone, the sort you might see in a 1980s movie.

Toby paused again, staring up at the flying saucer with a certain distrust. It resembled the large metal colander Clarissa used to drain her vegetables. The clickity-clack he'd been hearing came from that. Unseen mechanics inside. The monotony of the sound suggested a wheel or a cog slowly spinning and catching on something else as it did so.

The humming though?

Toby dropped his eyeline and shivered.

The humming came from the puppies.

Dozens of them. Curled up in cages. They slept on stained blankets, coiled in a circle like fat Cumberland sausages, their little eyes closed, their pretty eyelashes framing velvety eyelids.

The humming was the sound of puppies snoring.

"Whoa," Toby muttered. He hadn't reckoned on finding every puppy that had been stolen in the West Country over the past few months. Casting a furtive glance over his shoulder, he hummed and hawed. *How long till Larch comes back?* He doubted he'd be able to hear Pippin's warning from in here. The bunker's walls were thicker than he'd anticipated.

He tiptoed closer to the nearest cage. The puppy inside was a Samoyed, as pretty as a picture, perhaps twelve weeks old. Toby gently prodded her. "Hey," he whispered. "Hey. Wake up." The puppy stirred, her little nose creasing, her eyelids fluttering. "Mummy?" she asked, and snuggled down onto her blanket once more, fast asleep in a microsecond.

"That's not right," Toby told her. "Are you drugged?" He jabbed at the contraptions that fed her crate. One was a water dropper, the kind of thing you see in rodent cages. Another was a treat dispenser. Toby remembered the treats Larch had thrown at the dogs earlier. If anything was drugged, that's what it would be, surely?

Yanking at the treat dispenser with his teeth, he pulled it away from the cage. It dropped beside him and spilled its goodies. He leaned in to take a closer sniff. The faint tang of cheap chicken, too much salt, too much grain. Nothing chemical. But what did he know?

That left the remaining tube. This one was orange plastic, and it fell from the flying saucer on the ceiling and was inserted into the cage. It had some sort of funnel contraption attached to the end. Examining it more closely, Toby could see condensation lining the plastic.

Could this be air? Were the puppies being given oxygen?

"No!" Toby had an Einstein moment. "It must be sleeping gas. Right?" He peered around, as though someone somewhere would agree with him. "Right?"

Nobody answered. All he could hear were the snores of the furry prisoners.

"If I was to turn the gas off ..." he ruminated, examining the tube more closely. The flying saucer clickity-clacked above his head, and Toby noticed something interesting. The condensation ... was being sucked upwards.

Why would sleeping gas be sucked upwards? one half of Toby's brain questioned. He cocked his head as the other half answered, *It wouldn't, you great nit. There's no sleeping gas at all. The tubes are being used to suck something* out *of the cage.*

He paced along the bottom row of crates, examining the puppies he could see. There were golden retrievers, German shepherds, a Dalmatian, a labradoodle and a dozen or so mixed breeds. None of them were older than six months. That begged the question, what happened to the dogs when they grew older?

"Toby!" Troot's voice echoed above Toby's head. He glanced up, disorientated for a moment, spinning around and then around again.

"Up here!" Troot called.

Toby scuttled backwards. There was Troot, paws against the bars of one of the uppermost cages.

"I'm glad you came ... that you didn't leave it any later. I'm so sleepy, I might have missed you," Troot said, and yawned.

"Don't go to sleep!" Toby barked.

"I'll just close my eyes for one minute," Troot mumbled, slumping against the bars, his eyes beginning to droop.

"Did he hurt you, Troot?" Toby called up. "The man?"

"No." Troot's voice began to fade away. "Just ... really ... sleepy."

Frantic with worry, Toby jumped against the cages closest to him. The occupants inside stirred but did not fully wake. "Troot!" Toby called. "Troot?"

There was no answer.

What to do next? Toby could open the cage doors using magick, but how would he wake the puppies? And how could he get them down from those cages so far above his head? He could have a go at levitating them—the way he liked to do with his building blocks when he was learning to read—but it would take a lot of time, and time wasn't something he had a lot of.

Larch would be back imminently.

Helplessness settled on him, a millstone around his neck ...

Except, he already had something around his neck. "Mrs Crouch?" he whispered. "Mrs Crouch?"

"I'm here, Toby." Mrs Crouch's warm old lady voice seemed to fill the room. "How are you getting on?"

"I need your help," Toby told her. "Urgently."

"Tell me what you need me to do, Toby," she said.

"I've found the pu—huh!" Toby caught his breath. The door at the front of the building had opened.

"Bleedin' dogs!" Larch bellowed. "Taken a bleedin' lump out of me bleedin' arse!"

"Who's that?" Mrs Crouch asked.

"It's Mr Larch. He's a witch. I think he is. At least, he can understand me—"

"I'm going to find that dog and—"

Toby didn't catch the last part of Larch's threat because he disappeared into the lavatory and his voice became muffled.

"You'd better get out of there, Toby," Mrs Crouch said.

Toby grimaced, staring down the passageway. If he

timed his exit wrong, Larch would come out of the bathroom at the exact moment Toby walked past. "It's too risky," he said. "Unless I can distract him again."

Toby stared up at the desk and the telephone sitting on top. With one bound—and a little magickal oomph—he clambered up and examined the phone. "Mrs Crouch. I think I have an idea."

A clatter from the lavatory.

"But we have to be quick!"

Brrrurrrrruppp brrrurrrrrupp!

Brrrurrrrruppp brrrurrrrrupp!

Larch picked up the receiver and held it against his ear, almost tentatively. "Bushy Leaze 437."

Mrs Crouch's polite, albeit tinny voice, could be clearly discerned on the other end. "Good evening. Is that Mr Larch?"

Larch's forehead furrowed. "Who wants to know?"

"Hello there, Mr Larch. It's Isadora Sourjelly from the Ministry of Witches—"

Toby, hiding behind the door, one of Larch's note-books in his mouth, raised his eyebrows. *Sourjelly*? They were Mrs Crouch's favourite sweets. He kept a careful eye on Larch. The man was side on to him.

Chances were he would see Toby if the dog made a run for it now.

"Ministry of—" Larch gulped. "How did you get this number?"

Well, der! It's written on the telephone, Toby thought. *A bit of a giveaway. Such quaint ways, those old mid-twentieth-century folks had.*

"We have a record of all numbers, Mr Larch—"

"But I mean ..." Larch moved the receiver away from his ear to take a better look at it, then tucked the handset under his ear and pulled at the cord that came out of the phone at the back and—generally speaking—plugged into the socket in the wall. He kept tugging until the end of the cord hove into view. "The phone here isn't even connected."

"It's not connected to a *mundane* switchboard, Mr Larch." Mrs Crouch was thinking on her feet. "But here at the Ministry of Witches, we don't let a little thing like that stop us getting in touch with one of our own."

"One of your own?" There was no hiding the suspicion in his voice.

"Oh, indeed. We're very interested in what you have going on down there in Sunshine Valley."

"You are?" Larch puffed out his chest. "And so you

should be!" He turned his back to Toby. "You wouldn't believe what I've been inventing—"

Toby couldn't wait to hear any more. He dodged around the door and pitter-pattered as quietly as he could along the passageway that led to the main exit.

"I've been working on it for months—"

Past the lavatory door, then past the living area ...

"You ought to send someone down here, although you'll need to remember, it's top secret—"

"*Leniter aperta*!" Toby demanded, and the main door swung gently towards him. As soon as the gap was wide enough, he stole through. Dashing across the compound, he zoomed past the pile of black bin liners and dived under the chicken wire, scattering dust and grass seeds and floofs from the fuzzy cottony weeds everywhere. They floated off on the wisp of a breeze to drive human hay fever sufferers for miles around completely bonkers.

Dropping the notebook in relief, he turned to greet his friends.

The sun was falling, the light beginning to change. In the evening's golden glow, the halo of Pippin's fluffy head was a joy to behold. Beside her, Bryn and Jack hopped around in delight.

"I was beginning to get worried," Pippin told him and, before she could remember what a cool canine she actually was, licked his face appreciatively. "No sign of Troot?" she asked.

"He's fine! He's inside along with twenty or thirty other puppies," Toby told her.

Pippin gasped. "Twenty or thirty?"

"I didn't count them all—that's a pupstimate." Toby took a second to catch his breath. "But they're all alive and they seem perfectly okay. They're just ... sleeping."

"Troot is sleeping?" Pippin narrowed her eyes in suspicion. "He's just been pupnapped, and he's sleeping? That doesn't sound like Troot. I'd expect him to be beside himself."

"I agree. There's something odd going on—some contraptions and shenanigans inside—but I can't tell quite what." He nudged the notebook. "That's why I brought this out. It was on Larch's desk."

A rustle in the long grass close by alerted the dogs to incomers. Fortunately, it was only Sparky—looking incredibly pleased with himself—with Kimmy and Misty in tow.

"Good job, chaps!" Toby praised them. "A plan perfectly executed."

Sparky wagged his tail like a helicopter. "It was so much fun. We really had Larch on the run! He'll be scared to ever drive past Misty's cottage now!"

Misty's tongue rolled out of her mouth, her eyes alive with glee.

"Yo! Wotcha got there?" Kimmy asked, nudging the notebook.

"I'm hoping this might help us understand what's going on in there," Toby told her, flicking the cover of the worn exercise book over.

"There are thirty puppies inside!" Bryn told the newcomers, not that Misty could hear him. She only stared around in bemused befuzzlement. "And they're all asleep!"

"Thirty sleeping puppies? That's dope, y'all!" Kimmy hooted. "So now we gotta rescue them?"

"Of course!" Jack told her. "We've got friends inside."

"Every puppy belongs to someone," Bryn added.

Pippin pulled a face. "Not every puppy."

"What does it say?" Misty bellowed, hunkering down to get a better look at the notebook. She couldn't read the words, but the illustrations certainly looked interesting.

"Well ..." Toby flicked the pages over. "There are notes here that go back years. Many years. There's a date here. It says April 1979!"

"Wow!" Sparky slipped between Toby's paws to

get a better look. "I thought I was old, but that's ... that's last century!"

"If I'm reading this right—and I have to be honest, some of it is complete gobbledegook—it looks like our friend Larch has been trying to invent things since he was a schoolboy." Toby pawed at the book. "Trying to make his fortune by creating something no-one has come up with before." He flipped a page. Red lines had been scored across this side, driven so deep they'd torn through the next few pages.

"Without much luck," Sparky remarked.

"Indeed." Toby kept turning the pages. "He tried woodwork. He tried mechanics. He tried herbs ... but in every case, it seems his magick was at fault." Sitting back on his haunches, Toby raised his eyes to the sky, thinking. "He's a witch, but he's rubbish ..."

"What does that have to do with the puppies though?" Pippin asked impatiently.

"I'm getting to that." Toby returned his attention to the notes and kept turning pages. "He's started here on potions, and that ..."—*flip, flip*, went the pages; *flip, flip* —"... is where he's at." Toby scrutinised the drawing in front of him, the mathematical equations scrawled in the margins, some of them scrubbed out and reformulated.

"Is that an octopus?" Sparky wanted to know. He'd

often sat on his dad's lap watching nature programmes, so he knew what an octopus looked like.

"It's a machine," Toby said. Studying the drawing, he recognised the big flying saucer with all the tubes. "It's mounted to the ceiling and feeds from the cages ... because ..." He ran a claw along the page and caught his breath.

"What?" Pippin gasped, eyes on stalks. "What's he doing in there?"

"The machine sucks air out of the puppy cages and condenses it in the tubes." Toby indicated the long scribbles on the diagram, threading into the flying saucer, more of a jellyfish than an octopus. "Larch seems to imagine that he can create a concentrated liquid ..." He read on, trying to make head or tail of the complicated scrawl.

"He's using stale puppy breaths?" Sparky asked.

"Not to mention all da farts," Kimmy added. "Puppy food can be a bit rich at times."

"But what's he trying to concoct?" Pippin demanded to know.

Toby shook his head. "Sssh. Shh. I'm reading. Look. Here it is. Huh."

"What? What?" All of the dogs were on tenterhooks.

"Wizard Larch's Dilution of Puppy Eyes."

Pippin blinked. "You what?"

"That's what it says," Toby told her. "Wizard Larch's Dilution of Puppy Eyes. A Miraculous Cure-All designed to get you everything you want in life. Hand brewed in the deepest West Country using only the finest available puppies."

The dogs fell silent, digesting what Toby had read. Although not literally. Nobody tried to eat the notebook.

Pippin broke the silence. "He's barking."

Kimmy agreed. "Knitting with one needle."

"A banana short of a bunch, my dad would say," Sparky added.

Pippin snorted in derision. "There's no way that a dilution of puppy exhalation would work!"

"Not forgetting stinky chuffs—" Kimmy added.

"Although definitely trying to." Pippin rolled her eyes at the Labrador-thingie.

Toby flipped over the page, read the opening paragraph, swallowed audibly and looked back at the others. "There's more."

"More pseudo magick potion confectionery?" Pippin grumbled. "Spare us."

"Far worse than that. He's already decided the condensation and dilution method isn't working. It says here he tried to get a bank loan to bail out the pet shop on Draper's Row. He had an interview with the bank manager, so he smothered himself in his cutting-edge Wizard Larch's Dilution of Puppy Eyes Cure-All using a perfume mister—"

"Let me guess," Sparky sang. "It didn't work?"

"Not a flicker of interest from the bank manager, apparently, so Larch is moving on to something more extreme."

The dogs fell silent again, waiting for Toby to tell them, shifting uneasily. Above them, a cloud had rolled across the sun, the first cloud in the sky for days, but none of them noticed.

Toby swallowed. "He's going full-on vivisection. He wants to extract their eyes."

Pippin's eyebrows shot upwards. Kimmy smothered her shriek. Sparky dived beneath Pippin's legs. Bryn fainted. Misty, observing the reactions of the others in confusion, whimpered in anxiety while waiting for someone to explain.

"We have to get them out!" Pippin's voice shook with emotion.

"Oh, we're going to." Toby closed the exercise book with a resounding slap. "But not alone. We need help."

CHAPTER TWENTY

Twilight was falling ... and we all know what happens at twilight.

Dogs gather for a mass chat-in.

Tonight of all nights, this moment was more important than ever. Toby, along with his trusty band of followers, climbed to the top of the hill, away from Larch and the compound. In the distance, they could hear the deep woof of a large dog telling everyone what he'd had for dinner.

Toby's stomach growled. *When did I last eat? I'd kill for a sammich.*

To exacerbate the problem of lack of nourishment, the air was heavy with the scent of barbeques and pizza ovens. Toby's extra sensitive nostrils could even make out the fragrance of boiled onions.

"That's Griffin, the Great Dane," Sparky said, tilting his head to listen to the lone dog barking. "Lovely boy, but as dim as a nine-watt lightbulb."

"That's the problem with Great Danes," Jack said. "All that growing ... the cells run out by the time they reach the brain."

Pippin had carried the notebook up the hill. Now she placed it at Toby's front paws. "Let's get on with this," she said, her voice sharp.

Toby understood her anxiety. They couldn't know what timeline Larch had in mind to begin his new experimentation, but there was no point in leaving anything to chance.

"Misty," he said, addressing the deaf Border collie. "I need you to interrupt Griffin."

"Pardon me?" she asked. Sparky hastily intervened, standing on his back legs to nuzzle closely to Misty's earflap and yell, "Tell Griffin to shut the fluff up!"

"No problem," Misty said, and raised her head to howl. Sparky shot backwards, shaking his lugs.

"Boy, she's loud," Toby whispered, more in admiration than complaint, of course.

"Hush, Griffin," Misty sang. "We have important information to relay!"

Griffin's gruff bark came back straight away. "Can't it wait? I got here first."

"No!" Misty shouted back. "Shut your cakehole!"

Before Griffin could respond, Toby launched into his message. "Calling all dogs in the vicinity of Bushy Leaze! This is Toby, Spellbound Hound and friend of the underdog. I have an urgent message for you all! I have found the missing puppies, but I need your help! I can't rescue them alone. I am with six brave warriors, but I need more to answer this call. If you hear me, please make your way to the village and gather with us in the paddock behind Misty's crooked cottage. Over!"

One beat. Then two. Another. Toby shivered in anticipation, afraid that only silence would greet his plea. *Come on, come on*, he silently begged.

He opened his mouth to start again—perhaps he needed to bark louder—but suddenly Griffin sprang into action.

"Calling all dogs! Calling all dogs! Toby the Spellbound Hound needs you. Ship up, soldiers. Crooked Cottage paddock. As fast as you can." As soon as he finished his spiel, he started again.

Toby tilted his head, listening to the echo as Griffin's words were taken up by the next dog and the next, all the way from Bushy Leaze to the outskirts of Sunshine Valley.

The gem around Toby's neck began to vibrate. "Mrs Crouch?" Toby called.

Mrs Crouch's voice reverberated in his ears. "I take it you managed to get out safe and sound, Toby?"

He'd meant to call her back, but he'd been otherwise engaged with the notebook. "I did! Thanks for distracting Larch."

Mrs Crouch chuckled. "He's a gullible old so-and-so. Began telling me about his experiments and accused the Ministry of Witches of conspiring against his success. He's deluded. There's no way the Ministry of Witches would give him the time of day—"

"Let's hope so," Toby said.

"I suggested that the Ministry of Witches would love to pay him a visit and discuss his latest research," Mrs Crouch tittered. "He's expecting a visit any minute."

"Is that so?" Toby could use that to his advantage.

"It is," Mrs Crouch said. "Oooh. You're a big boy."

Toby frowned. "Huh?"

"Not you. I'm sitting here and an enormous Great Dane just strolled past me with a little white thingummy-poodley-type friend. Is that you doing that, Toby? Setting all those dogs to barking?"

"It is, Mrs Crouch," Toby told her.

"They all sound a little frantic—"

"We've got some important business to attend to. I'm going to have to go."

"Is it safe?" Mrs Crouch sounded alarmed now. "Should I walk down?"

"No, no. You stay there," Toby urged her.

"If anything happens to you, Clarissa will never forgive me," Mrs Crouch said.

"I'll be fine, I promise."

Bryn whistled. "Wow."

Toby turned to see what the puppy was looking at, and there, streaming in through the paddock gate, came the first few soldiers. Griffin the Great Dane surrounded by half a dozen friends.

"Are you sure?" Mrs Crouch was asking.

"Absolutely." Toby smiled. "The cavalry has arrived. United we stand."

At full dark, Toby directed his nose at the door of the bunker and barked sharply. "*Ostium pulsans,*" he ordered, and an invisible hand rapped hard on the wood. Pippin and Jack had surveyed the area a few minutes ago and found the door secured. Larch had evidently locked up after finishing his call with Mrs Crouch.

Toby couldn't help wondering what he'd thought when he found the door wide open. Perhaps he assumed he hadn't closed it properly. Larch didn't seem like the sharpest knife in the drawer.

Sitting directly in front of the door, paws neatly aligned, eyes wide, bright and appealing, Toby waited. It wasn't long before he heard Larch drawing back the locks. "Gawd. Gawd. Gawd. Who could this be?" he grumbled. "Not the Ministry of Witches. Not this quickly ..."

Cracking open the door, one eye glared directly out. When he couldn't see anyone at eye level, he pulled the door open a little more and dropped his gaze. "You! The handsome little pupster!" he cried, rubbing his hands in delight. "I certainly wasn't expecting you. I thought you'd run home for your tea."

Chance would be a fine thing, thought Toby, maintaining eye contact with Loopy Larch. *I'm not going anywhere until all of the puppies you're holding inside are free.*

"Good evening, Mr Larch," Toby said, using his best telephone voice.

"Weeeeee!" Larch began to applaud. "The talking doggie! I'd forgotten you could talk!"

"My name is Toby Page. I'm from the Ministry of Witches." Toby wagged his tail, keeping it friendly.

"You are?" Larch's brow crumpled. "That was quick. To be honest, I wasn't expecting a dog." His eyes flickered nervously, his body turning slightly, angled towards his laboratory. "You were hanging around earlier."

"I have been conducting fieldwork in East Devon on behalf of the Ministry for the past few days. Given my local proximity to you, I have been tasked with the initial visit before they send the ... erm ... principals along." Toby was hoofing it. He hoped it didn't sound too amateurish.

"But a dog?" Larch plainly wasn't keen—not entirely surprising, given the nature of his experiments. "I'm not sure it's ... er ... appropriate."

"I can assure you it's all entirely above board," Toby replied, jovial and efficient. "No judgement here. A quick in and out and a message to my superiors, and then we're done."

Larch considered his options. Toby could see the consternation and doubt scrolling across the witch's face. Turn Toby away and miss out on recognition from the Ministry of Witches? Or let a dog witness what he was doing to other dogs?

"Very well." He didn't sound thrilled, but moved away from the door anyway, ambition winning out over discretion.

Toby stepped back from the door. "Enter!" he yelled.

Larch dropped his head as a streak of light—the dog formally known as Sparky—shot between his legs. "This way, men!" Sparky shrieked, leading the onslaught down the passage.

"Hey!" Larch protested, but the word was hardly out of his mouth before Griffin and Kimmy, working in tandem, leapt at him, each aiming for a shoulder, and brought him down. The moment he was lying flat out, Misty jumped onto his chest, and a number of smaller dogs each took a hand—or even a finger—or a foot or a piece of tatty robe or worn shoe, and held on to them for dear life. When there was absolutely no chance of Larch moving, Misty began conversing with him in her friendly bellow. Larch tried to turn his head away, but a pair of Dobermanns named Peach and Posy had that eventuality covered. They snapped and snarled at Larch every time he tried to edge away from Misty's impressive vocal talent.

How was Larch to know that the Dobermanns were foster parents to a litter of kittens and loved nothing better than sleeping snuggled up to their mum's slippers? All that mattered for now were appearances.

Toby joined the throng of adult dogs surging into

the passageway. Some took the first door on the left, some the first door on the right. Toby had given orders for everything that wasn't bolted down to be destroyed. Chewed up and torn apart, thrown around, smashed to smithereens. Whatever it took.

But the room at the end? The laboratory? That was a different kettle of fish.

Toby hurried through, pleased to see that every-doggy had adhered to his instructions. Out of respect for the sleeping puppies they had massed calmly, standing in orderly lines in front of the cages. They peered into the lower cages, aw-ing and cooing at the fluffy little angels snoring softly inside. From the direction of the passageway came the snarling of the Dobermanns, Misty's ferocious bark ... and Larch's terrified pleas for mercy.

Vaulting onto the top of the desk, Toby regarded the papers, pens, books, plans and drawings piled up there, making sure there was nothing he wanted, then began to scatter it all, directing it to the ground to be set upon by Jack, Sparky, Pippin and Bryn. He meant to ensure that everything was destroyed. Larch must never be allowed to repeat the experiments he'd been engaging in, nor must he be permitted to proceed with fresh ones. Toby's trusted friends took immediate and great delight in shredding the paper to sawdust and the biros and pencils into fluff and plastic fragments.

Finally, Toby turned his attention to the cages. Slowly pivoting while drawing energy up from the earth, he began envisioning the doors of each cage opening. The power flowed, his paws tingling as he channelled more and more of it, up into his chest and his heart and onwards to his mind.

Big Dom had been teaching Toby magick, and he'd recently been learning more complicated composite spells. If ever there was a need for one of those, it was now.

"*Aquastillante*," he whispered. "*Exominisexcito*!" Over and over. "*Aquastillante, exominisexcito*."

One by one the water bottles began to leak, the water seeping into the cages. Blankets became sodden, the sudden discomfort disturbing the puppies. They started to sit up and take a little more interest in their surroundings, yawning and licking their soft pink lips, sleep buried in the corner of their eyes.

"Shhhhhh, shhhhh, shhhhh," Pippin cooed as a puppy, two crates up, began to whimper. "Be brave, baby. It won't be long."

Toby had decided they needed to get the puppies out of their cages as quickly as possible. He didn't want to risk them noticing the treats and attempting to eat those. Toby didn't know whether it had been the consumption of water or the boringly bland biscuit that had doped the puppies, but he didn't want to take any chances.

He wouldn't risk it for a biscuit.

He changed the emphasis of the spell, readjusted his intent. The cage doors began to pop open. *Click, snip, pop*!

Instantly, the waiting dogs became more alert. Each of them had been tasked to puppysit a single cage. It was their job to ensure that the puppy inside was brought out safe and sound. Where the puppies in the bottom crates were concerned, this was easy, but the higher up the allotted cage was situated, the more complicated it became.

The second their cage doors sprang open, those puppies who were sufficiently awake began to do what all puppies, curious and fearless, enjoy doing the most. They began investigating. Straight away, a disaster had to be averted when a bulldog puppy from an uppermost cage decided she could fly. She poked her head out of her cage door, spotted the dogs below, wagged her tail with enthusiasm and overbalanced, tumbling headfirst. Pippin made a dive and caught the puppy in her soft jaws.

"Phew," Pippin said, depositing the bulldog on the

floor among the torn paper and shredded plastic. "That was lucky."

The bulldog giggled. "That was so fun! Can I do it again? Can I? Can I?"

"No." Pippin curled her lip in disbelief. "What's your name, honey?" she asked.

"Winnie," said Winnie.

"Well, Winnie, let me put it this way—if you ever try and jump from that height again, I'll bite your bum and sew your ears together. Do you understand?"

Winnie's bottom lip trembled. "You're mean."

"You've got that right," Pippin told her.

"Why are you so mean?" Winnie pouted.

"Because I have to be," Pippin told the pup, because wasn't that the truth. How else would she survive, living on the streets the way she did?

"I don't like you. I want to go back to my mammy." Tears welled up in Winnie's eyes. "Mammy Andrea. She'll sort you out!"

Awww! Pippin's heart melted. "Don't worry," she soothed, nuzzling the little dog's head.

"I want my mammy!" Winnie wailed.

"We'll find your hooman," Pippin promised. She had no idea how, but perhaps Toby had a plan for that too.

By now Toby was supervising the rescue. The

cold, hard floor of the laboratory was growing thick with dogs: older dogs who'd heeded Toby's call and puppies who'd been freed. Griffin and Kimmy, as the tallest dogs, were in charge of releasing the puppies from the highest cages.

The problem was, even they couldn't reach the uppermost tier. Not all of the puppies up there were prepared to take a tumble the way little Winnie had.

Toby lay his head to the side, thinking. *What if … what if …*

"What if," he said, "we pretend we're the fire service?"

"Find a ladder, you mean?" someone asked.

"Find a ladder!" Someone else took up the cry.

"There's no ladder in here!" came an answering yell.

"No need for a ladder," Toby said, still directing proceedings from on top of the desk. "All we need is a medium-sized dog to be the fireperson, to stand on a larger dog who acts as the ladder, and everyone else to form a canine canopy below."

"Got it!" shouted Pippin, retrieving one of the damp blankets from the nearest cage. "If three others take a corner with me, the puppies can jump into this, with a little help from their rescuer."

"I so want to have a go at that!" Winnie shouted

gleefully, her tears miraculously drying up. "Let me! Let me!"

"Someone needs to tell that little girl that not everything is a game," Sparky said.

"But ... but ... let me!" she cried as Sparky shepherded the bulldog puppy, already bigger than him, out of the way.

"I need three assistants," cried Pippin. The words were no sooner out of her mouth and three eager volunteers grabbed the corners of her blanket while a medium-sized poodle was given several noses up, helping her climb onto Griffin's back.

"Ooh-ya," he said. "Someone needs their claws clipping."

"Soz," said the poodle, wobbling a little and fighting to hold her balance. "I haven't been to the beautician's for a while."

"Nah, don't worry, hun," Griffin said. "Let's do this."

Pippin and her three deputies angled themselves as close to Griffin as possible, while the poodle reached for the first puppy. She gently hauled him out using her teeth, then, before she could overbalance, dropped him into the waiting blanket. The plan worked like a charm. The puppy hit the blanket, bounced once, and was caught by an attentive bichon frise.

As the poodle balanced precariously atop Griffin, he navigated his way to the next cage and they repeated the process. Grab the puppy, drop, bounce, catch!

Puppy after puppy found themselves quickly freed from their cages until only one remained.

Troot.

Toby gazed up at Troot as he manoeuvred to the edge of the cage. "I can jump by myself," he called.

"No, you can't," the poodle told him. "You're in the wrong place for the blanket. Let me—"

But she didn't have time to finish. Troot, ever the daredevil, made a leap for freedom. He jumped too wide, the arc sending him outwards, way beyond the reach of the blanket, with the bichon frise out of position. Disaster was inevitable. Toby had a nanosecond to consider a levitating spell, but everything was happening too quickly.

Not for Pippin though. She dropped her corner of the blanket and threw herself sideways. As Troot hurtled towards the hard floor, she opened her jaws and snatched him from certain injury. They rolled together for a moment until Pippin extricated herself.

"You saved me!" Troot cried in triumph.

"I'm going to kill you myself," she told the puppy, but he only laughed and nuzzled into her neck.

"Well done, everyone!" Toby shouted. "Now, let's tear this place apart!"

The dogs launched themselves at the cages, the plastic tubes, the water droppers, the blankets, anything and everything. The air was filled with the sounds of chomping and cracking, splintering and tearing.

When Griffin started on the table legs, Toby decided to vacate his hallowed ground. As he did so, the crystal on his collar began to vibrate. "Mrs Crouch?" he said.

"Toby!" she hissed. "You need to get out of there quickly. According to the barman here, someone has reported screaming and now the police have turned up mob-handed. They seem to think someone is being murdered!"

"Consider it done," he told Mrs Crouch. "Over and out!"

He stared around what had once been Larch's laboratory. There had to be fifty dogs in here, fur flying, tails wagging, growling, barking, giggling, chatting, singing, having the most destructive and wonderful time of their lives.

"Hey, guys! Gals! Hey, everyone," Toby called, trying to make himself heard. "Operation P!"

The cry was picked up by none other than Griffin. "Operation P!" he relayed. "Operation P!"

"Then, everyone out!" Toby ordered and began to lead some of the puppies away from the mayhem.

"P?" Troot asked.

"Yes, pee," said Griffin, and cocked a leg against the splintered remnants of the table.

Mission accomplished, thought Toby, and grinned.

CHAPTER TWENTY-ONE

"Catch that one, DC Plum! There! What are you, a fool? By your legs!"

Half a dozen uniformed police officers along with a handful of plainclothes detectives were scurrying around after puppies. The puppies, relieved to be free after so long in confinement, and full of boisterous puppy energy, refused to be detained. Toby could hardly contain his mirth.

"Toby," Mrs Crouch scolded him, but even she was holding back giggles. She'd followed the police convoy down the lane, hobbling on her stick and stopping for a breather every now and again, but fortified by a gin and tonic or two and a few hours with the racy novel she'd been reading, she'd somehow found the energy.

She'd arrived just in time to see the police helping Larch into the back of a van. Not that they'd had to manhandle him. He couldn't escape the jaws of Peaches and Posy—still snapping at his heels—fast enough.

She'd stood by the open gate, bemused by the number of dogs dashing around here, there and everywhere, especially the puppies, chasing each other and wrestling each other to the ground, only to roll through the dust, collide with something, shake it off and start again.

Now DC Plum pulled open the back door of his car to victoriously stow a young Border terrier-mash-up-thingie inside. His triumph was short-lived. "Wheeeeeeeee!" Winnie the bulldog, still keen on learning to jump from heights, launched herself from his back seat and onto the long grass. As the young detective made a grab for her, she skipped off, just out of reach, looking for something else to climb.

Toby snorted and Mrs Crouch clutched her sides. "Oh my," she said. "I'm going to wet myself in a minute. An occupational hazard when you get to my age."

DC Plum, his brow shiny with sweat, shot Toby a look of sheer exasperation. "Can't you do something?" he asked. "I know you're behind this somehow!"

"I don't know what you mean," Toby replied haughtily, not that poor Ed could understand. "What can he mean?" he asked Mrs Crouch.

Eyes twinkling, she reached down to stroke Toby's head. "You know, if we ever want to get home tonight, perhaps you should help poor DC Plum sort the puppies out."

"I suppose." Toby vacated Mrs Crouch's side to track down Griffin, who was standing around, shooting the night breeze with Sparky. Misty looked on, nodding occasionally but not with any clue as to what they were saying.

"I think it's time we sent everyone home," Toby told the Great Dane. "Would you do the honours, please? One last time."

Griffin nodded, his face serious. "It's been a pleasure working with you, Toby."

"The pleasure was all mine," Toby assured him, bumping noses with the three Bushy Leaze dogs. "Thanks for all you've done!" He winked at Sparky. "Especially you, nipper! You're a force to be reckoned with."

Sparky beamed with pride. "Thank you, Toby! I shall have to tell my dad that."

"I'm sure he already knows," Toby said, tail wagging as they began to walk away.

Griffin barked out orders and quickly rounded up all the adult dogs who'd come to Toby's aid. Then, bearing far more resemblance to a crowd of football fans than a battalion of orderly soldiers, they ducked out of the compound and trotted merrily up the lane, singing the song of their people as they went.

Arrrroooo, roooo, roo roo roo rooooooooooo!

Arrrroooo, roooo, roo roo roo rooooooooooo!

Arrrroooo, roooo, roo roo roo rooooooooooo!

The police stood by helplessly, watching the mass exodus. "Are we going after them, Sarge?" a young female officer asked.

"Do they look like they know where they're going, PC Mayweather?"

"They kind of do, sir," she ventured.

"Then let's leave them to it. We're not the bloomin' RSPCA. Just concentrate on the puppies."

Under Toby's—and especially Pippin's—watchful eye, the puppies were brought under control and one by one loaded into the back of police cars. Toby observed as Bryn followed Bron voluntarily, his tail wagging, his ears flapping, eager to be with his sister. Jack too, after a quick tail wag in Toby's direction, had snuck inside the back of a car alongside Alphonse, eager for a lift home.

"What will happen to them?" Pippin asked, licking her lips anxiously.

"I overheard one of the officers say they'd be taken to the emergency vet to be checked," Toby told her. "If they have microchips, that will speed up the process of reunion with all their worried hoomans."

"They'd better not try and scan my microchip!" Pippin darted backwards. "I haven't got one and I don't want one."

Hmmm. Toby realised he had a problem. How would he get Pippin and Troot away from here without the police suspecting anything and dumping them in a rescue kennel?

"But it's fine. I can walk back to town," Pippin told him, slinking into the shadows. "What is it? Eight miles? Ten?"

"I'll come with you," volunteered Troot.

"Don't be silly," Toby said. "We can all get the bus again, can't we, Mrs Crouch?"

Mrs Crouch shook her head. "Catch the bus? At this time of night? I doubt they're running, Toby."

PC Mayweather was approaching, her eye on Troot.

"But we can't let the police get their hands on Pippin or Troot!" Toby cried, casting around for a solution.

He found it parked just a few feet away. "You drive, don't you, Mrs Crouch?"

"I do." She followed his gaze to the pink Fiat. Ducking her head, she stared into the driver's side. "The keys are in the ignition ..."

"Come on then," PC Mayweather sang. "You're the last three pooches I need to round up—"

Mrs Crouch straightened her back and smiled at Mayweather. "These are my dogs, officer," she said.

"All three?"

"Yes, yes. Cute, aren't they? Thank you for finding them." She opened the passenger door of the little car. "Hop in," she told the dogs. Pippin didn't need telling twice. She jumped onto the passenger seat and slipped through to the rear, where she hunkered down and avoided Mayweather's curious eye. Toby indicated Troot should go next, before jumping in last of all and settling down on the passenger seat.

DC Plum wandered over and clocked Mrs Crouch as she inserted a leg into the pink Fiat. He narrowed his eyes but held his tongue.

"We'll be off then," Mrs Crouch said, and, admittedly with a little difficulty, squeezed her rump through the narrow driver's door, settled herself and turned the key in the ignition. The Fiat didn't so much roar into life as wheeze, but at least it started.

PC Mayweather tipped a salute and drifted away, but DC Plum leaned down and tapped on the passenger window. Mrs Crouch rolled it down.

"What *is* going on?" he asked. "First of all I have Clarissa looking for lost puppies, then she's asking about stolen Fiats, and now *I* have a panda car with a back seat full of puppies, and Clarissa's neighbour is driving off in a pink Fiat."

"It's all a coincidence, I can assure you," Mrs Crouch told him.

DC Plum studied Toby. "I doubt that somehow."

"Do you know what?" Mrs Crouch revved the engine. "If I were you, I'd have a chat with Clarissa about it."

"Maybe I'll do that," DC Plum agreed, his voice glum. "Not that she wants to talk to me ..."

"That might change given that she's currently immobile. If I know Clarissa, she'll appreciate the opportunity to chat. You'll find her in the Royal Devon and Exeter for the foreseeable future."

"What?" Not-so-dead-to-me Ed performed a comical double take. "She's in the hospital?"

"You hadn't heard?" Mrs Crouch asked innocently. "She broke her leg earlier today."

"No! Poor Clarissa. I'll definitely go and see her,"

DC Plum promised. "But she has her boyfriend staying. I don't want to get in the way."

"Oh, pur-lease." Toby rolled his eyes.

"You'll be doing us all a favour if you do," said Mrs Crouch. "Now hop to it, boy. Time and tide wait for no man." With that, she threw the Fiat into reverse and, much like Nikki and her boyfriend had earlier, screeched out of the compound at top speed.

Toby, righting himself after being thrown backwards, sat up and clung to the door for dear life. "I didn't know you were a Formula One driver, Mrs Crouch!"

"There are many things you don't know about me, Toby!" she laughed. "Let's go home!"

EPILOGUE

Gormless Gordon and his Crapmobile were toast.

Toby wasn't privy to exactly what had gone on in the hospital, but the day after the Great Puppy Escape, Mrs Crouch had visited Clarissa. She'd taken the bus all the way into Exeter, because, although she'd driven the bright pink Fiat 500 home from Bushy Leaze, it hadn't been on the drive when Toby woke up the following morning.

He'd spent a very cosy night on a blanket on Mrs Crouch's sofa after a smashing dinner of smoked haddock—deboned by Mrs Crouch using magick because who can be bothered with deboning fish that late at night?—and rice. Despite Mrs Crouch's urging, Pippin and Troot had elected not to stay over. Troot had headed back to the marketplace, hopeful of catching his friend Bourgie just as soon as the stall-holders arrived and began to unpack, while Pippin had gone to wherever it was that Pippin went to.

It felt odd to Toby to wake up somewhere other than his own basket, without the sound of Clarissa tippity-tapping on her laptop—and, after a few days of intense activity, it seemed weirdly quiet not knowing when he'd see all his canine friends again.

Quiet apart from the rock music that had been blaring out from next door since first thing this morning, that is.

Toby had pressed his nose against Mrs Crouch's big bay window. What was Grubby Gordon up to in the Page house? It belonged to Old Joe, and Clarissa, and Toby. Not some shabby opportunistic squatter with a stinky attitude and boxer shorts to match.

But, when it came to love, comfort and snacks aplenty, Mrs Crouch was well on the case. "Ignore him," she'd said. "He just wants to provoke a reaction. He's a little boy in a man's body crying out for attention. He's not mature enough to realise he's going about it all wrong."

"What happened to the car, Mrs Crouch?" Toby had asked as he'd watched her crochet. She was making some sort of blanket in bright rainbow shades.

Her knobbly fingers moved like lightning, so fast he could hardly make them out.

"I sent it on its way, Toby," she'd replied. "Back to its real owner."

"Wow." Toby had wondered at that, a driverless car on the roads of Sunshine Valley. Truly. Mrs Crouch had impressive skills. He must pick her brain and see if he could learn a few more of them.

After lunch, she'd headed off on the Number 9 bus to Exeter and by all accounts had had to explain to Clarissa why Toby was staying with an elderly neighbour and not Gruesome Gordon. Clarissa had, apparently, taken rather a dim view of this behaviour, especially given that Grotty Gordon hadn't bothered to visit her or bring her a nightshirt or any of the bathroom products she'd needed.

When Mrs Crouch had returned from the hospital, she'd fed Toby a couple of extra treats and sang as she pottered in the kitchen with him glued to her ankles.

"You're in a good mood, Mrs Crouch," Toby had observed. He'd been mining her for information about Clarissa but there hadn't been much she could tell him, except that his young mistress had sent him all her love and that he was to stay with Mrs Crouch and under *no circumstances* venture inside their home where Grotesque Gordon was holed up.

"Am I?" Mrs Crouch had beamed down at him. "I suppose I am. Did I mention that just as I was leaving the hospital, the extraordinarily handsome DC Plum was nipping in to visit Clarissa?"

"Not-so-dead-to-me Ed?" Toby had asked. So he *had* found the cahonies to call into the hospital after all. Brave man. "Is he handsome?"

Mrs Crouch had fanned herself. It was rather hot in the kitchen. "Oh yes. Very pleasing. Fine, upright gentleman with a good future."

Toby had nodded, pleased that DC Plum would not be popping his clogs anytime soon, because presumably Mrs Crouch would have foreseen such a thing.

"He was bringing flowers," Mrs Crouch had continued. "Such a sweet young man."

"Mmm." Toby was of the opinion that firstly only he could be the most handsome man in Clarissa's life and secondly, she didn't need any other man but him!

"I hope they rekindle that little flame that had started to burn there ..." Mrs Crouch had said, closing the lid on her treats jar and leading him into the front room.

"But how's she going to get Grubby Gordon to

move out?" Toby had asked, returning to his place at the window and anxiously watching for the slightest activity next door.

"I expect a broken-down boiler, a lack of hot water —or indeed any water—blind mice in the pantry, fleas in his bed, bats in the belfry and ants in his pants might persuade him that Clarissa's house isn't the one for him."

Toby had watched doubtfully, and yet, the very next day, South West Water had turned up and then, after shaking their heads and frowning, consulting each other and their clipboards, and making a few phone calls, just as quickly left again.

Environmental Health from Sunshine Valley Town Council had been next to pay a visit. And had just as quickly departed.

The next day, finally, Grimy Gordon had packed up the Crapmobile and vacated the house.

Toast!

Ten days later, Clarissa was allowed home from hospital and funnily enough, guess who drove her? Yes, Mr Extraordinarily Handsome himself.

No, dear reader, not Toby but DC Plum.

Mrs Crouch threw a little tea party in the garden for Clarissa, who lounged in a comfortable chair with her broken leg held aloft by a pile of cushions stacked onto a coffee table. She wore sunglasses and a big floppy hat. DC Plum—Ed—draped her in a blanket as the shadows began to lengthen. Summer was nearly over and the air was cooler now. Toby could smell bonfires and chimneys rather than barbeques and pizza ovens. And there was the scent of autumn in the air: leaves on the turn, undergrowth beginning to die back, plants drawing their energy back into the soil. In Bucklebeare Wood in the Blackdown Hills, the squizzels would be hard at work hiding their nuts.

"Look who's come to see you, Toby!" Mrs Crouch called, and Toby, lying on Clarissa's good foot, blinked out of his reverie and scooted around to see.

"Hi, Toby!" Troot called excitedly. "We brought all our friends with us!"

Pippin, Bryn, Bron, Troot and Bourgie, Jack and Alphonse were waiting politely at the gate for a sign they were welcome.

"Awww, the puppies!" Clarissa clapped her hands.

"We came to say thank you," Bron said, dipping her head shyly.

"Come in! Come in!" breezed Mrs Crouch. "The more, the merrier. We have lots of treats and lots of water. Let me grab a few more bowls." She toddled off to the kitchen.

"Really?" Ed asked, mooching over to open the gate and escort the dogs through. He counted them as they passed. "Where do they all come from? How do they multiply so quickly? We're letting *all* of these dogs in?"

"Yes, we are," Clarissa replied firmly.

"Don't they have homes?" DC Plum asked.

Clarissa removed her sunglasses so she could direct one of her 'looks' at him.

"Fair enough," said Ed, holding his hands up in mock surrender.

"They're Toby's mates," Clarissa informed him, replacing her sunglasses.

"Of course. Any friend of Toby's is a friend of mine," he reassured her.

Toby nodded approvingly. Ed was learning fast. Pleasing Clarissa seemed to have become his number one priority in life.

Scooting back to where Mrs Crouch had piled Toby's toys, Ed called, "Hey, guys! Let's have a game of football. Come on! Who wants to play?"

Everyone wanted to play! Of course they did! In seconds, Mrs Crouch's gloriously kempt garden was alive with the sound of dogs barking and tails wagging. Ed tripped over one of the corgis and was instantly covered in dogs trying to lick his face and nip his elbows and pull his hair. Clarissa, with Toby by her side, laughed fit to burst.

"Aren't you going to play, Toby?" Mrs Crouch asked as she returned with two bowls of water. Toby ambled over to take a sip.

"I'm caring for Clarissa," he told her. "Being doctor."

Mrs Crouch stroked his head. "Get on with you," she chided gently. "Clarissa's fine. See how happy she is?"

So Toby looked. Clarissa, with her enormous smile and open heart, was sitting comfortably and giggling at Ed and the puppies.

"You can run and play, Toby. She'll get well quickly now," Mrs Crouch told him. "Laughter is the best medicine."

And so he did.

Because it is.

PLEASE LEAVE A REVIEW

If you enjoyed *Master of Puppies* please consider leaving a review. This is especially important with this series as although it is the one I am most often asked about, it isn't as popular as the other books I write.

If you'd like to see *Up, Pup and Away* featuring Toby and friends hit the shelves at the end of the year, let me know!

Thanks so much!

OUT NOW

Dead as a Dodo: A Paranormal Cozy Witch Mystery (Wonderland Detective Agency Book 1

From the Amazon bestselling author of the Wonky Inn books comes a brand-new magical fantasy witch detective series.

Dodo was dead. And there the matter should have rested.

At least for DS Elise Liddell.

Emotionally burnt out, she considers herself retired from police work.

By rights it has nothing to do with her, but someone killed the poor man and, as Elise can resist everything except a good puzzle (and a shot of Blue Goblin vodka), here she is tangled up in a murder case.

When a petty thief hands himself into the Ministry of Witches Police Department, Elise's ex-colleagues consider it an open and shut case.

She's less convinced.

Revitalized by the investigation, she takes the suspect on as the first client of her new paranormal detective agency. What would this insignificant wretch have to gain by murdering the cantankerous old wizard? Elise knows full well, by uncovering the motive she can reveal the true killer.

But she forgets, in Tumble Town even the shadows are alive ... and now someone or something is hunting her.

The Wonderland Detective Agency Series is a paranormal cozy mystery series, set in the same Wonkyverse that readers have already fallen in love with. While some of the characters and places will be instantly familiar, Wycherley effortlessly casts her spell so that her zany new friends quickly become ours too.

Packed full of witches, wizards, warlocks, ghosts, shadow people and more, you'll love this glimpse into the dark side.

Take a walk in Tumble Town today!

ALSO BY JEANNIE WYCHERLEY

Spellbound Hound

Ain't Nothing but a Pound Dog: Spellbound Hound Magic and Mystery Book 1

A Curse, a Coven and a Canine: Spellbound Hound Magic and Mystery Book 2

Bark Side of the Moon: Spellbound Hound Magic and Mystery Book 3

Master of Puppies: Spellbound Hound Magic and Mystery Book 4

The Complete Wonky Inn Series

(*in chronological reading order*)

The Wonkiest Witch: Wonky Inn Book 1

The Ghosts of Wonky Inn: Wonky Inn Book 2

Weird Wedding at Wonky Inn: Wonky Inn Book 3

The Witch Who Killed Christmas: Wonky Inn Christmas Special

Fearful Fortunes and Terrible Tarot: Wonky Inn Book 4

The Mystery of the Marsh Malaise: Wonky Inn Book 5

The Mysterious Mr Wylie: Wonky Inn Book 6

The Great Witchy Cake Off: Wonky Inn Book 7

Vengeful Vampire at Wonky Inn: Wonky Inn Book 8

Witching in a Winter Wonkyland: A Wonky Inn Christmas Cozy Special

A Gaggle of Ghastly Grandmamas: Wonky Inn Book 9

Magic, Murder and a Movie Star: Wonky Inn Book 10

O' Witchy Town of Whittlecombe: A Wonky Inn Christmas Cozy Special

Judge, Jury and Jailhouse Rockcakes: Wonky Inn Book 11

A Midsummer Night's Wonky: Wonky Inn Book 12

Halloween Heebie-Geebies: Wonky Inn Book 13

Owl I want for Witchmas is Hoo: A Wonky Inn Christmas Cozy Mystery

Oh Mummy!: Wonky Inn Book 14

Pieces of Hate: Wonky Inn Book 15

A Barbarous Band of Blood Brothers: Wonky Inn Book 16 (Release date TBC)

Wonderland Detective Agency

Dead as a Dodo: Wonderland Detective Agency Book 1

The Rabbit Hole Murders: Wonderland Detective Agency

Book 2

Tweedledumb and Tweedledie: Wonderland Detective Agency Book 3

The Curious Incident at the Pig and Pepper: Wonderland Detective Agency Book 4

A Tragic Tea Party: Wonderland Detective Agency Book 5 (July 29th 2022)

The Municipality of Lost Souls

Midnight Garden: The Extra Ordinary World Novella Series Book 1

Beyond the Veil

Crone

A Concerto for the Dead and Dying

Deadly Encounters: A collection of short stories

Keepers of the Flame: A love story

Non-Fiction

Thoughtful support for those affected by dog bereavement or pet loss

Losing my best Friend

Follow Jeannie Wycherley

Find out more at on the website

www.jeanniewycherley.co.uk

You can tweet Jeannie

twitter.com/Thecushionlady

Or visit her on Facebook for her fiction

www.facebook.com/jeanniewycherley

Follow Jeannie on Instagram

(for bears and books)

www.instagram.com/jeanniewycherley

Sign up for Jeannie's newsletter on her website

www.subscribepage.com/JeannieWycherleyWonky

Printed in Great Britain
by Amazon

22308948R00199